Travelers Along the Way

A Robin Hood Remix

TRAVELERS ALONG THE WAY

A ROBIN HOOD REMIX

AMINAH MAE SAFI

FEIWEL AND FRIENDS

NEW YORK

A FEIWEL AND FRIENDS BOOK
An imprint of Macmillan Publishing Group, LLC
120 Broadway, New York, NY 10271
fiercereads.com

Library of Congress Cataloging-in-Publication Data is available.

First edition, 2022
Book design by Michelle Gengaro-Kokmen
Feiwel and Friends logo designed by Filomena Tuosto
Printed in the United States of America by LSC Communications

ISBN 978-1-250-77127-8 (hardcover)
1   3   5   7   9   10   8   6   4   2

For Selina

The sister of my heart—

I always wanted to grow up and be just like you

"Regard the Franj! Behold with what obstinacy they fight for their religion, while we, the Muslims, show no enthusiasm for waging holy war."

—Yusuf,
son of Ayyub the Victorious

"The Crusades were a tragic and destructive episode. There was so much courage and so little honor, so much devotion and so little understanding."

—Steven Runciman,
A History of the Crusades

My dear reader,

*They say that history is a record of what has happened. Facts, dates, people. The rulers and fighters and doers of old. The things that we know **happened**.*

But I disagree.

*I think history might be a record of what did **not** happen.*

*The Franks, who invaded the eastern shores of the Mediterranean starting in 1096 CE—they did **not** stay at home.*
*They were **not** rebuffed.*

*There is no version of history where the Crusader states do not exist. No version where the Crusades **never** happened.*

I say this, reader, so that you might think.

*The following is a story that perhaps we cannot say **did** happen.*
We have no proof that such a girl as Rahma ever existed.
*But neither can we say that the following did **not** happen.*
*We cannot say that she **never** existed.*

And if I encourage you in anything, it is to go looking for the stories—the histories—that are possible but not definite.

History is a record of what did not happen.

What did happen—that's another story altogether . . .

THE AFTER

Outside Jerusalem:
No-Man's-Land

Sha'ban, 587 Hijri—
Early Winter,
Anno Domini 1192

A Rivalry of Kings

IN THE STORIES OF THE DAYS OF OLD, THERE WAS ONCE not a king, but a thief.

But perhaps we are getting behind of ourselves. We must start a little after that.

We must start in the tent.

Yusuf watched the man across from him. The man watched him back.

It was a long, tense silence.

Then the man abruptly turned his attention to the translator. The translator began to speak, taking what Yusuf had said and speaking the words as they might be understood in the other man's tongue. Yusuf watched the interaction attentively.

Here, before Yusuf, was his enemy.

He smiled. He was an old man now. He had campaigned for many long years and he knew, the way he knew many things, that his body would fail him soon.

Yusuf was dying.

But the man across from him did not need to know this.

He waited as the translator conveyed what he had just said, watched as the king across from him listened.

His enemy was young and, though weakened with illness, still full of life. He was tall, with long limbs and canny, pale eyes. He had hair the color of sand, hair that took on the redness of the sun in the firelight.

Yusuf was very unlike this man. He told himself this, and yet he still saw himself in his opponent. He was his enemy, and his enemy was him.

They were two men of God. Two men fighting for the same slice of holy land. Two men trying to outwit each other. Two warriors at cross purposes. Perhaps it had been ordained, was always meant to be so—Yusuf staring across the table as his enemy sat on one side of the carpet and he on the other.

Earlier, before this meeting, his enemy had offered a sister—with the Kingdom of Jerusalem as his bride price. It was a trick, Yusuf knew. To get him, the sultan, to refuse. But Yusuf was clever, too. He understood his enemy's ruthlessness. For he was his enemy, and his enemy was him. So Yusuf accepted the bride and the bride price. Jerusalem for the Faranji king's sister. His enemy, the Faranji king, had retreated then.

The pale king claimed that his sister had been sent back home without his knowledge.

There would be no marriage.

Yusuf had smiled when the messenger returned.

Two foxes trying to outwit each other. Two warriors, both trying to outwait the other.

His enemy nodded when the translator was finished. He turned his gaze on Yusuf. Pale eyes met black ones. Yusuf knew there was little in his own eyes, little in his own expression.

There was little there in the King of Faranj's looks as well.

They were two men who played this game well. But the Faranji did not belong here. They took land and they refused culture. They were ruthless and ill-disciplined, though cunning warriors. At least, when they weren't sending their peasants into cities, to club and eat the remains of the local populace.

Ah, it was something—for a little while at least—to have a worthy enemy.

Yusuf could not tell if he had the Faranji king cornered yet. He knew from the reports that the patience of Faranji's vassals and knights was wearing thin with this waiting. That the king himself grew sicker. Some of his men were headed back to their homeland. Others, frustrated that their king would not attack the holy city and take her by force again, were making their own plans. Brewing their own rebellions.

But this king was stubborn, as Yusuf himself was stubborn. Perhaps this pale king would wager it all, just to continue his own fight in the name of God. That was not outside of the realm of possibility.

So, Yusuf waited. And he smiled. The Faranji king smiled back.

His enemy said nothing back to the translator. It was another long moment of silence.

It really had been good, for a little while, to have a worthy enemy.

The translator held her breath. For she—she was our thief.

And her story is just as startling as that of the kings.

In the Midst

Earlier, at the fall of Akko

The former dominion of
Yusuf ibn Ayyub, al-Nasir,
sultan of Egypt and Syria
(or, to his enemies, Saladin)
Jumada al-Thani

587 Hijri—
Summer,
AD 1191

CHAPTER ONE

Oo-De-Lally

THE WALLS OF THE CITY OF AKKO ARE NOT HIGH, BUT they're high enough.

I can see that now.

I've still got one handhold on the wall and I watch as my legs swing freely, high in the air. Dizzying, to say the least.

Terrifying, to say the most.

I suppose I should tell you why I'm dangling from the walls of the fallen city, but I haven't much time. Zeena is already halfway down. She likes to remind me that though we've both been climbing date palms since we could walk, she is older and she, therefore, has more experience. Personally, I refuse to admit to her that she's any better than I am.

But the truth is, she's the better climber. I'm better with a bow.

That won't help me here, though.

These city walls were not built for scaling. A statement of the perfectly obvious, I know. But they really, really weren't. The stones were placed precisely in such a way to keep anyone from doing exactly what we are. My arms are sore and my legs are stretched to their limits. Getting from one brick to the next would be difficult even in the daylight, much less with three quarters of a moon as the only source of light. There are campfires not too far in the distance, but those provide little comfort to me—they belong to the very people I don't want to notice me or my sister.

So, when my boot slipped earlier on one of the stones . . . well, now you know why I'm hanging by one arm, scrambling for purchase against the walls.

The scrape of boots against rock, of course, causes Zeena to look up and hiss. I already bit back a curse when I missed the brick, and there's no other way to find my foothold again without a little bit of noise.

But it doesn't matter; Zeena is not reasonable. She cannot possibly resist the urge to silence me, as though I might have missed the stakes in this dangerous game. As though I think we are currently racing down the spine of a palm tree to see who could bring Baba back a fresh date first.

As though her hissing were any less noisy than my one—extremely small—slip-up.

I can hear her warning in my mind: *Silence and invisibility are our one advantage*. Thank you for that sage advice, Zeena. Truly thoughtful and supportive and exactly what I needed this very moment. Could not do this without you, my shining and guiding light. Please, hush me again so that we might draw further notice to our climbing out of a city during a siege in the middle of the night.

My foot, mercifully, finds the next stone. I ignore the burning ache in my limbs as they beg for relief, pleading with me to relax for just one tiny moment. *That* feeling is a lie. Giving in to it would get us caught or killed. Akko fell—is falling—and its walls are not ones that I would dare scale in any other situation.

The Faranji came by the sea; we had to get out the hard way. To be a captive soldier is always a risk, but we did not have the safety of being men. If we were discovered, we would be too far from home for our name or our tribe to mean anything to these strange invaders. The men we fought alongside with for months had told us in no uncertain terms: The Faranji were barbarians. We would not be afforded the honor of being soldiers by *them*.

Zeena had balked at the thought of deserting our comrades, but Omar had ordered us: *Leave now, and do not turn back*. A direct command from our captain. I think he told Zeena to go on and defend Jerusalem, but we knew that part of the order didn't matter as much.

We had to run.

The only thing left in our way is the city's famous walls.

And a Faranji siege.

And, also, the siege of al-Nasir that surrounds that.

And, of course, the invaders who would be reaching the city's port by now, attacking the other side of Akko and potentially breaching the inside and spurring any troops on this side of the wall to approach.

And, not to mention, still surviving this climb.

Simple, right?

A laugh bubbles up in the back of my throat, and I bite my tongue in order to keep it from escaping. Mostly to avoid Zeena's glare again.

Focus.

One handhold and one foothold at a time. Finding the rhythm is always the tricky bit. Doesn't matter if you're scaling trees or walls, you've got to set a pace. Hand to foot to hand to foot. The movement must stay smooth. The movement must be balanced. The movement doesn't have to be fast, just consistent.

I keep moving.

A small thud sounds below me. Zeena's made it down, mashallah.

The rest of my climb is mercifully uneventful. I make it down without thinking further of Zeena's frustration or the expression in Omar's eyes as he ordered us to abandon our company. He was the only one who would look at us; the rest averted their gaze, knowing that this would never have been asked of them. I try not to think of the cast of rage on Zeena's face as I pulled her away from our fellow soldiers.

I try not to think much of anything at all anymore.

As my own feet touch the soft earth, I say a short prayer, in the smallest of whispers. "Allahu Akbar."

"Save it," says Zeena. "We've only just done the easy bit."

I hate her for saying it. Mostly, I hate that she's right. *Again*.

CHAPTER TWO

A Tale of Two Sieges

"WHY DID YOU HAVE TO INSIST ON THAT GREEN cloak?" asks Zeena.

It's her constant complaint. She's crouching behind a rock and I know she's cursing that I don't wear black to match the cover of the night and the color of her soul. That the green of my mantle, though dark, is still just enough color to be spotted by the invaders in the firelight of their camp.

She's not wrong, but I only have one reply at this point: "Green is my color."

"You are vain," says Zeena.

She's not wrong about that, either, but that's not why I bought this cloak, dyed extravagantly and deeply green. It reminded me of home, though I've never told her that. It's the color of the rushes that grow on the banks of the Tigris and the groves of date palms, their lush tops swaying in the breeze. I wanted a piece of our home—verdant and alive.

But I let her think I bought it because the color favors my olive skin and dark hair. She's the reason we left our land, and I try not to remind her of how much I long for home. For rice fields and date orchards and the smell of orange blossoms.

A cool night breeze washes over my face and brings me back to the present.

Zeena's watching the rhythm of the Faranji campsite, looking for the edges of darkness that we can use to skirt around. It's not a bad plan, as far as plans go.

But I've just spotted a soldier sleeping on his own, and I've one idea better than hers.

"We cannot sneak," I say.

"We must," she replies.

"No," I say. "It's too far. We'll never make it. Not without a single soul spotting us. They have ten thousand men, at least."

Zeena looks at me, catching the glint in my eye, and shakes her head. "No."

"You haven't even heard my idea," I say.

"I don't need to. I know your ideas, Rahma. They're ridiculous. Each one is worse than the last." Zeena raises a single eyebrow like she's taken a piece from me in a game of backgammon.

But I know I'm right. I know I've given up that small piece to win the game at large, so I say, "Look at that knight over there. He's already sleeping."

"Let the lion at rest stay at rest, sister."

"But we could just knock him out, steal his armor."

Zeena is unimpressed, and she crosses her arms to show me so. "And then what? There's one of him and two of us."

"And then," I say, adding a little dramatic pause because though I know she hates it, I also know that it works on her, "we walk through camp, with you as my prisoner."

"Don't be ridiculous," says Zeena, frustration in her voice.

"I'm not being ridiculous," I say. "You're short. I'm tall. I wear the knight's armor and I take you as my prisoner."

"I won't do it," says Zeena, not realizing she's raised her voice. "It's degrading. Like doing Please Good Sir I've Lost My Camel."

"We'll do what we have to, Zeena, to get out of here alive." I try to keep my voice to a whisper.

"I will not be your prisoner." Zeena's voice is firm. Resolute. She's mad, still, about being ordered to abandon our post. She came here to fight, to defend the land with her dying breath. That Omar has robbed her of this makes her testier than usual.

I am, on the whole, much less frustrated by Omar's order. I only signed up to come along with Zeena so she *wouldn't* give up her last breath for this land. I'm here for her and her alone.

I've never told Zeena that, either. She's so used to being the elder and my following her to the ends of the Earth that she's never asked.

I'm about to argue further when I hear a noise.

The knight has been roused from his slumber; our raised voices must have woken him. His heavier armor is set to his side, but he's wearing his jupon and he's got a dagger in hand. He's standing now and he looks around, scanning the landscape.

Zeena and I both duck behind the rock and stay as silent and still as we can. I pray that the knight walks toward the small cove of trees to his left.

But . . . no. He's headed toward us.

His movements grow louder as his steps draw closer. I'm almost impressed with how accurately he's identified the source of the sound. Or perhaps he saw us duck behind the rock. I can't exactly look up to check.

But I can hear the crunch of his boots; he's almost to the rock.

I have no choice. Zeena yanks on my sleeve to keep me still, but she can't pull me down once I'm in motion.

I stand and bow before the knight is close enough to strike.

15

"Please, good sir," I say in my best Faranji. I've learned it from listening to the men as they blasted holes in the city walls. "Have you seen my camel? I seem to have lost her."

The knight stops short for a moment, still brandishing his dagger. He's obviously confused by the question, or maybe by my mere presence. Or perhaps simply stunned that I was bold enough to confront him first.

I don't blame him. He's meant to be confused. I am the bait, after all. I can only hope Zeena does not draw his notice.

"None of your sorcery, infidel," he growls. "I'm taking you back to camp." He's identified me by the outline of my clothing alone; it's too dark, even with the moon shining full, to make out faces. He's big—tall, but also made of corded, thick muscles. He'd have to be, wearing the heavy armor the Faranji sport day in and day out. He's looking right at me, pointing his dagger in the direction of my throat. But he's not close enough to grab hold of me . . . not yet.

I step back, trying to keep out of his range. It's trickier than it sounds when your opponent is a good head taller than you and believes you're in league with the devil, as most of these Faranjis do.

"But . . . good sir . . . my camel?" I say. I've only a few more moments before I'm in real trouble, but I keep the plaintive tone in my voice.

The man steps forward. He's in striking distance now. "If you say one more word about your camel—"

But he never gets to finish his sentence. From behind, Zeena smashes him over the head with a rock. He falls down, hard and fast.

Zeena tosses the rock away. "I don't like this."

When I approach him, he's breathing, but he's going to be out for a long while. I don't envy the pain he'll have in his head, either.

"You don't have to like it," I say. "Just find some rope to loosely bind your hands together."

I begin by taking his belt and his jupon. I leave him his hose and his short boots—people rarely look down at your feet, and I could practically stuff my own, taller boots inside his. Besides, there's something about taking the shoes off a man's feet that, no matter what he's done to me, seems immoral.

Why that is the line I have drawn in this war zone is beyond my own understanding. But we've all got to stand for what we believe in.

And I believe in leaving a man his shoes.

CHAPTER THREE

Just Seen a Face

I'M IN THE KNIGHT'S CLOTHES, MY OWN DAGGER IN hand, when another set of footsteps approaches.

"Who goes there?" calls out a voice.

"This one," I say, trying to make my voice as deep as it can go and kicking Zeena in front of me. I spit on the ground beside her for good measure. "Caught her skulking over there."

I point to the boulder where Zeena and I have hidden the other knight's body. We had to lay him out longwise so that nobody could see him from the camp.

The Faranji soldier steps closer—too close to Zeena for my liking. But I don't bristle. I can't. I have to keep my face in the shadows. I've got my mantle back from my shoulders, but the hood is over my face.

He needs to focus on Zeena. He needs to only see that I wear the proper jupon with the proper coat of arms and the proper colors. I pray to God that he doesn't look down at my feet and see my boots. I hope he doesn't recognize the kind of bow I've got strapped to my back. They're a dead giveaway that I'm not one of them. My heart is thumping so loudly I can feel it beating from my scalp to my toes.

The soldier is watching us, trying to decide if he believes me or not. I'm not known to him, but I've got on enough familiar markers to make him *want* to believe my story.

Zeena starts yelling at me, in the tone of a defiant prisoner. "I really hate this, you know. Next time, *I'm* the one who's lost her camels and *you're* the captive girl!"

It's a risk, her speaking like this. The Faranji could perhaps understand her, could speak the common tongue. But this Faranji, he tilts his head, confusion written across his features. He doesn't know our language.

I step closer to Zeena, my face still shadowed by the hood, and brandish the dagger at her. "Silence," I say in Faranji.

She shouldn't be able to understand my words in our little theatrical production. But knives and weapons are a universal language, the tongue of violence. So Zeena, as my fake prisoner, stops yelling at once.

The performance is all for this invading man's benefit and he believes it, alhamdulillah. He jerks his head behind him. "Take her to the captain."

I spit again and then nod. I shove Zeena from behind and she pretends to trip a little, though I know she was expecting it. I keep marching. I've got to wait until we're out of sight of the man.

I can feel his eyes on us, but I haul Zeena straight into the camp.

"We're going to get caught," she hisses.

"Hush," I say.

I feel we've gone far enough into the camp that the soldier can no longer see us. The rest of the soldiers must be sleeping. There's a little activity on the edges, but the center we've walked into—which holds a large tent and a dying campfire—is lulled by the night.

We just need to not be seen. I'm not sure how long I can keep up that Zeena is my prisoner and I'm taking her to be turned in. You can only run the same ruse so many times before it becomes stale in your mouth and an obvious lie to those you must convince. Perhaps Zeena was right and this was a bad idea after all.

I still won't tell her she was right, though.

I shove her a little and she growls. We're to the edges of the light from this campfire now. We really could be out of sight and stay that way.

Of course, that's when I see the soldier.

He's staring straight at me, his posture relaxed. He's sitting, reclined, on the ground with his feet kicked up against a rock.

But he's alert—I can tell from the tilt of his head. And his eyes . . . watchful.

I don't wait for him to speak, finding my Faranji tongue again. "Who goes there?"

"I could ask the same of you," he says. "More so, too, for I'm the one who's sitting and you're the one who's going."

"Don't be clever," I say.

"That I cannot help." Though his face is mostly in the dark, I can see that the edges of his eyes crinkle, as though he is smiling.

"Do you mock me?" I ask.

"I'd never dare mock one who keeps to the shadows," he says. There's a light accent to his own Faranji that I cannot place. Perhaps he's a local soldier, fighting for the Nasrani cause. Though most of them defected to the sultan after a hundred years under Faranji rule. He's definitely from the mountains due east. Or perhaps that's the accent of the west, of Rum.

"Why do the shadows matter?" I cannot explain why I am still speaking with him. His voice reminds me of a memory, of a piece of home I cannot quite place. Something familiar I lost long ago. A song, perhaps? I hear the whisper of a laugh as it dances through my mind, but still, I do not know why this man by the campfire seems so strange and so known at once.

I can feel Zeena grow tense beside me. She wants me to quit stalling.

"The shadows matter," he says, knowing that I am leaning in and still listening, though my face is cloaked in the cover of darkness, "because they hide what we have always known."

"And what is that?" I ask, my breath catching. I don't realize until it's too late that I've stepped into the light.

"That is between you and the shadows."

I am drawn toward him. And the memory solidifies—Majid, the boy from our childhood and the only one aside from Zeena who could draw me into a battle without question.

But Majid left with his father long ago. And I am here, half a world away from home. The memory's distracted me. It takes me a moment before I realize that he hasn't replied in Faranji. He's speaking the common tongue. My tongue. And he's speaking it without any accent at all.

He's spotted me. Seen me for what I really am.

Zeena freezes. Perhaps she's been frozen the whole time.

Or maybe I'm the one who gave myself away. Had I started speaking my own language, relaxing into the speech when I was searching for that memory?

He gets up and takes a step closer. "Ah, but I'd know those eyes anywhere."

I take a step back and raise my bow toward him. But it doesn't matter, for our gazes are still locked and his own expression is still aimed with lethal intent. "What eyes?"

"Al-Hud brown."

I lower my bow. "Distant cousins," I hedge.

"Perhaps. It is possible. The family strike does seem so consistent—regardless if you're in the south by where the two rivers meet, or up north, in Baghdad. I've known enough al-Huds to know that they were a prolific bunch." He leans in, his breath tickling my ear. "But I only knew one al-Hud with flecks of gold in her eyes."

My breath catches. I stare at him. "Majid Mirza."

I shouldn't say it, shouldn't acknowledge it. But he can see the truth in my eyes just as I can see the truth in his.

He smirks, his own concession. It's a devastating expression. I remember admiring it as a child, remember loving to watch him inflict it on others. "Do you still steal dates off of people's plates when they aren't looking?"

It's such an old, familiar memory that I say automatically, "Do you still cheat at backgammon?"

He grins, knowing he's bested me. Knowing I've just admitted all.

But somehow, I know—the way I know that Zeena will always hiss at me—that he will not betray me in this moment. That my secret is his secret now. *Our* secret.

What a strange thing to know.

He winks, steps back. Then he bows, his hand on his heart. He's back to Faranji when he says, "Fare thee well. I pray God keeps you well on your journey." He nods to Zeena, then to me. "Perhaps we shall meet again."

And then he's gone. His footsteps are so light as he melts into the shadows that I cannot hear him after a pace or two. I'd almost think I'd imagined him, but for the expression on Zeena's face when I look at her.

"We're found out." Her voice is hoarse.

"No," I say. I stow my arrow and strap my bow across my back. "I think he has his own secrets, too."

"That's ridiculous," she says. "I think your bow gave you away, until you confessed all. I saw him take notice of it before he spoke Arabic."

There's a small relief, at least, that it was not I who used the language first. It's a scarce consolation, for we're still well in danger. I refuse to acknowledge my worry to Zeena, though. I'm going to keep our morale up, the way I have this entire time. Perhaps I am full of wild ideas, but I'm also the better of the two of us at not losing my head to cynicism or sorrow.

"We're only one campsite over from al-Nasir," I say. "You think he has not sent his own spies here? You think we are the only ones hiding amongst the enemy?"

That gives Zeena pause. It's a less outlandish theory than she realized. We both remember why Majid's father was banished from our own father's diwan—perhaps the son has grown to be more like the father. It has been years since I've seen Majid. He could be anyone now.

I press my advantage. "Lead on. We mustn't get caught again."

Zeena doesn't bother to argue. I follow her through the shadows to the far edges of the camp, and together we vanish into the night.

CHAPTER FOUR

A Horse with No Name

SNEAKING THROUGH ONE CAMPSITE IS BAD ENOUGH. Sneaking through two in the same evening feels like some great cosmic joke.

I will spare you the details of working our way through a second siege camp. I will not insult your intelligence and say that it is easier to sneak through a camp of your own compatriots, for the men of al-Nasir's camp were not really our own. They did not know us. They had never fought alongside us. We were still intruders here.

We continue to stick to the shadows, particularly because I was still dressed as an enemy soldier. I know deep in my heart that Zeena will never let me live that down. Inshallah, I will be an old khala one day, and she will still be reminding me about the time I was foolish enough to dress up like a Faranji knight and escort her through their camp as though I was holding her prisoner.

The soldiers here now know their siege of many months is lost. We overhear the conversations as we move through camp. And I can feel the soldiers' frustration, their sense of loss. Nobody wants to abandon Akko. It's too important of a port. It's been too long fought over. But still, in one way or another, giving up the city is what we must all do.

We keep our heads down and try to stay beyond anyone's notice. A man in defeat is the most dangerous kind of creature. They have nothing to lose and a swell of hot anger in their hearts.

It's the same anger beating through Zeena. To be forced into a retreat that no man would ask of another man . . . It makes her feel less-than, I know. To not be allowed the right to die alongside her fellow soldiers. Zeena has always been an idealist like that.

I might be younger than her, but I was forced into pragmatism at an early age, having followed my sister into enough fights of honor. Back home, Zeena used to hunt snakes with her bare hands; I think she started doing it to scare not just the village boys but any potential suitors, too. I know the fact that she doesn't get to die with honor behind the walls of Akko is eating her alive right now.

Honor is everything to her.

"Why did you have to insist on wearing that Faranji knight's equipment?" Her voice is barely a whisper, but I can hear the censure in her tone. "If we are caught here, there will be hell to pay."

"There will already be hell to pay if we are caught, regardless of the knight's garb that I've stolen," I whisper back. "At least this way, we're prepared for the next time we must disguise ourselves."

Zeena snorts. She hates disguises. She wants to win by brute force and cunning alone. I, meanwhile, would dress up like the Faranji king himself if it would get me out of trouble. Have I mentioned that it's been a long year in the Holy Land?

The last edge of al-Nasir's camp is not quiet. Dawn is breaking, and the men are rousing from their sleep and their tents, preparing themselves for the day ahead. Some look ready to fight. Others—the ones who were already up and have heard the news—are packing their armor and their provisions. A soldier's way of accepting that the order to live to fight another day is coming.

25

Three Faranji kings have landed on the shores of Akko, and with them fresh soldiers. Not even al-Nasir—Salah-a-Din—can save the city now.

But this kind of activity is good. Everyone is focused on their own tasks. This is better than the whispers of defeat and the murmur of anger from earlier. Even though the breaking light could betray us, nobody notices two slight, smaller soldiers as we make it to the edge of camp.

There is only one flaw in our otherwise brilliant escape. It occurs to me now, for I had no idea we would make it this far. We've taken a thousand risks tonight, and as we stand at the outskirts of the camp, I know it's this one, this thousand and first risk, that will likely ruin it all.

"We need a horse," I say.

Zeena looks up. "Are you out of your senses?"

I shake my head. "Actually, we need two horses."

Zeena's nostrils look as though they might take flight, they're flaring so. "Why didn't we take one of the Faranji horses?"

"I don't think walking two Faranji horses through the defender's siege would have been inconspicuous," I say.

Zeena just glares.

I go on, belaboring the point. "Their horses aren't built for the desert. They're heavy and slow and brutish, just like the soldiers they carry. We need good, light horses. Our horses are built to endure. They have strong bones and they are only outlasted by camels."

"I don't need another one of your lectures on horses," says Zeena. "We are not thieves. We're soldiers. We have *honor*, in case you've already forgotten."

I know that she's itching for a fight—and she's refusing to speak of Omar, which means she's still furious about his sending us away. Zeena in defeat is no different from any man in this camp. I can see it in the way her stance has shifted, the way her eyes have narrowed and her brow is furrowed. She's dangerous. She wants to be dangerous.

She *needs* to be dangerous, right now.

So rather than give her the retort that is on the tip of my tongue, instead I say, "I've forgotten nothing. We're lucky to be alive."

Zeena snorts.

"It's time, sister," I say. "We must go home."

"We have to go to the Site of Holiness," says Zeena. "That's what Omar told us to do. I am *not* a deserter. I will stay and fight till the end. *Sister*."

She means Jerusalem. What we came here to fight for. The city taken by the Faranji and held as their captive for a hundred years. The city reclaimed by al-Nasir a mere year ago. The city all these Faranji have come by sea to recapture, the crown jewel of their stolen states.

"We have to get home," I say. "We've been gone too long."

"We have not done what we set out to do!" Zeena is shouting now.

I know from this outburst that she's really on the edge of tears, that she's so sad, she's angry. That she cannot believe she was not allowed to stay with her compatriots. That Omar did not do her the honor of allowing her to fight to the last breath. I've always known Zeena best of anyone, being second in age to her of all our sisters. But after this past year of fighting alongside her, I can read her moods the way old men can tell a sandstorm is approaching. The way they know the khamsin winds are about to blow.

"We do not have that luxury," I say. And it's true.

"Because we are girls," Zeena spits.

"Because we are strangers here, sister!" Now I'm shouting, too. "Do you not understand? We were never meant to be here. But you heard the call of war and you ran. As though the drumbeats could not carry you away from home fast enough!"

"The war still calls. We must go. The Sacred City. That city is next." She points due south, as though her body was born knowing the lay of the land, even though we've only been here for the past year. "The Faranji will not give it up without another fight. The False Queen Isabella would never let them."

"We just survived a siege and you want to go and insert yourself into another one? Have you lost all sense?" I want to shake her, but I resist the urge. Barely.

"Have you lost all honor?" Her voice is so cold it's nearly cruel.

I cannot tell you what I would have done next, for I'm suddenly distracted by the noise of light stamping. I look over and find a horse, standing placidly beside a rock at the very edge of the camp. Like she was waiting for me there the entire time.

I stop arguing with Zeena, too entranced to ignore the creature. "Why hello there, friend."

The mare is deep red—so red she almost looks brown, like the rich bark of a tree trunk. But as first light shines on her coat, I see that she's got little white speckles across her frame. Out of her four hooves, she sports three white boots, and on her muzzle is a continuation of those white speckles that fleck her body. She's so short, she's nearly a pony. But she's not a pony, she's a full-grown horse. She's simply stout, sturdy, and obviously very strong. I approach the mare, keeping my footsteps gentle and my movements slow.

I reach out and she allows me to stroke her face. She nuzzles my hand back.

"Rahma!" shouts Zeena. "We do not have time for this!"

I ignore my sister. The mare's got a saddle that I've seen only a few times before: high in the front and low in the back. The stirrups are short, with round disks attached to the ends. The tack is set on top of a soft felted blanket. Draped across the pommel of the saddle is a belt holding a quiver and a bow. From that alone I know I should take caution that this horse's rider is nearby. No one leaves a weapon unattended for long.

"We must go," commands Zeena. She must have also drawn the same conclusion from the bow and quiver. "Now."

It's the demand in her tone that brings out my stubborn side. I take the horse's reins in hand for safety and continue to pet her. I'd say from the bow she carries that this is a horse of the high steppe to the east, but her build, so solid and sure-footed, makes me think that she's trekked all the way from the mountains even farther north. A true traveler. She's tied loosely to a boulder and her hooves look rough—she's not been shod, possibly not ever. But I can tell this is not a lapse on the part of the rider, but intentional. The horse's hooves look hearty, intentionally calloused the way my own feet are in my riding boots.

What a tough, sturdy little thing she is. I cannot help but admire her. She has seen so much more of the world than I.

Of course, I can't steal her, this horse. She's too well cared for. Too loved. Too noble and cosmopolitan. She's glossy and adventurous and though I'm desperate enough right now, I'd never take a well-cared-for creature out of good hands. I could certainly never lay claim to a horse with the kind of courage to travel so far from her own homeland and into a foreign warzone. It's too bad, though; she seems like an excellent companion. I'd like to know her better.

"You are a brave, pretty thing," I coo. "What is your name?"

"Red," says a voice.

I turn around, and for the first time in my life, I meet a girl who is taller than I am. Her hair is long, dark, and braided in two plaits tied through and wrapped in red ribbons. Her eyes kiss in the corners and she's sturdy and broad-shouldered. At first, I think the girl is wearing a kaftan that falls clean to her ankles.

But then I see that the garment wraps around her torso so that it's fastened with three ties near her right shoulder and belted with leather around the waist, creating a large pocket across her chest. It's a beautiful, deep crimson color. She's smiling, but then I see the look in her eyes. I wonder for a moment if this is what people feel when they find themselves caught in Zeena's gaze before she decides to strike them.

I'm so startled, there's only one thing I think to say. "That's her color."

"We call them by their colors," says the girl. She's looking at me intently. Sizing me up. Assessing. "She's the red of the fire when the earth and the sky split from one another."

"That's not really a name, though, is it? Sounds nearly like a destiny to me." I run my mouth when I don't know how I might get out of a sticky situation. And this is shaping up to be a sticky situation.

The girl shrugs, as though she is not here for the philosophical merits of whether calling a horse by their color is really a name at all.

Zeena has none of my charm, none of my stall tactics. When she senses a threat, she dives in like it's already a melee. I say this so you understand what comes next.

"Who the hell are you?" Zeena's about half the girl's size, but she's already taking her longest strides, trying to put her body between mine and the girl's.

I really love Omar as a brother, but for a moment I'm angry with him. That he left me to deal with Zeena after putting her in such a mood.

I put my arm up before Zeena can step in front of me. "What can I do for you, stranger?"

The girl quirks her smile. "I was just curious if you were about to steal my horse?"

I suddenly see what this looks like. I put on my most guileless face, dropping the reins and moving back from the horse. "Me? Steal a horse?"

The girl nods, the smile not quite gone from her eyes. "Yes. Especially since horse thieving is punishable by death." The girl pauses, looking us both up and down. "So is desertion."

This has Zeena absolutely fuming. I knew better than to lower my arm earlier, and honestly, it's the only thing keeping her back right now.

"Desertion is an ugly word to bring up, friend," I say. "Do you think so poorly of your fellow man?"

"War brings out the ugliest in all men."

We're near a large stream, what could perhaps even be called a small river—Nahr Na'mein. The name floats to me like it came from another lifetime ago. I remember Omar telling me that it flanked the northwest side of the city. He gave us a sense of the geography as we came into Akko—not that it had done us much good. We'd spent most of our time holed up in the city, waiting as the siege blasted holes in our defenses and the city's walls. Then waiting as al-Nasir surrounded the Faranji siege with one of his own.

I hadn't seen this river, in any case, as we'd come to Akko by the east, farther from the coast. It's a pretty, placid kind of stream. We're on the side with low brush and grassy meadows. But the other side of the stream looks like dense forest. I spot a small footbridge. If we can just make it across that bridge, I know we can hide in the woods.

But this girl . . . she seems to know the lay of the land quite well. She's keeping her back toward the bridge.

She's blocking me.

I return her earlier half smile.

We both have swords strapped to our belts. There's also my bow. Praise Allah that *her* bow is out of her reach and on her horse. She's got a small whip, but I'm quite sure that's only for riding the horse. I imagine she's got daggers hidden in that long pocket of hers, the same way I've got knives stashed in my tall, soft boots. But neither of us reaches for our weapons.

Not yet.

There's still a performance to be done.

CHAPTER FIVE

Teeny Teni

ZEENA IS STILL BEHIND ME. I CAN FEEL HER ANGER and frustration radiating off her in waves. She's ready for this fight.

But this tall girl is biding her time. So, I bide mine.

The sun is just reaching the horizon and the first hazy light of day is giving way to a real flood of illumination. The girl keeps her body between me and the bridge. She picks up a nearby spear, as though the gesture is the most natural thing in the world. She's holding the weapon like it's a walking stick, but I know if she lifts it at just the right angle, she could break the bones in my chest. Or spear me straight through the gut.

Depends if she decides to use the pointy end or not.

There's a large, solid-looking branch leaning up against a nearby tree. I grab it and do a little twirl. I could use my bow, but the weapon is precious enough to me that I'd rather not break it in a fight with a staff. Then I mimic my opponent's walking stick posture. "What shall we talk about, friend? The weather?"

"How can we be friends if I do not know your name?" she says, like she has been very clever and set a trap that I will have to find my own way out of. I must either tell her my name or declare her to be my enemy.

But I am proud of my name. I claim it quite often, even in disguise.

I take my free hand, press it to my heart, bow slightly, then take that same hand, kiss the tips of my fingers, touch my forehead, touch the sky. It is a slow and elaborate gesture, but it tells her exactly where I am from and how my people worship.

Her eyes widen in surprise that I would give away so much. But I'm not done yet.

"Rahma bint Ammar bin Ali al-Hud, at your service," I say in my most gallant of tones. "As-salamu alaykum." *May peace be upon you.*

The girl does not return the greeting. "Are you a fool?"

Zeena snorts. "She has your number, sister."

"Good," I say. For I know that I've confused her enough to take the advantage—I've maneuvered so that my opponent is no longer keeping her back to the bridge. My foot reaches the edge of the first plank. Zeena is still behind me. It's a relief to know that even if I lose, Zeena will be able to run to safety. Not that she would, but she *could.* "Then it shall be a fair fight."

My words unlock something in my new opponent. She raises her spear like the weapon that it is. Blunt end first. Humdulillah for small mercies.

"Zeena," I say, raising my own. "Please stay back."

My sister would normally not listen to a word I say. But she's been eyeing the girl as much as the girl has been eyeing us. Zeena has taken on men twice her own size, and even several that are twice this girl's size. But there, Zeena had had the advantage: Men always underestimate her. This girl, we can see, will underestimate neither of us. So Zeena backs away, properly listening this time. She's halfway across the bridge when the girl strikes her first blow.

I hope Zeena finishes crossing and runs far from this spot. Knowing my sister, she won't. But it's a dream I hold on to as I parry, blocking the strike at my head.

The girl is fast, but I'm faster.

But.

There's always a *but*, isn't there?

But eventually, I will tire. Eventually, the girl will score at least a glancing blow to my arms or my shoulders. Or, if I'm very unlucky, to the crown of my head.

I'm good. I'm better than good. But even greatness can run out of luck eventually.

Thwack.

Her spear comes crashing down beside me. By God, that was close.

The fact that I've dodged that blow has caused her to rethink her strategy. I watch as a new idea flashes across her eyes, and I know I'm in for it now.

She starts throwing elbows, and I take one across the cheek. My teeth rattle with the force of the hit. This girl knows her power. And if I'm being frank with myself, she's probably only using a third of her strength.

I am strong, but this girl is stronger.

"Rahma, draw your damned bow." That's Zeena from behind me. Confirming that, as I suspected, she's returned to this side of the bridge and not gone all the way across like I asked.

She's probably correct, of course, about the bow. Zeena is always correct about these things.

"You know, I must admit. That doesn't seem like the right thing to do." I jump over a low swing of the spear. This time the pointed end was swung my way. Not a good sign, as far as signs go. The fight is ramping up and I'm learning the more frustrated my opponent is, the more bloodthirsty she grows.

It's nice to learn we do have something in common, though.

My opponent is switching up her technique. She's found a beautiful way to break her own rhythm of attacks. I'd admire her syncopation more if I weren't its target.

Her spear comes crashing overhead. I half expect the branch I've chosen as my weapon to split in two, the blow rattles through my arms so. But my makeshift staff holds, for the moment.

My opponent smiles. It's a convivial expression. If she weren't attacking me here, I'd think we were fast on our way to becoming compatriots. "That stick won't last forever," she says.

I return her smile with a lopsided grin of my own. "Doesn't have to last forever. Just for long enough."

"You're quite something, for a deserter," she says.

These words unlock something in Zeena and she runs, charging full bore toward the girl, who dodges easily enough.

Zeena is now swinging from the girl's back. The girl just laughs and flips Zeena over easily, placing her spear to my sister's throat.

Damn. The game is over.

I lift both my arms and drop my makeshift staff to the side.

"You stay put," the girl says to Zeena. "I will not show such restraint next time."

My sister huffs.

"Zeena," I say, not taking my eyes off of my opponent. "This is my fight."

The girl looks to my dropped staff and shakes her head. "You give up too easily."

I shrug. "Sisters in peril have that effect."

The girl does a double take. She's still in an attack stance, but she's taking in the look of us as if for the first time. She scans Zeena, with her short stature, her deep golden hair in a single long plait down her back. She's not wearing a helmet, but her head is still covered, wrapped the way the other soldiers cover their heads. Then there's me, with my height and my darker skin and my black eyebrows. The only thing we have in common are the same brown eyes. The girl seems to register this after a long look.

"Is that the only family trait?" she asks. "The eyes?"

"Yes," I say. "Those eyes and the stubbornness of a camel. That's the mark of the sons of al-Hud."

She does a twirl with her spear. It's a beautiful, flourishing move that keeps the weapon on both of us, ready for an attack at any angle. "You are not a son."

"No," I say, grinning again. "Baba only had daughters, four of us in all. But we all have the family strike—the eyes and the stubbornness. I think he was glad to have Zeena and me off his hands when we left for the war. He did not want us to go, of course. But he was relieved, too."

The girl takes another step closer. "And why is that, Rahma al-Hud?"

"Hard to find stubborn girls a husband." I grin, trying to pull her focus.

I only have one chance now. So far, I've kept myself more than three paces away. But I've no weapon and she's got the advantage of size and strength. At exactly the right moment, I have to get underneath her arms before she notices what I'm doing.

She grins back.

I wait. And wait. Seconds linger like dripping honey. And then—

She lunges.

I duck and charge. I'm under her in a moment. She's moving

forward and I take her momentum and grasp her wrists. I pull her forward and she has enough training to not fight the motion. That at least spares her wrists from breaking.

Ah, but of course, she knows how to wrestle, too. She's keeping the momentum going so that I might land flat on my back. I sweep her leg. She grabs for my neck with her free hand. But I block with my elbow just in time and get her spear in one hand.

She's on her back and now I've got her pinned with her own spear. My knees hold the wooden shaft to her chest. I grab her collar with my free hand. "Check," I say, like we are playing a friendly game of chess.

"Checkmate," she says. And then I realize she's grabbed one of those knives that I suspected was in the pocket at her chest, and she's pressing the blade to my throat. "Now release my deel, if you please."

I smile. She's really *very* good. I let go of my hold on the collar of her garment.

"Call it a draw," I say. My glance flickers down to the arrow I grabbed from the pouch at my side as I swept her leg. The arrowhead digs into the soft part of her belly.

And then the girl laughs. A deep laugh, jostling against the point of my arrow.

She pulls the knife from my throat, and I pull my arrow from her gut.

"What now?" I ask as I shuffle backward, allowing her to get up as I stand myself.

"I don't know," she confesses.

"Where is your company?" I say as I toss her spear back.

She catches it. "I was sent as a diplomatic attachment from the Altai mountains, though my clan hails from elsewhere originally. The mountains are our clan's refuge for now. There are but a few of us here. They mean to ride home."

I watch her for a moment. She's not easy to read, but I sense a restlessness not unlike Zeena's. I remove my helmet. "And do you want to return home with them?"

"What would I do, were I not to go home?"

"We are on marching orders from the captain of the Akko guard," I say. "Apparently the Faranji do not recognize girls as soldiers."

Zeena sucks her teeth. "We should have been allowed to die honorably with our fellow men at arms."

"A pity you did not," says the girl. It's difficult to tell if she's serious or not. "To where do you march?"

I lock eyes with Zeena briefly, but her expression shutters.

"Jerusalem," I say.

I regret it as soon as I say it. But it's done now. Hope kindles in Zeena's eyes. It's my turn to shutter my expression from her.

"I doubt we can offer you anything that your kin could," I say. "Or the safety in numbers of the al-Nasir camp. But there is one thing we can offer."

"And what is that?" asks the girl.

I grin. "Adventure."

The girl nods, then bows briefly. "They call me Teni."

"Teeny?" I ask.

"Te-ni," she repeats.

And that is how we end up three girls and a horse, on our way to the Sacred City.

Chapter Six

My Backpack, My Pony, and Me

Zeena is still not over Teni calling us both deserters.

I can tell by the way she is walking. Her shoulders are stiff, she's clenching her jaw, and she's generally giving off the kind of air she uses when she walks into a space packed with soldiers and other rough-and-tumble sorts.

I know it's because she feels Omar *made* her desert. She'd never admit this, of course. But there are things we know about each other that we'd never say aloud.

Zeena has always been small, but she's learned to compensate for her size with sheer willpower and bristle. She was only six by the time all the children living within our father's diwan were aware that she was terrifying and never to be antagonized under any circumstances.

Teni has not gotten this warning, obviously. Then again, Teni looks like she's had to prove her toughness on many an occasion herself. But a fair warning is a fair warning.

I look over. "Zeena is protective of what is hers."

This seems like a kind way to say what I mean, while also saying the truth. I know who my sister is. But she's still *my sister*, and I would defend her unto the ends of the Earth. It's why I'm here in this cursed place, after all.

"Yes," says Teni. "I can see that."

Zeena snorts.

"And allow me to apologize," says Teni, as though such things are too precious to put off. As though the cost of admitting fault is worth it for her, when dealing with those she rides with. "I should not have called you a deserter earlier. You—and your sister, too—appear to be made of honor and nobility."

Zeena stops walking for a moment. Red stops behind her. It's a little cascading effect of *arrêts*, as the Faranji might say. My sister looks Teni in the eye, judging the sincerity of her apology. She must be satisfied, for she nods.

"I thank you," says Zeena. "And to be fair . . . I would have thought the same had I encountered us on the edge of camp as well."

I blink. That is a huge concession, coming from Zeena.

Teni, by the way, does seem to understand this. She places her hand on her heart and nods. "I respect you for your truth."

Zeena sniffs, but it's a mollified sort of sniff. The kind where she says she accepts your apology without ever really acknowledging it. Teni seems to understand this as well. I wonder about her and her family and her tribe. That she would apologize with such grace and with so little misunderstanding.

We continue marching on at our earlier pace in a companionable silence for a little while. Teni has largely been leading us. She has an uncanny sense of direction, as though she was made to know where south was at all times. The woods are thick enough to provide shade and cover, but not so dense that we cannot walk two or three across. The air is a little damp, and sweet with decay in the way only a forest can be.

41

But something Teni said earlier caught my attention and I am unable to let it go. "We are not noble," I feel the need to clarify. "Our people do hold land in the south of the Tigris. The land of the two rivers, they call it sometimes. The marshland, they call it, too. The Sawad. South of Baghdad."

Teni nods. "I have never seen the river you speak of, but I have heard of its wonders and long to see it one day. We did not go through that city or any of the land to the south. We traveled from our mountains, down through the desert, and then across the steppe. We saw the Great Salt Desert and then went north, across that extraordinary inland sea, though I would not recommend traveling with horses that way ever again. We were meant to send men on north. They call it Byzantium and you call it Rum. But instead we trekked back through the mountains and then we traveled east through the wadis and farmland before we turned south to Akko. And there we met."

"Truly?" I ask, breathless at the wide world that Teni has seen on her journeys. "You have traveled so much farther than I ever have."

"And yet there is still so much of the world to see."

I'm fully grinning before I realize it. "Then we must go after we are done in the Sacred City. Date palms and orange trees as far as the eye can see." I try my best not to sigh just thinking about it, but I can hear that I'm unsuccessful. "We're an unruly tribe, by everyone else's account. But we keep the peace and we keep the order. And Baba holds court over them all, making sure the dates are distributed fairly and the water goes to whom it must."

"How many are you?" asks Teni.

"A thousand," I say with a laugh. I have no idea if it's true. But that's how it's always felt. And some things, I've learned, *are* true if they *feel* true. I'm desperate to ask her of her own people, but I can tell she must know more of me before she'd reveal anything of herself. "But of the sisters, there's four of us. Zeena, then me, then Hala, then Noor."

"And no boys?" asks Teni, looking to me to see if she's remembered correctly.

"Not one," I say. I wait, watching her, but she gives nothing away. "Do your people value boys as well?"

Teni shrugs. "We cannot get by without everyone doing their part. Our girls are not chattel or pawns in games of war. Not since Temujin took the reins of our clan. Though it feels as though I've been fighting my whole life, for I love the spirit of it. I do not love war. But to ride a swift horse as I fire arrows? To wrestle until my body is spent? Perhaps it is unwise, but I am drawn to that kind of a fight. I relish such adventure."

I laugh again. "Then you are in good company."

Teni nods. "Did your father not take another wife?"

"No," I say quite simply. "It's not done in our family."

"But in your religion? Are you not sartaq?" And that's how I know that she's not just traveled a good amount of the world, but that Teni has paid attention to those unlike herself. Learned which customs are like her own people's and which are foreign. She's listened enough to know the different faiths by some of their rules.

"True enough. But not in our family. Not even when my mother died." I wonder if her own people allow a man to take more than one wife. The Faranji say they do not, but then the false queen of Jerusalem was married off to a man who already had a wife—one who was alive and well and a Princess of Rum.

"He must have loved her very much." Teni says this so simply for such a romantic notion.

"That," says Zeena, deigning to join the conversation, "and we told him we would kill his new bride in her sleep if he tried to marry again."

Teni grins. "I think I'm starting to understand why second marriages are not done in your family."

"Yes, you're getting the idea, aren't you?" I say, chuckling. There's a clearing just in front of us—a space where the forest trail opens wide. A nice patch of green. I think perhaps we will have a spot to camp for the night.

We stop short. All of us run into one another, back to front. All except for Red—she's got enough sense to have seen the collision coming and taken a step to the side.

Up ahead, there's tents and mules and camels and horses. Several lit fires dot the side of the road, and the air is thick with the smell of dried, roasted meat. And with the stench of travel—of a mass of humans moving throughout the day and unable, or unwilling, to bathe in the evening. It's as enticing as it is revolting.

It's a Faranji campsite, set up directly in the middle of the clearing ahead. I could identify one by scent alone at this point. And it's a large one, too. It's not the first time I've prayed for the Faranji to take up the custom of hammams. The smell of their stale flesh on the other side of the wall of Akko is not one I will forget for a long while.

"Damn it all," says Zeena.

"Can we not go around?" Teni asks.

"We could . . . ," I hedge. "But there's more desert in either direction and God knows how safe the wilderness is at the moment."

"We certainly can't go through," says Teni, stating the absolute obvious.

"I do still have that knight's jupon—" I start.

"We are *not* doing Please Good Sir I've Lost My Camel again," Zeena states flatly, crossing her arms.

"All right," I say. "We wait until nightfall. Then we'll skirt around them."

I hope that I've managed to keep the nerves out of my voice.

From the looks on both of their faces, I haven't.

CHAPTER SEVEN

Rhyming and Stealing

THE NIGHT IS YOUR FRIEND WHEN YOU'RE USED TO sneaking about. But the truth is, all this secrecy and silence and sneaking makes me long for the heat and sunshine of the day. I was raised for a fair fight. An honest fight.

I know now, the way I know many things, that there's no such thing. Not really. But I hold on to the idea that there *could be*. That there is fairness and honor in the world. That wherever it's been hidden, it's worth fighting for.

It's worth preserving, even in some small corner of myself.

I know I'm probably fooling myself. But I'd rather be a fool than a cynic. Perhaps that makes me a little bit like Zeena, but she's too rigid in her idealism and her beliefs for me. Zeena leaves no room for ambiguity in anything.

Which is why she's steaming with frustration as we're trying to stay silent, us three girls and a horse, as we skim along the edges of this camp. The Faranji typically post sentries around their campsites, but there are so many soldiers dotting the perimeter of this one that I think we've stumbled upon a truly important caravan. It's practically its own caravanserai, with makeshift walls and guards and checkpoints.

"I don't like this," I say to Zeena. I'm watching as a few of the men in the camp collect food and goods from local villagers paying a tithe. This camp is just passing through, and yet they seem to have the right to collect an inordinate amount of produce and goods from the nearby farmers.

There's power, and then there's the willingness to abuse that power. Both are on display in this large campsite.

"Me neither," mutters Teni.

I'm already starting to learn Teni. She's direct. Confident, but never without reason. If she's concerned, she'll tell you. If she's sure of herself, she'll tell you that, too. So, she's not hedging. I respect this immensely. Right now, her confirmation of my fears, well . . . it brings the slight taste of bile to my throat.

"Look, I know there's too many guards," I start to say.

"Hush," says Zeena. She's trying to take charge, but I can hear the underlying tension in her voice. It is not merely Teni and me who are afraid.

I hear footfalls nearby. I grab both of them and pull us behind some nearby brush. Humdulillah that Red is such a short, stout horse, or she'd never be hidden. I cannot thank Teni or her clever horse aloud, though: The source of the footfalls has arrived and stands no more than a couple of arms' lengths away from us.

Another guard. He's walking at an easy but alert pace. Like this is his post, not like he's searching for the source of a sound that he's heard. I slow my breathing, counting long inhales and slow, steady exhales. It takes everything in my willpower to not hold my breath, to not panic. Holding your breath is another illusion, letting you think that you are being quiet and safe. But what it really means is that I'll exhale on a sigh and then we'll be caught.

Slow and steady rhythms. That's the way to hide in plain sight.

That's the way to stay alive. The guard might not have noticed us yet, but he's still alert. I pray that the horse makes no noise. She's a smart creature, Red, and I believe she knows when to hold her tongue.

After a minute, the guard continues his arc and walks away from our hiding spot. He'll pass back this way eventually. I'm not sure how long their rounds are. We can't have more than a few minutes, given the number of soldiers along this perimeter.

"We're going to get caught," I say.

"If we keep talking, yes," Zeena snaps.

Teni looks at us both for a moment. "No argument here. We're sitting ducks if we stay here chatting. If they don't spot us, they'll spot my horse soon, for sure." She returns to watching, not taking her eyes off the landscape above us. "This is some caravan we've stumbled upon."

"We need a plan," I say. I don't want her finishing her thought—I don't *want* to know how important this caravan is. I just want to get out and around and make it through to the other side. I've been telling myself this since we arrived at Akko a year ago: *Make it to the other side.* As though a new danger does not loom beyond it. As though once I am safe, I am safe for good. It's one of those lies I have to keep telling myself. "Those guards aren't just posted, they're prowling."

Zeena glares at me. She hates when I'm right. "What do you propose we do, then? Strip naked and do an authentic little Faranji jig through the campsite?"

"Careful, sister. If we make it out of this alive, I will put that on the permanent list of ideas."

Zeena snaps her mouth shut.

Teni snorts. She claps a hand over her mouth, silencing her barely contained laughter. After a moment she speaks. "I should not find it so funny. We are clearly going to die here. But you're such a merry party. I'd rather die here with you two bickering than with an army of serious men on the front."

"We are just as serious as the men." Zeena glowers.

Now it's my turn to bite back a laugh, though I do so better than Teni. We might be just as serious in our purpose, but we are not as serious in our means. And I, for one, think our means and our humor allow us to survive better than them. The laughter has kept me going far longer than the tears.

Footsteps approach again. We all quiet down, aware of how precarious our position is. If this new guard approaches from the wrong angle, we'll be spotted at once. Even Red goes still again. Bless that horse. Honestly, I'll buy her a dozen fresh carrots after this is over, no matter the cost.

I peer over the brush. I want to see my death if it's coming for me. But luckily, the new intruder in our midst is not a guard. He's armed, but he has an old, worn jupon that he's clearly inherited from someone else. And the sword at his hip is rusty, as though it's not one he's used much, or plans on using much. More citizen, then, than official soldier. He's holding a horse just behind him. He's handling her roughly, tugging her by the reins and dragging at her bit.

The horse whinnies and tosses her head. He just keeps pulling back, heedless of her mood and her wishes.

She's a jumpy, frightened thing. The man either does not notice this or does not care. "Come here, you worthless brute," he shouts. He pulls harder on the reins, clearly having no respect for the creature that is supposed to be in his care. "I've got to get you brushed down and fed and you've already run off once. Quit your whining."

He's a harsh, brutal man. Or perhaps he will be punished harshly and brutally for leaving this task unfinished. Either way the results are the same: He's cruel to the beast when he ought to be kind.

And as the horse moves into the moonlight, I can see that she's got little cuts in her hindquarters. Someone's used metal to spur her on, to make her go faster. It's an abominable practice.

In an instant, Zeena takes hold of my arm. "Don't you dare."

But I must dare. From the size and shape of her, the horse looks like an Asil, and an Asil has to run. They are not collectible, the way the Faranji see them. Not prizes of the East. Not exotic treasures to display. They are free beasts and they have spirit.

The Asils are horses that have been bred to run, to live comfortably with the Bedouin of the deserts and keep pace with camels. Hearty, beautiful, long-distance creatures. I can tell by the way she's pulling and shaking her head, she needs the wind in her hair as much as I need the air in my lungs.

But this poor horse looks as though she's being kept to impress—to do a ceremonial march. As though she's only occasionally ridden. A creature made to bear an armor-laden Faranji on her back, to show her owner's ruthless dominion over this land and then be sent back to a pen.

I wait, watching. The man is distracted by the horse. He is crouched low, pulling with all his might. His crouch is my advantage.

I move out from behind the brush.

Zeena—as usual—hisses at me. I flap my hands, gesturing for her and Teni to stay back. Red, I see, actually listens to me.

The man hears nothing. He is still crouched and pulling, the horse doing her best to resist. I'm able to come up from behind him. Unseen. Unfelt.

I clap my hands over his mouth and swing my arm around his

neck to get him into a choke hold. He doesn't even have a chance to let out a surprised squeak. I plug his nose and keep my arm crooked around his neck.

The horse startles at this, though, and the man loosens his grip on the reins in response to my attack. Luckily, Teni has ignored my earlier order. She is already there beside me, gently grabbing the reins of the skittish horse to keep her from bolting.

The man passes out within a minute; but it's a long, tense minute. It's a difficult hold to maintain and I don't recommend choking another if you can avoid it. I can still feel his pulse beneath my arm, but he's gone slack. I let go and double-check for his pulse. Still there, humdulillah. I might have thought he deserved death for mistreating the horse, but now is not the time to mete out my punishment to those I feel deserve it. Nor is it truly my place. I've seen enough of death.

"Wonderful," says Zeena as she approaches me and Teni. "Now either he will awaken and alert the whole campsite to our presence, or the other guard will return from his patrol and we will be found out then. All for this horse."

But I ignore Zeena. The horse is scared and I'm doing my best to calm her.

So, too, is Teni. She is singing a soft, lulling song. It's soothing to my ears and it's having a calming, nearly soporific effect on the horse. She stops pulling. Teni gives her reins some slack.

The horse senses that we are not here to fight her. That we are not here to master her. She stops resisting and watches us, cautious and skeptical.

I don't blame her.

"Don't you dare call her by her color," I say. I don't even look at Teni, but she knows I'm speaking to her.

"I wouldn't dream of it," says Teni.

"I'm taking her." I'm not sure who I'm telling this to.

"Are you mad?" says Zeena. "That horse is fit for a king. Or a queen."

"She's not my queen," I say. We all know of whom I speak, though I refuse to say her name here. "And she's certainly not our sultan."

Teni chuckles. "You have a point there."

"We don't need to draw any further attention to ourselves," Zeena snaps. "We need to get to Jerusalem. We need to get out of this campsite before anything else can go wrong. We do not need what looks like the most beautiful horse in Dar al-Tawhid in tow."

"We'll get there faster with two horses." I've got one hand outstretched to the Asil, but I won't force her to accept my touch. She's not backing away from me now, and I'm using my calmest tones. *I'm your friend. I'm here to help.*

"Not with two to feed, we won't. And we can't ride them the whole way—we have to save their strength." Zeena is positively obstinate about this. But, then again, when is she not? When you're obstinate about everything, it renders your opinions meaningless, to some degree.

And in any case, I don't care what Zeena says. I stroke the horse's nose. It's a lovely, soft thing. "Hello, sweetheart."

The horse snorts her approval.

The deepest recesses of my heart warm. "I won't leave you. I promise, habibti."

"We cannot steal a horse from this camp," insists Zeena.

"We ought not, but actually, we *can*," I say. "We've knocked the guard out and there is no one to stop us."

"*I* am here to stop you."

"No, I came along to stop *you* from getting yourself killed,"

I retort, digging my heels in. "And so did Omar. You cannot stop me from protecting this creature."

Zeena pinches the bridge of her nose. "Why must you meddle in everyone's business?"

"Did you really just ask that? You, who traveled from the land where the two rivers meet all the way to this place in order to fight off the Faranji invaders?" I say, incredulous. "Did you just ask why *I* must meddle in everyone's business?"

Zeena says nothing. She maintains a dignified silence.

For a moment, I turn my attention away from the Asil and look her dead in the eye. "Tell me, why did you decide we must go to the Sacred City?"

Zeena stamps her feet in frustration. "Because I must."

"And I must steal this horse, to protect her from a life in a cage. Surely you can understand that, sister," I say.

Zeena glowers but says nothing in response.

The horse nuzzles into my touch and Teni hands me the reins.

"I shall call you Fouzia," I tell the Asil. "For you are triumphant against all of your foes."

The horse snorts. It's just the sort of approval Zeena would give, though my sister's now marching back into the darkness beyond the camp and ignoring us all. I've got Fouzia in hand as I follow.

Eventually the soldiers here will discover the unconscious man. Eventually they will realize this horse is missing. We cannot break for camp, not for a long while now. Sleep is always a specter when you're on the road—a winking mirage, lulling you into a false sense of security and hope—but I've just made it an impossibility.

"Have you two always been like this?" asks Teni. "Or is this just the by-product of war?"

"Always," I say. "War has nothing to do with it."

Zeena says nothing. She continues on in her mood, silently moving ahead of us as though we don't exist. The world could be ending and Zeena would continue in her mood. That is her way. She's at least maintaining a pace that we can keep up with, even with the two horses.

My way is that I take advantage of her moody silence to steal a mistreated horse without further argument.

"I cannot imagine how they cut into her flesh like that," says Teni. She's looking at Fouzia's hindquarters.

She comes from horse people—we are so different, but that is immediately a thing I know we have in common. That she uses her whip only on the back quarters of her horse, and that those little flicks leave no lasting mark. That she probably lets the horses under her care choose their own pace, as they have a right to do.

"She's meant to roam free," I say.

"Indeed," she says.

I remember the strange reins on her horse. The way she had not tied Red down, not really; the horse could have pulled free of that boulder if she'd wished. The way Teni lets Red lead as we walk along. What the Faranji have always misunderstood about the great horse masters in this part of the world is that we do not actually master the horses. We build a relationship of trust and respect with the animal. Horses might grant one the ability to conquer the known world, but one ought never conquer a horse.

But then again, the Faranji are barbarians and brutes. They conquered a land and discarded its customs. They killed their fellow believers, the local Nasrani, and called it a mercy when they arrived on these shores a hundred years ago. Said they were sending the dead to heaven to let God decide who was a heretic and who was saved through their belief in the Lord Almighty. I can't expect them to respect a horse.

Fouzia whinnies. She's wary of humans and has learned to not trust anyone for long. Her instincts have been tampered with by mishandling. I lull her, soothe her. "There, girl. I am not here to hurt you."

This quiets her down, at least for now.

We'll have to double back and go the long way around. But it'll be worth it, I know it will be. To have saved a creature from a life of mistreatment and mishandling, even if she's not rideable anymore. I could set her free once I find a herd of wild horses in a nearby wadi. I could give her freedom if that's what she wishes.

She's deep brown, so brown she almost looks black. But as the moonlight shines on her coat, I see she's that rich color only the most beautiful horses can be. She's all one color—hooves and mane and tail and coat. Except for her face—down her nose is a cream stripe.

She's so lovely my heart sings. Knowing she's free of that horrible man and that horrible camp is a small consolation.

I have saved the horse. But I have possibly doomed us all.

The camp
of the
queen of Jerusalem

CHAPTER EIGHT

A Pox on the Phony King of England

RICHARD OF INFERNAL BLOOD!

A warrior king if there ever was one—and she meant no compliment by it. Richard, the king of England, had arrived. And like all the men before him, he meant to use Isabella as a pawn for her own birthright.

She, who was descended from the kings of Byzantium. She, who could claim kinship with the Holy Roman Emperor himself. And now to be pushed off her rightful throne by yet another man?

It was too much this time.

They had all gone too far. Her adviser and godfather, Balian of Ibelin. All the other men who were meant to be her councillors but really just used her as a gateway to power. A vessel for the throne. Even her mother, who had forced her to leave her first husband and marry another. And of course, Conrad, her new husband.

Her king. Sitting on *her* throne by right of *their* marriage.

The man who had saved Tyre, gifted the bride of Jerusalem as thanks for his service to the land.

Conrad, who was supposed to be a man of action. A handsome man. A charming man.

But by the time Isabella had been given him as a husband, Conrad was too old for her to see him as handsome, and he was too used to his own way to feel he needed to charm his new bride.

And now the king of England—Richard the Lionheart—had landed at Akko and decided that he would give Isabella's throne to Guy of Lusignan. Guy, who had failed to protect Isabella's sister during the siege at Akko. Guy, who didn't even hold power by proxy through anyone anymore.

Then again, he didn't have to. He was man.

Richard. Guy. Conrad. All felt they could decide Isabella's fate for her. As though she were still a child.

As though being a child had stopped them from marrying her off eight years ago, when she was a girl of eleven who hadn't even started her monthly cycles. As though being a child had stopped them from using her as a pawn in their games of power.

She was not yet twenty and had a second husband. She was no longer a child. She had not been one for a long while.

And this would not do.

They had come by sea to save Jerusalem from the infidels. A relief, at first. The Franks and the Normans already had Akko within their grasp. The dog Saladin had retreated then. He'd gone running when the true Christian men had shown up to fight. He'd been *routed*. Soon, she knew, he'd be crushed to the bone. Until there was nothing left of him and his men but rivers of blood to wade through and piles of flesh to burn.

And then the men had called a council without her. To decide her fate once more.

Isabella, queen of Jerusalem, was shut out from the discussion. Shut out of the halls of power. But if they were to hold power in her name, then by God, Isabella was going to have a seat in that room.

It was time to act.

58

"My lords and councillors—" she started as she walked into the tent occupied by her privy council. The men all started. Stared. Then they remembered their place and bowed.

Well, all but one. Conrad simply stared.

Isabella kept walking. She saw an empty seat beside her husband. She would have it. "My lord king," she said on a nod.

He had to acknowledge her now. "My lady queen, what brings you here?"

Isabella sat in her chair, then turned to Conrad. "I was told the privy council to the throne was to meet. We are here. The throne. To meet."

A few men shifted uncomfortably as they straightened. Conrad did not break eye contact for a long moment. But then he turned back to the council.

Ignoring her, the bastard.

"King Philip returns to France," said Balian. "In him we have lost a powerful ally to your cause, sire."

They were all politely ignoring Isabella, taking the king's cue.

Conrad smiled. A crooked smile that perhaps must have been something to look at when he was nearer to Isabella's age rather than twice it. "Yes, we have lost an ally. But we have gained a few rewards."

"My lord?" asked Balian. All eyes were on Conrad now.

"Philip returns, but he ensured our coffers were full."

"How much?" asked Isabella.

Only Conrad turned to her. "Half of what he acquired in the siege at Akko."

"So half of what he plundered from our own lands, you mean," said Isabella.

"Patience, wife," said Conrad. "He also gave me his prisoners."

Now the room went still. Even Isabella couldn't resist the impulse at first, but she found her voice quick enough. "Which prisoners?"

"The valuable ones. A free company that guarded the citadel. And many of those who call Saladin kin." Conrad's smile was gone, but his eyes glittered.

"Then we need not fold to Richard's demands," she remarked. Hope bloomed outward—starting in Isabella's chest and giving her whole body a feeling of lightness. Her first hope since she'd learned that her only ally, King Philip, was leaving.

They could reclaim her throne. For *her.*

"Careful, wife," said Conrad. "Richard leads the fight now, with Philip gone. We cannot act like petulant children. Holding a hasty bargain over our liege's head so that we might snatch at power that is not ours to command."

It was a censure. And the hope that had flowered and unfurled in her chest died in an instant, in a flash of rage so pure, Isabella felt sure that it was *she* who had infernal blood. It burned her every inner hope to the ground.

"You mean to give them to Richard," said Isabella. It was not a question.

"I hope not to," said Conrad. It sounded true enough. "I hope to hold on to the prisoners for as long as I might, until Richard sees reason. That I am the rightful king of this land."

"True," said Isabella, barely containing the rage in her voice. She knew Conrad would do what he liked with the prisoners, and that he would cave to Richard eventually. Probably without even securing the throne. *Her throne.* "For you are *my* husband."

But an unusual thing happened next, preventing any further censure from Conrad—a new man crashed into the room. The entire council turned and stared.

"Your Majesty—" The stranger was panting, huffing and puffing. He was not a noble, not a member of the council. He wore her livery, so he was part of her house by some means. But she did not recognize him. Nor could she expect to, not when she had kept so many safe within the walls of Tyre and Akko and the roads in between. They were on the move now, and it was hard to keep track of all the comings and goings of those who served her. He was a messenger, the poor bastard. He must have important news, then, to have entered so abruptly.

Despite his uncouth and unprecedented manner of entering the room, he waited for Isabella to acknowledge him.

Isabella, with one flick of the wrist, summoned him closer. The man scuttled forward, still bent over in a bow.

Her father's blood gave her the right to the throne, though he was an upstart compared to her mother's line. The blood in her own veins could be traced all the way back to Byzantium. But at least she'd been granted the ruthlessness of her father's Norman blood.

The men who had been in Father's employ, particularly the ones she had inherited, were even worse. Thieves and barbarians, the lot of them, as evidenced by Guy's paltry claim on the throne of Jerusalem. Descended from those who had sacked all of Byzantium. They were animals in their hearts. But they were useful animals, and as such, Isabella kept them close.

This man, this messenger, was no different. He was one of those sniveling, obsequious types. They all were. Peasants, the lot of them, as far as she was concerned. And aside from his livery, the rest of his clothes were shabby and old. As he bowed before her, his fear was evident. At least one man in this room feared her.

Good.

"Speak." Isabella, queen of Jerusalem, never had a quaver in her voice. That was for lesser men. And since she was neither lesser nor a man, *she* could never show weakness.

That had been her lovestruck sister's mistake from the start. *Half* sister. But still, a sister. More kin than that brother of hers had been. They were both dead now, in any case. And she was left to clean up the mess that her sister's widower had left behind. Guy had liked his taste of power and he would not give it up now.

The man before her stammered, unable to form coherent words. Then he finally managed to clear his throat. "Your Majesty," he said, bowing deeper.

"I am aware of my title," Isabella snapped. "What I am unaware of is, *why you are here?*"

The man knew enough to keep his eyes trained on Isabella's feet. But still, he froze.

"Loosen your tongue, or lose your tongue. The choice is yours."

"A horse has been stolen," the man said. He somehow bowed even lower, his spine seeming to break in two. "*Your* horse, my queen."

"*My* horse?" Isabella would admit, at least to herself, that she was startled by that news. Who would dare steal her horse?

"Yes," said the man. "The Asil. The one from your father's own stock."

"Has any other been taken?"

"No, Your Majesty."

He sounded relieved. He was more of a fool than she'd realized.

"And why," asked Isabella, her rage finally seeping into her voice, "was only *my* horse taken? Why were the greatest protections not afforded to *my* horse? Why were the other horses safe, but my horse, and mine alone, was left at risk?"

Isabella stood. The man shuffled backward, still bent over. "There were, my queen. Protections, I mean—"

"Obviously not, or the horse would not have been stolen." Isabella let the violence of her mood thread through her words.

The man quaked in his ill-fitting boots, and a chill hush fell over the council.

Isabella walked up to the messenger. "I will spare you, boy, if you can tell me anything of use. You have seconds."

"A green hood," replied the man. "The thief wore a mantle of green, like the black forest itself. And a hood to match."

Isabella nodded. "Go."

The man fled, not needing to be told twice.

She looked to her advisers, who were all staring, aghast at this interruption. Aghast at her for taking the lead. She did not care. She was beyond caring. "Put a reward on the man with the green hood. I want him brought before me *alive*. I would like to look such a man in the eye before he meets his maker. A hundred bezants—captured alive. No bandit gets away with such a slight. Am I understood?"

Balian looked mutinous. "My queen, that's a king's ransom! And the war—"

"Yes," she said, silencing his argument. "We must win the war. We must convince King Richard to open back up the gates of the Heavenly City for us, to take our side and not that of the usurper Guy. We must use Richard's forces to battle with these heathen invaders who follow the false sultan, and to stem the tide of upstarts who come from the Occident to take what is not theirs. We must use the prisoners we have at our disposal to make Richard see reason."

Isabella paused, waiting to see if any of her councillors would dare interrupt her.

They dared not.

But her husband, Conrad, did. He looked at Isabella and said, "But wars must also be won by belief, as you have seen. We came to these

63

shores a hundred years ago. We had no provisions and were in a hostile land. And yet, God Himself was on our side. Providence gave us victory after victory. We should have all starved to death. But instead, God placed me here, as king. And, as your king, it is my right to decide how we treat with Richard and with the prisoners bestowed in *our* care by Philip."

There were murmurs of agreement from the council. Isabella scanned the room for a loyal face. She saw but one—all the way in the back. He was a pretty foreigner from the outskirts of Byzantium. She had always supposed him to be a spy, but perhaps he could be of use.

Later. She would call upon him later.

For now—the rest of them were her husband's men, through and through. Even Balian, one of her oldest and most trusted councillors. Her godfather.

"But have your ransom, my queen," said Conrad, his eyes never leaving Isabella's. "And never say that I have not been a generous husband."

Isabella had been outmaneuvered. She dipped her head prettily in a nod of acquiescence. The next words brought bile to her throat but she said them nonetheless. "Thank you, my lord king."

Balian of Ibelin spoke up. "If I may, my queen."

"You may not," she said, turning to him, for she could tell from his tone that he meant to soothe her like she was a petulant toddler, rather than a queen in her own right. "Not today."

Balian nodded, a tacit acknowledgment.

Isabella stood. She was not done yet, but she had lost the battle today. "Bring me that thief. I want to put his head on a pike myself. Are we understood?"

Balian nodded. "Yes, my queen."

She knew they had to march toward Jerusalem. They had to be ready to take the city. Ready for when Richard approached. Ready to make sure that the crown stayed in *her* hands. In *her* bloodline. She knew that she had to keep those prisoners out of Richard's hands.

That was why Isabella had taken the keys to the holiest of holy churches as she'd fled Jerusalem all those months ago. The ones that opened the doors to the most sacred of churches.

Isabella had fled the Holy City when Saladin the usurper had come. He'd conquered his own people—taken land from the man who was supposed to be his own king—and then the monster had sought what was hers. He had come for Jerusalem. And he'd won. Taken the lands from God-fearing Christians.

But she would not allow him to keep it.

That was the vow Isabella had made when she'd fled Jerusalem. That God's kingdom here on Earth would be back in Christian hands.

In *her* hands.

And so she had taken the keys to the Holy Sepulchre. They were meant to be in the hands of the ancient line of Georgians who kept the church. But Isabella had retrieved them in the chaos. Her last bargaining chip. She had told no one. The men—Richard, Guy, her husband, Conrad—all believed the keys were in Saladin's possession. They thought the sultan denied Christian pilgrims the privilege of prayer at the holiest of tombs out of his own religious pride and fervor. They were waging war over those keys. Over that rite.

The keys were the only thing that Richard had cared about. The Holy City and the Holy Mother Church, where Christ had been crucified and resurrected, back in Christian hands. The pilgrims able to make their holy trek.

But Isabella had another plan for those keys.

Now she wanted to be within striking distance of the Holy

City—*her* Holy City—when the Franks, the Normans, the English, and all those of her blood swept back to victory. Came back to reclaim *her* inheritance. Before Richard could hand it over to yet another man.

Jerusalem would be Isabella's again.

She would not fail this time.

No man would stop her.

The desert foothills

CHAPTER NINE

The Long and Winding Road

IF YOU'VE NEVER EXPERIENCED THE SUN OVERHEAD ON a hot desert day, I think you ought to count your blessings. We've left the cooling river and the shade of the forest for the dirt and heat of the nearby foothills. We're even avoiding the farmland.

Normally I would break for the heat, move to the shade of a shrub and have a morsel of food. But Zeena wants to keep a breakneck pace, so convinced is she that we have an army of Faranji at our heels over a single horse. I feel grumpy and resentful about it; we should be preserving the horses' energy and our own. We shouldn't be marching in the blazing heat of midday.

I am trying to be grateful about this, about clean air and the wafting scent of salt from the sea. There was always something burning in Akko, always smoke billowing from somewhere. I'd forgotten that air could taste like this. Fresh. New.

But still.

We should be cooling off in the shade, or by the waters of a stream. If there were a stream, I would wash and pray. But I can't waste the water we have to drink on praying. Not when it's so hot and not when we travel. At least we're not riding the horses, though that's sparing them more than ourselves. But I'll take the consolations that I can get.

Teni just continues taking one stride after another, like walking beside us in this heat with her robes on is nothing in the world to her. She's unflappable, Teni. I'm learning this about her. She's the best of all traveling companions—all she needs is some food, sunshine, perhaps a little water, and her horse, and she'll be all right.

Red keeps apace of us and Fouzia ambles beside her. She is a proud horse, underneath all her mistrust, but she seems to understand we're her herd now. Or maybe she's just decided we're as good a set of companions as any, and far better than her last one. I can't really tell yet. But we're not forcing her to go along with us. I saw some wild horses a little farther back in the valley, and she did not run to join them. Though she fought her other captors, with us she's not trying to flee. And she's not picking fights with Red, who has accepted her with friendly grace. She's chosen us as much as we chose her. That's another cheering thought.

If it weren't for the dust and the heat, I'd be fine. But there's lots of dust and lots of heat and I'm damned miserable. The truth is, I'm used to being uncomfortable. It's not really the dust and it's not really the heat—it's the heavy silence between Zeena and me. The kind I know means something to her. I want to break it, make us merry again.

I know that she would not break this silence for the whole of the Kingdom of Jerusalem.

I begin to whistle a tune. I'm trying to find the words. Back at camp, Omar used to sing folk songs. Easygoing music. The kind you learned so young, you can't quite think of the words so much as remember them as you sing. And when he couldn't remember, he'd make up the lyrics and just tell an old folktale about a love long lost. A silly thing, at the time. After a few moments of whistling, I find the lyrics, or at least an approximation of them that I like well enough.

"Ah, once I knew a pretty girl. They say that I'm Majnun. But Leila was a pretty girl and this night, I'll see her by the moon—"

"I hate that song," Zeena barks. "And those aren't the words."

I never said it was a *good* folk song. But it's at least passable for our current circumstances. And it's gotten Zeena speaking to me, which is even better than I dared expect so soon.

"Do you?" I am positively guileless. She is annoyed because the song reminds her of Omar. He was always singing as we waited between battles or when he sat on watch. And Zeena, she still refuses to speak about him—they had been comrades, and when he ordered us out of Akko, she felt betrayed. I wonder when her anger will cool and we can share happy memories again. I wonder if she will ever forgive him. Few can carry such an enduring flame of rage in their hearts as Zeena can.

"Yes. It's ridiculous. Besides, you're singing it off-key." She huffs because she knows that when I act all innocent, I'm up to some kind of trick. But I'm not mad at her huffing.

The bickering is nice, honestly. It reminds me that she's my sister and that nothing changes our bond. Not war, not siege, and certainly not a hot, unholy day. Or the theft of a horse.

It is nice to know that war cannot compete with sisterhood.

"Ah, once I knew a pretty girl," I sing again.

This time Teni understands my purpose, and she joins in the singing. "They say that I'm majnoon."

If I am singing off-key, then I'm not sure what to call Teni's voice. It's in an entirely different musical tone, so perhaps it's not off-key so

70

much as simply musically off-kilter. We're musically incompatible. And yet we sing together anyway. There's a joy in that.

"But Leila was a pretty girl," I sing.

And together we create one of the worst harmonies on this earth as we sing, "And this night, I'll see her by the moon."

"Ya Allah," says Zeena. "You'll wake the dead."

"They'd be merrier than you," says Teni, snickering.

It's very difficult to not join in the laughter. But Zeena is frowning and she's looking angrier than before.

And that is when we come upon the girl.

Actually, what I should say is—that is when the girl comes upon us. She was traveling in our direction and she simply passed alongside us and kept walking down the path.

Perhaps it was my whistling. Or the bickering with Zeena. Or the singing. But I certainly didn't hear her coming. And from the shock on everyone else's faces, no one else did, either. Even the horses appear startled.

I do have to admit that the surprise *might* have stemmed from the fact that, aside from a necklace around her neck, this girl is totally nude.

Zeena averts her eyes immediately. Teni and I look at each other. Then back to the girl. Then at each other.

I mean . . . I can't say *nothing*. I cough. "Excuse me."

The girl stops and turns around, tilting her head but keeping her posture erect. "Yes?" Her accent in the common tongue is local, though not from Akko. Her tone is perfectly polite. Extremely even-keeled—almost as if she expects someone to pour a little tea soon so we can all have a nice chat in the diwan. "May I help you?"

Teni cocks her head, mimicking the girl's body language. "Are you all right?"

The girl nods. "Certainly," she says.

I feel now is the time to interject. "But you've got no clothes."

She looks down. Assesses her own situation. Then nods again. "Yes."

I'm not sure why I expected her to be surprised by her own nakedness. Perhaps that was my own fault. "Is that by choice?"

"The nakedness?" she asks.

"What else?" I retort.

"Did God not make us naked?" she asks.

That's not an answer.

"Aye," says Teni. "But the gods also gave us the hands and skills to create clothing."

The girl assesses Teni. "I have never met a sky-worshipper before. Salaam." Her tone is flat but lacking any judgment. She's peculiarly well-mannered, this naked girl.

She's in some kind of constant state of assessing, I notice. Always observing, but not in the way of a soldier. She's precise. Mathematical. Dispassionate. Even naked and covered in cuts and scrapes and mud and blisters. Her hair is still braided back as neatly as she may have been able to get. Her posture is still straight.

Pride. Ah, she's a girl with pride. I can admire that in anyone, truly I can. But in a naked girl, trudging down the road to Jerusalem, I think I more than admire such pride. She seems formidable. And I would certainly like to have a formidable girl on my side.

Zeena, by the way, is still staring at the sky, not acknowledging anyone or anything. I've never seen her in such a way before.

But I digress—I have to follow up with my initial instincts. I have to understand this girl's cool, detached character. "Do you have a problem with those of other faiths?"

"No. My apologies. I was merely observing." The girl is still dispassionate as ever.

"Observations," I say, "are dangerous in this time in and this place."

"Yes," she agrees. A hint of a smile plays at her lips, but she doesn't give in to the expression. "But I would be little without my observing. So I continue to observe. And I continue to march on. Hopeful that God shall eventually deliver me from my plight."

"That is optimistic," says Teni.

The girl catches sight of Zeena refusing to look at her. Her earlier near-smile cracks across her face. I say cracks because the ash on her face really does have to crack and break through the crust a bit in order to allow her face a full range of motion.

"Death is also deliverance," says the girl.

"You're quite young to be such a cynic," I say, and I regret it instantly.

Her eyes grow sharp, harsh. It's the first real expression I've seen on her, even more real than her smile. "And has this time and place made an idealist out of you?"

"No," I say. "But what has this time and place made of *you*?"

"A girl in need of clothing." She looks to Teni. "And you?"

Teni laughs. She has such a hearty laugh. It's hard to be sad or concerned when I hear it. "I am too practical to have ever been an idealist. But that's for every woman to decide herself."

The girl's expression shifts back to that dispassionate thoughtfulness. "True. A girl does not get much leeway to be idealistic, does she?"

Teni shakes her head in agreement. "No, indeed."

The girl looks away, her gaze now going skyward. "Guay de mi. What is God in such a time? When men kill in Their name and make pawns of us all?"

I have no answer for her. It's a question I've been asking myself too many times of late. But luckily, it seems to have been rhetorical.

The girl looks over at Zeena, pointing. "What's wrong with her?"

There are so many ways to answer the question, I surprise myself when I say, "Oh, she *is* an idealist. The oldest kind."

"I see." The girl sizes up Zeena quickly enough. Looks her up and down, quirks a brief smile, then goes back to her unyielding, observant expression.

Zeena's nostrils flare but she still says nothing and continues to train her eyes on the sky. I would have flinched under the power of such a stare. The girl makes it seem as though Zeena is the one who has been naked all along.

The girl turns to me. "Ijo de ken sos tu?"

I stare blankly back at her. It was a test of some kind, though I cannot make out the language. It is not a dialect of Arabic or Faranji. I look to Teni, but she merely shrugs.

The girl sighs, for a moment almost melancholy that I do not understand her. Then she takes in my person, our horses. She registers something, her eyes alight with a new keenness. "And you are?"

I feel as though I must be on my guard, but I'm not sure why. "I am of the Akko Guard. The free company. Or I was. We both were." I gesture to Zeena.

The girl does not accuse me of desertion. Instead she's looking at my robes so intensely, I want to squirm. "That is quite the mantle you sport."

I'm not exactly sure where she's going with this. But I can tell she means to identify me somehow. I can feel the sand slipping out from beneath my feet, and it's not a feeling I like all that well, despite how familiar I am with the sensation. "Yes."

"You know, there is a reward out right now. For a thief." She's

74

watching me very carefully now. "A hundred bezants to whoever finds them."

"Is there?" I ask, keeping my voice as casual as possible.

"Nobody knows for certain who they are. But they stole a prized horse from the queen of Jerusalem."

We've covered Fouzia with a mottled-looking blanket, but she's unmistakably conspicuous. That cream stripe down her nose is distinctive. She looks like a royal horse, if ever there was one.

I look back at the girl. "How fascinating. Did they say what kind of horse went missing? One of those Faranji warhorses, I would imagine."

The girl smirks. "No, an Asil. Gifted to the queen herself from the bloodline of one of the horses that belonged to her grandfather, al-Bardawil."

At this, Zeena and I both spit.

"I see," says the girl.

"Indeed," I say.

She pauses, as though she chooses her next words very carefully. "The thing about the reward is, they've got an eye to catching the thief alive. The queen wants to look her robber in the eye before she sends them to God."

"Good luck to them," I say.

"And the only defining feature," says the girl, "is that the thief has a hood of deepest green."

She looks at my mantle. I look back at her.

For a long while, we are all very, very still.

Zeena moves lightning fast. Suddenly she's eye to eye and nose to nose with the naked girl, and she's got a dagger to the girl's throat. "I would choose my next words very carefully, were I you."

There is a long, tense moment. I notice that the pendant hanging from the girl's necklace is silver metal in the shape of a hand, on the palm of which is a blue stone inlay in the shape of an eye.

"For the good Lord's sake," says the girl, but her voice has none of the urgency of the moment. She's more annoyed than scared, if her tone is anything to go by. "I don't want to betray you."

Zeena does not relent. "Then what do you want?"

"Clothes. A bath. Some food. If you provide even one of those, I will go with you as far as you are going. The ends of the earth if need be. To the Devil himself at this point."

"There's no need to go to the Devil," I say. "It's hell enough here."

At this, Zeena growls at me. She gets mad about blasphemy, to say the least. She still has her knife to the girl, but she's staring directly at me. "You had to go steal a horse from *the queen of Jerusalem.* Couldn't have stolen an ordinary horse, could you? Or not stolen a horse at all!"

"I'm not interested in an ordinary horse," I reply mildly. "And besides, this one was being mistreated." And then I turn my attention back to the naked girl with the great pride and the keen, observing eye. "And who are you, that we might trust you?"

"Who am I?" The girl snorts. "I am the daughter of Zachariah."

"And who is he to us?" I ask.

"I am Viva," she says, smiling like she's told herself her own private joke. "I come from a long line of the Abravanel family. We are found in many places. But we are no longer in Grenada. We tried our luck in Tripoli, but there was no luck in Tripoli, either."

And I know at once: She's Jewish, and her people hail from all the way across the sea—in Al-Andalus. That even if she herself did not see it, her parents and her people saw an unspeakable horror, the kind that makes my time in Akko seem like a visit to a delightful pleasure garden by the sea. Even I, all the way in the Sawad, had heard of it. The massacre at Grenada. The fall of Tripoli. It was all before my

76

time. Before Viva's time as well. But people's memories are long, and scars like that run deep.

This much I do know: It was a slaughter in Al-Andalus. And it has been an unending wave of violence here since the Faranji arrived, killing all those in their path on their way to claim Jerusalem as their own.

"Your people survived?" I ask. It feels almost impossible that despite all of this, she still walks through this earth. A wanderer with her head held high in the face of all that had been taken from her.

She laughs again, the laugh of one who has seen death and decided it did not frighten her. "Yes, they survived, and called me Viva to prove it. *Alive*, they called me. During Las Fadas, when they introduced me and blessed me, they said, 'You are alive.' And then they fled Tripoli, which was meant to be safe. But it was not safe, not since the invaders came. So I was left to live here in this place, wandering on my own, in a land invaded by the Faranji and then every warlord from the Roman Sea to the land of the Hindus."

I nod to Zeena. She removes the knife.

"I am Rahma al-Hud," I tell her. "Do you mind explaining why you're wandering the desert without any clothes?"

"I had a little place of my own, outside a village just north of here. But it wasn't far enough outside of the village, it seems."

"And why is that?" I ask.

"A few of the Nasrani villagers caught sight of me in my own home and decided I was a witch." Her voice is still laced with that calm, unflappable politesse, but her eyes challenge each of us in turn.

"And *are* you a witch?" I ask.

"No," she says. "Just an alchemist devoted to her studies. I was saying a prayer just as I finished an equation. And, well, you can imagine the rest."

I crack a smile. "You are quite lucky to be alive, then. How did you manage it?"

Viva smiles. "I managed to keep one last trick up my sleeve. A bit of my own invention—I've been trying to replicate the ancient recipes for Greek fire."

"But you don't *have* any sleeves," says Teni placidly.

The girl coughs and looks almost embarrassed for the first time. "My clothes were an unfortunate casualty in my escape plan. The good news is, I managed to get away before they could shear my hair."

"You burned your own clothes?" I ask.

"Not intentionally," she says.

And perhaps it's the primness in her tone, but I burst out laughing thinking about this girl, with her pride and her scientific mind, scaring a bunch of local villagers, saving her own life, and burning her clothes off in the process. Lucky for me, Viva begins to laugh, too. Soon we're all laughing—except for Zeena, who is still pointedly staring at the sky.

I pull out a knife from my boot and toss it Viva's way. "You may ride with us now."

She doesn't catch it, letting it fall to the ground. She gingerly picks it from the dirt, observing the weapon carefully, then dusts it off lightly against her hands. "You're going to arm me?"

"I'm certainly not going to clothe you and leave you without a weapon. Not here, in the land with too many names for God," I say.

Perhaps I am a fool to trust a stranger so readily, but I can tell she means us no harm. And while I might have gotten Zeena and myself in and out of many scrapes in our time, I've never been a bad judge of character.

"You are strange, Rahma al-Hud," says Viva. "But I will ride with you. And if you have any need of alchemy along the way, my knowledge is at your disposal."

"I accept," I say, and then gesture toward Teni and my sister. "I'm sure we all do."

Viva's smiling again, this time in the direction of Zeena. "And she is?"

I laugh. "That is my sister, Zeena. She is very proud and disagreeable. And that," I say, pointing, "is Teni. She's a mighty horsewoman and has the best sense of direction I've ever seen."

Viva does a nod that could also be taken for a slight bow. "A pleasure."

I move toward the pack I'd slung over Fouzia's back. I grab some clothing and toss them toward her. "I'm sorry, Viva, that we cannot provide you a proper bath on the road. When you're dressed, you can ride her."

Viva looks at the Asil—the horse that once belonged to the queen of Jerusalem but now keeps company with us. "Deal."

Between Akko and Jaffa

In the camp of the queen
of Jerusalem

CHAPTER TEN

The Boy with Kaleidoscope Eyes

"YOU REQUESTED MY PRESENCE, YOUR HIGHNESS?"

Isabella looked up from her weaving. The beautiful foreigner had entered her tent, dipping into a practiced bow. Her lady-in-waiting, Marie d'Anjou, sucked in a breath. *Understandable,* Isabella thought as she took in the sight of his elegant and handsome person. He had dark, glittering eyes dusted with thick lashes. His beard was close-cropped, his head covered, and he wore a black wool coat—high necked and flared outward from the waist, with buttons down the middle. His appearance was neat, like many military men. But it was all so . . . intentional. Isabella couldn't help but think of a wolf, dressed in another wolf's clothing.

"I did," she said.

He stood, a smile at the edges of his lips that did not touch his eyes. "I confess I was surprised. I was sent to your husband's court, but you and I have never been introduced."

"And we still have not," said Isabella. "Nor will we be."

An expression that Isabella could not name danced across his features. But the expression was gone again just as quickly. He said nothing further.

Isabella smiled. He was more than just a handsome face. "I have a task for you."

The young man dipped his head in acknowledgment but maintained his silence.

"But I have a question first," said Isabella.

He looked up.

"Are you a spy?" Isabella did not so much as blink as she said it.

To her surprise, the young man's smile finally reached his eyes. "We are all spies, Your Royal Highness, in one way or another. I think you are smart enough to ask a better question of me."

He was not patronizing as he said it—that much Isabella would give him credit for. "Where do your loyalties lie—to the prince who sent you to this court?"

"Aye," said the young man. "But what you wish to know is how loyal my prince is to your king. Or how loyal my prince is to Richard, le qour de lion."

"I know by your dress that you come from the edges of Byzantium, perhaps even just outside."

The young man bowed again, the tails of his coat fluttering as he did so. "Your Royal Highness is most wise."

"And I know, as my mother's people ruled the Eastern Empire, that not all those of Byzantium are loyal to the Frankish crown."

The young man put his hand over his heart. It was a most winning gesture. "As you say, there are those who have grown tired of foreign rule, who prefer the respect of the locals to the disdain of their fellow Christians. But I would not be so bold as to claim myself amongst them."

"And what of your prince?" Isabella took in his coat again. The very shape of it was enough to tell her that he came from the mountains that lay between the two seas. "Those at the foothills of the great mountains would hardly prefer retreat to a fair fight."

"If you have an offer for my prince, I am more than happy to hear what message the queen of Jerusalem would send to him."

Isabella stood and approached him. "I do have a message for your prince. But first I have one for you. Bring me the Green Hood, and I will double your reward. For both you and your prince."

"The Green Hood?" asked the young man. "Did not your husband say that he would put a reward on that thief's head?"

"My husband did, yes." Isabella thought for a moment. "What do you know of my husband?"

"That he is a canny prince, traveled from Italy, Your Highness."

"Speak plainly with me, and I will deal plainly with you."

He thought for a moment. "Then I would say this: Your mother forced you to annul your marriage with your beloved first husband. Perhaps your first husband was not a true husband, as they might have hoped, but he had been a true friend. And you were bartered to an old warrior with an eye for your throne."

"Good," said Isabella. "Bring me the Green Hood, and I'll know I can trust you. Bring the Green Hood—to me and no one else—and I will treat with your prince."

"And how can I know that when we treat with you, we will not be betrayed by your husband?"

"Because I mean to reclaim my throne, and my husband has not the stomach for it."

Because Isabella knew she had the keys to the Holy Sepulchre. Because Isabella had her ladies watching Conrad's men. Because Isabella would intercept any treaty that Conrad sent out, before it could get to Richard or Saladin.

The young man paused for a moment. Then he bowed. "Then I shall endeavor to find a way to be sent on an errand, for it seems I have a thief to catch."

The young man took his leave.

And hope bloomed again in the queen of Jerusalem's chest.

Just outside Haifa,
to the north

CHAPTER ELEVEN

A City by the Sea

HAIFA IS ONE OF THOSE COASTAL CITIES THAT GENTLY slope into the sea. It has that easy, sunny energy about it, like everything that needs to get done will be done in good enough time. I'm so used to the hushed tension of Akko, I'd forgotten that a city could feel this relaxed. Bustling with quiet energy. Calm, warm days under a merry sun. As though the sea breeze and a shady spot were all anyone needed in this life.

I'd forgotten about joy. And for a brief moment, just seeing the city ahead of us gives me a pang of longing for that which I hadn't even realized I'd been missing.

We're waiting atop a hill and looking down on the city.

"It's beautiful," I say.

"We have lakes," says Teni. "They are the clearest blue you will ever see. They freeze in the winter and are so sturdy you can travel across them like land. But nothing like this."

She stares out at the sea and I cannot help but agree with her. We have the Tigris and the Euphrates, but we, too, don't have a sea like this back home. So blue it glitters like lapis lazuli. So vast it looks as though it could be an ocean. It feels like the edge of the world, though I know that there is still more land beyond its shores.

"Looks like there's no caravanserai outside this city," says Teni. She's been our guide the whole way along—not only does she have a keen sense of the cardinal directions, she's a natural scout and makes a quick study of any landscape we encounter. We've been taking turns hunting for dinner with our bows.

"Shall we risk going inside?" I ask.

"I don't see why not," says Teni.

Zeena snorts. I roll my eyes at her, then look to Viva.

"Don't ask me," she says. "If you need a compound to set fire to a city, I'm your girl. But I'm the one who picked the wrong house to run alchemical experiments in and got labeled a witch, so . . . I don't like making decisions like this anymore."

"Fair enough." I look back down at the city. "I say we risk it."

I turn and look at the group, to see if Zeena is going to fight me.

And that's when a low voice says, "I wouldn't if I were you."

But it wasn't Zeena. Or Viva. Or Teni.

I whip back around.

"*You*," I say, for I have no other words.

And then he pulls back his hood, and I cannot help but gasp. "'Tis I. But I think you meant something else, didn't you, Rahma?"

"Majid." Outside of Akko, the night and the firelight had obscured his features. But I can see him clearly now. His face has lost the soft, round looks of boyhood and transformed into the harder, more angular planes of a man. But I'd know that dimpled smile anywhere. It's the smile of a fellow mischief maker. But looking at him now is making me light-headed and a little dizzy in a way I never was as a child. Then we were two little rogues against the world of adults. Now I'm not sure what we are. I'm trying to remember if he always had such thick eyelashes. And I'd never thought about how he'd be older and grow a beard one day. I'm in such a state of shock that I take a step forward.

Teni grabs my arm, stopping my movement. In her other hand is her sword, long and curved. Not as curved as the swords Zeena and I use, but there's still a slope to the blade. It's a beautiful weapon with a jade-colored handle and a bronze guard. "And who is this Majid?"

Majid laughs and, despite being two octaves deeper than his laugh in my memory, it's such a familiar sound that I'm almost startled. He does a flourishing little bow. "Majid Mirza, at your service."

That does nothing for Teni; she keeps her sword raised. Meanwhile it's all I can do to not reach out and dazedly touch his face. I'm not sure where my wits have gone, but they've fled at the sight of him.

Majid starts over. "We were kids together. Rahma and me. And Zeena. Where is your sister? Still wrestling snakes?"

Zeena steps forward, putting her body between Majid and Viva. "And what exactly are you doing here? Following us?"

"Zeena!" I say.

"Sister," says Zeena. "It is a fair question. You might have asked it, too, if you weren't so dazzled by his pretty face."

"He does have a very symmetrical face," says Viva from behind my sister. She speaks as though she's stating something obvious, like where the sun currently hangs in the sky. She tosses a wink at Zeena, who's moderately flustered by the expression.

"Why am I here?" Majid says. "I'm here to stop you from entering Haifa—there's a reward on your head."

"We know about that," says Zeena. "Viva told us."

Viva does a little wave from behind her.

Majid touches his hand to his heart and bows his head as though he has just been introduced properly to her. "Then you know that if you enter a city, they'll be on the lookout for a thief with a green hood."

"It's not as though we would have entered the city without a disguise." This, surprisingly enough, is from Zeena. Who—as you now know—would prefer to throw every piece of clothing I use for a disguise into the great Middle Sea rather than do another version of Please Good Sir I've Lost My Camel.

"And how, may I ask, did you plan to disguise the horse?" Majid is staring right at Fouzia.

"Dirt," I say. I'm not sure what compelled me. It's not a terrible idea, but I haven't seen Majid since I was ten years old and now the next word out of my mouth—aside from his name and my sister's name—is *dirt*. I feel foolish somehow, but I can't understand why.

Majid begins to laugh, and I'm not sure whether I'm pleased or whether I'd like for the entire mountain range to swallow me whole.

Luckily, Teni hasn't missed a beat. "That doesn't explain why you're here."

"I am here," says Majid, followed by a dramatic pause. Everyone—including Zeena—has leaned in to await the rest of his story. He's always been a charmer, Majid. "Because the queen of Jerusalem personally asked me to bring back the Green Hood so she might put the thief's head on a pike. And I remembered that I ran into a green hood, funnily enough, just outside the siege of Akko."

Teni steps closer, raising her weapon a fraction higher.

Majid holds up his arms. "I have no intention of bringing any of you to her."

"How can we know that?" Zeena hisses.

"How did you find us?" asks Teni before he can answer.

"You're joking, right?" He looks at each of us, eyebrow quirked. "All I had to do was start walking south and ask villagers along the way. They would tell me of an unusual band of foreigners traveling in one another's company. You're a conspicuous motley crew, you know."

"Why did you come?" I ask, finally finding my voice again.

"I came to warn you." Majid looks right at me, and maybe I'm imagining it, but his eyes seem to soften again. "And, perhaps, to see you again. It has been a long time, Rahma al-Hud."

My face heats even though I'm standing in a bit of shade. But now that I've found my tongue again, I can at least spot the truth. He's wearing a frock coat that does not belong to his people, who are from just east of my own homeland. Nor does the garment belong to the Faranji—it's from those who live at the border of the sultanate of Rum, the mountain dwellers. He's playing a role.

"You're spying, aren't you?" I say. "For your father."

"Always the clever one," he replies. "Yes. I am spying for my father."

After all, that was why Majid left my father's diwan all those years ago. His father had been sent packing, accused of espionage, and my father had declared banishment a mercy.

"I should have known you'd turn sneak," Zeena growls.

Majid seemingly takes no offense to this. "We cannot all run away and sign up for a war halfway across the world. Some of us have duties we cannot shirk."

Zeena bristles, but Viva, somehow already prescient of my sister's moods, interjects before my sister can throw a true fit. "What are we to do? We cannot enter the city, for someone will be looking for Rahma and the horse. We cannot stay here, for we need shelter and food and rest. And we cannot go with the pretty boy, for he is not trustworthy."

Majid laughs again, but he makes no move to go.

"Teni, lower your weapon," I say, and she complies. I have to think, and between Majid and the hostile tension of the group, I cannot. "We must go in disguise, as I said before."

Perhaps I rely so heavily on disguises so that no one can see me, so that I can make them look where they think they want to look. So that I can decide another's opinion of me, just by changing my robe and the way I cover my head.

90

"We only have one jupon and I am not doing Captured Soldier again," says Zeena, crossing her arms over her chest.

"But I'm the only one who *has* a jupon. There's no other explanation if only *one* of us has a jupon."

I keep mentioning the garment, but I'm not sure that I've told you what they actually are. Silly of me.

A jupon is armor for those without mail, or for underneath the mail. It's padded and quilted with rows of stitching. A difficult garment to make, but it's the first line of defense against a cut or a slice. It won't stop you from being skewered, of course, but it'll keep you from all of those thousands of cuts and gashes that go septic and cause men to lose limbs. It's a useful garment. Our people have them, too. But ours are different from the Faranji's. The same idea, but constructed in a different shape. They make long bars of the quilting; ours are in squares or diamond patterns.

"And we cannot pretend to have lost camels when we have two horses. That would simply be silly." At this point, I'm the insistent one.

"I'm the oldest. I'm in charge. I'll capture *you*." Zeena's argument is too fragmented to make sense to anyone but me. I know all she wants is to win, and refuses to show weakness.

"We've already been through this, Zeena. The jupon fits *me*," I say. It's a bit big on me, that much is true, but it would positively swallow Zeena. I look like I inherited the garment from an older and larger family member. She looks like she might get lost in the quilted fabric and never find her way out again.

"We cannot go disguised as Faranji," says Teni. "Not when it's so light out. They will know we are not one of them at once."

My heart sinks hearing it. Teni's not wrong, of course. The Faranji have invaded these shores for nearly one hundred years, but still they keep to themselves. A few have married with royalty and nobility of

91

Rum. But the rest . . . they are as fair and as separate as the day they arrived on these shores a hundred years ago. They do not mix, they do not intermingle, not even with their fellow Nasrani.

They disdain anyone who is not of themselves. And even then, they disdain those who are not immediately of their kin. Of anyone who is not of their faith, anyone who is not Nasrani, they are suspicious. The local Nasrani, though they are of the Faranji's faith, are *also* considered suspicious. Their loyalties are seen as split between their homeland and their god.

The problem, I'm suspecting, with being so ruthless and warlike is that you move through the world assuming everyone is as you are: a menace.

Though the local Nasrani were happy enough at first when the Faranji arrived—they were looking forward to rulers who shared their faith and their ideology—now they've grown weary of being treated as suspect and contaminated by those in charge. Too local for the foreign rulers and too Christian for the local rulers. They exist in a disgruntled, in-between state where no one is safe and no one is sure of them.

"Then what shall we be?" I ask. "We must rest. We must feed our horses. We must recover before heading farther south."

I suppose we could make camp outside the city walls. But within them seems safer than without. A nice caravanserai with food and drink means we wouldn't have to hunt or forage or make our own fire. I confess I grow weary of taking out my bow to kill small creatures for food along the road. And the idea of getting to spend the night in a city filled with calm, everyday energy is too much temptation to bear.

The wind blows a warm sea breeze our way and that pang of longing hits even harder than it did the first time.

"Look," I say to Viva and Teni. "I'm the one who got us into this mess. I stole the horse. If you would like to try your luck alone, I don't feel as though I can make the demand of you that we stick together."

"Are you turning us away?" asks Teni.

"No, of course not."

"Then I for one shall stay," she says.

"You have a strange sense of honor, Rahma al-Hud," says Viva. "But I told you I'd ride with you to the Devil himself. And I meant it. I stay."

I look at Majid.

"Oh, I'm not leaving," he says. "Not yet."

"Then I confess, I'm not sure what to do," I say. "Aside from disguises."

It is a long beat before Viva finally speaks. "I have an idea."

Then she looks to Majid. "And it requires you to prove you *are* here to help us."

CHAPTER TWELVE

My Friend Elias

I WATCH AS THEY DECIDE WHO THEY'RE LETTING through at the city's gate and who they're deciding to turn away.

My stomach churns as I think of the peace I felt looking at this city from atop the hills above. Those who already live in the city are allowed to pass through. Merchants are being questioned, but ultimately let through as well. And those seeking sanctuary—those who have fled the surrounding regions, attempting to escape the conflict that has raged all up and down this coastline—are being turned away based on their faith. Some of the Christians are let through. But only if they look right. Not if they look too poor or too hungry. Not if they look like they'll be a burden.

I have to tamp down the rage I feel for the gatekeeper as he makes his decisions.

Such is the nature of war: Men seek to make a name for themselves, and the rest who work the land to live are caught up in the great sweep of violence.

The Christians often fled to Rum, and the Jewish people to Tripoli. Or they would before Tripoli, too, was conquered by the invaders. But every city is under a new dominion every few months.

Sometimes the Muslim men are sent from the city. Sometimes the women and children flee before the invaders arrive.

There seems to be no such thing as home in a war.

Sometimes I wonder if even my memory of home is an illusion. An idea that can be taken away at a moment's notice.

You've got to pay attention, to every city and each and every time you try to enter. The rules are ever changing, ever undulating beneath our feet. Like a sand dune or the tide. Every time a city changes hands, who they *will admit* and *won't admit* shifts. Sometimes all the Christians must leave. Other times, all the Jewish people will flee for fear of the invaders. Given that the Faranji swept through the countryside eating people, no matter their faith, the first time they passed through, it's not an illogical reaction. Then the Muslims are kicked out, or sometimes they're killed. Sometimes they're enslaved and sold—depending on the mood of the ruler, truth be told.

For now, Haifa is in Faranji hands, and they're turning away anyone seeking sanctuary in their city. Such is the cost of their ease. They do not want to see that which would disturb *their* peace.

A group of knights jostles a family as they're turned away. They have on white robes with a big red cross on their chest that I can see even from here.

Templars.

I move to help the woman in the family, who's been kicked over by one of the knights—he is laughing now. But Majid grabs for my hand.

I stare at his hand for a long moment, then at him. He releases his hold.

"I know you would fight every battle if you could," he murmurs. "But let's get inside before you fight that one."

I blink at Majid. "How could you know if that's still true?"

He smiles. Not a grin, but a quiet, private expression. "Because you're still here. Following your sister to the ends of the earth rather than leaving her to fight all alone. You have always been thus."

I'm not sure what to say to that. So I turn and look at the people in front of us in line, avoiding Majid's gaze.

As we form part of the line to enter the city, I watch the others in front of us. One man has been turned away for claiming to be a merchant, but he has no way of paying the city's taxes on his goods. It's the one irrefutable law of commerce and we forgot it, wholesale.

The flaw in our plan becomes immediately apparent. "We cannot pretend to be merchants," I say.

"You say this now?" Zeena stares, wide-eyed. "We're already in line! It's too late."

She's right, of course. We're already penned into the line with two horses in tow. There's no way we're getting out of this line until we reach the very front. We're also already dressed as we are. We cannot back out now.

"But we are going to be taxed," I say. "On the goods we sell. And we have no goods. And we have no money to pay taxes."

Viva stares, a little bit shocked. "I might have forgotten that we needed goods to sell in order to be merchants."

"How can you forget that?" asks Zeena. She is, surprisingly, not hissing. She sounds more baffled than anything else. "That's only the most essential job of being a merchant. Goods and taxes. Those are the core of the job. Buy, sell, trade. Be taxed by the cities so they let you buy and sell and trade."

"I was just thinking in terms of the disguise." Viva shrugs, as though she misses essential details like this all the time. "It's not like any of you remembered that before we got in the line."

Zeena just stares at Viva, like she can't quite believe that someone who's so brilliant could also be so obtuse. Or perhaps she just likes to stare at Viva—my sister's been doing such odd things around her, it's hard to say. Viva, for her part, stares back at my sister.

"What shall we do?" asks Teni. There's real concern in her voice.

Her words seem to break whatever spell was cast over Viva's mind; she stops looking at my sister and says, "That is why our plan relies on Majid's charm."

He laughs. "Don't worry, then."

We all stare at him.

"That's not exactly possible," I say.

"Just wait." And, to underscore his point, he winks at me.

I turn abruptly from him. I watch more of the carts, horses, merchants, farmers, and city dwellers being waved through after they've paid their fees to get inside. Some seem to know the guard, calling out to him as they pass. Thank Allah for these little details and these small greetings, for I have learned the gatekeeper's name. I see that Majid has registered the name as well.

You can do a lot with just a name. Then again, Majid can do a lot with a mere wink.

"Hello, my friend!" Majid calls out to the guard at the gates, before he has time to ask us a question. Or assess the wares we do not have. Or closely assess our horses. "My dear Elias!"

He jolts back, a little startled. "Excuse me, sir, what is your business?"

"My heart! You forget me!" Majid puts his hand over his heart, as though he is at a true loss for this great misunderstanding. "After I fed you at my sister's wedding! Elias, how could you?"

The gatekeeper has the grace to look shamefaced. "My apologies, dear friend."

He's so distracted, he's not looking at me or at Zeena or Viva or Teni. He barely registers that we've got two horses with us, though he's been checking the beasts that every other envoy and caravan has come through with. People, I've found, are often so focused on themselves that if you give them reason to worry about themselves further, they'll forget that they're meant to pay attention to you. It's the best sleight of hand there is. Majid seems to know this, too.

Majid just needs to worry the gatekeeper so that he's more concerned about his own social standing and less about the fact that we're a group of merchants with no good to sell and no money to pay taxes.

And that only one of us has a beard.

Oh, and our two horses. One of which is very stolen.

"You call me friend, yet you forget me! I would even wager you have forgotten my name." Majid presses the hand over his heart and bows a little, feigning great sorrow.

It's a deeply endearing gesture and I'm not surprised that the gatekeeper is affected by it.

"I would never," the gatekeeper cries. He's got to defend his honor now.

I stare at him, one eyebrow raised. I hold his gaze and I wait.

"My dear friend," Elias says, clearly stalling. "My friend . . . Khalil!"

"Khalil!" Majid cries. "Ya Allah! Khalil!"

Now he turns to me. The move draws attention to me but the gatekeeper is still too nervous to really register that I'm anything other than a young man and potentially a distant kinsman of Majid's.

"He thinks my name is Khalil!" Majid cries again. "When I have always been Davit!"

I tsk. I don't look at the gatekeeper—to play my role, I don't have to. I just need to express my deepest disapproval.

"My sincerest apologies, Davit," Elias says. He must be a little suspicious now, with all of Majid's theatrics, for he adds, "Shall I expect to see you at mass on Sunday?"

"Mass on Sunday!" Majid's voice takes on a lyrical quality. He does not shout, but there is such a true lament in his voice as he practically slumps against me in despair. "When you know I go back to the Church of the Transfiguration in two days to pray for my sick mother! All the way back to Mount Tabor. This, he asks of me. After I fed him at my only sister's wedding!"

Zeena snorts. Her snorts are a marvelous thing—in one quick puff of sound, she can imply that Davit should not have fed Elias at his sister's wedding, to say the very least.

"Your mother?" he asks, looking truly worried now. "Umm Davit?"

Here Majid nods, as though the gatekeeper has at least remembered correctly that he is the eldest of all his fake siblings in this scenario. "I must pray for her body. And failing that, for her soul."

"My condolences," says Elias, handing over a scroll and some papers. "Please, take these."

Majid takes them from his hands. But before he can speak—

"Go in, go in," says the gatekeeper. He's relieved that he's gotten something right, and he wants to be rid of us before he can ruin the effect of his good guess. "And rest yourself and your horses before you must go out again in the world."

"Thank you, Elias." Majid claps his hand on the gatekeeper's shoulder. "Thank you."

As soon as we are out of earshot, I let out a sigh. Majid simply laughs.

"That seemed like more risk than was strictly necessary," says Zeena.

Majid shrugs. "You asked for my help."

"If you haven't noticed," Zeena says, "asking for help is different than taking more risks than are strictly necessary. That's how we end up with my sister stealing horses from the queen of Jerusalem."

I shush her. "Keep your voice down!"

"She's right," Majid says mildly. "We don't know who can hear us, and we don't want to draw any further attention to ourselves."

"Says the boy who pretended to be kin with the gatekeeper." Zeena has turned away from both of us, delivering her joke directly to Viva.

Viva smirks. Traitor.

Zeena, of course, beams at eliciting such a response.

"Now what?" asks Teni, as though Zeena and I have not been bickering the entire time we've been in her presence. Bless Teni for being as easygoing as they come.

"Now we must find a way to earn our bread and a roof over our heads for the evening," I reply. "Not to mention a stable."

"Have we no money?" asks Viva.

"A little," I say. "We'll be able to stable the horses at the caravanserai, but that's about it. It's not like they pay you when you're sent packing from a city under siege."

Viva groans. "Out of one fire and into another. I should have known. I might have clothes, but now I'm surrounded by bloodthirsty Nasrani."

"First of all," I say, pulling all of them into a deserted little alleyway, "no one is going to set you on fire. Not this time. And no one is going to discover who we really are. We are four merchants just returned home. We are good friends with the gatekeeper Elias. Majid goes to pray for his sick mother in two days' time at the Church of the Transfiguration. We are no one. We could blend into the darkness and the shadows if we so wished."

100

"That is a lie," says Zeena.

"And we must all believe it, if we are to make it out of this city alive," I say. "Come. We'll meet our fate regardless. Much better to face it head-on."

The others follow me out into the streets of Haifa. Our caravanserai awaits.

CHAPTER THIRTEEN

The Boys Are Back Inn Town

THEY SAY THE CARAVANSERAI WERE BUILT TO PROTECT against bandits along the roads that lead east, the ones bringing silk and spices and paper from as far as al-Seen. Anywhere merchants go, you'll find them, always a day's ride from one another. Always a place to trade and to gossip and to stable your horses and camels. The Faranji call them hostels or guesthouses, sometimes inns. Usually they're located just outside a town, with their own walls and their own fortifications. A city unto themselves.

The one inside Haifa is modest, perhaps because it is inside the city's walls—you can really never tell with a caravanserai. And for as much as people will tell you about caravanserais, and as much as each is like another, they are also governed by rules that belong only to themselves. They are at once methodical and haphazard.

It is a place, I think, the jinn like to make mischief.

In the lower courtyard Teni and I pass Red and Fouzia to the stable hands with a few bits of coin. It's almost the last of our funds and I'm sure the horses will eat better than we shall. I count our remaining coins and the situation looks grim. Of course, that's when a breeze blows by with the scent of bread baking in the oven. The kitchen is down here as well; as the smell of the hearth mingles with the scent of the stables, I'm reminded of the campfires shared around Akko. I think of Omar, laughing and telling a story about the girl he loves back home, in the cedar forests north of here, and how he'll marry her when he comes back from war. Her name is Zeyneb, and she's got eyes as black as the night. He says her hair must be just as dark, but he's never seen it.

It's a pretty tale. And at the end of a day of fighting and defending the city walls, we all needed food and a pretty tale.

Omar once asked if I'd ever been in love. I shrugged and told him about the boy I used to follow around constantly when we were children. I hadn't been in love with Majid back then. But he was the only boy I'd found tolerable and we decided we could marry one day. I thought if I were to marry anyone, I could marry a friend.

When I told Baba, I'd never seen someone throw a fit so fast.

It's not my fondest memory of Baba. About how Shia and Sunni are all believers, but we're different sorts, and so we cannot marry each other. Majid's people, by the by, are Shias. Dissenters to my father. Instead of telling Omar all of that, I just said the boy had beautiful eyes and long lashes, and I would race him through the village to beat him back home.

Omar had said that was no way for a girl to win a boy's heart. I told him I hadn't been *trying* to win his heart. I simply needed to best him more than I'd needed to best anyone in my whole life. I'd spent my childhood either trying to keep up with Majid or trailing after Zeena.

That hot, dry summer, Majid became my confidant and friend while his father was staying with us. We would play backgammon until we were yelled at by one khala or another. Majid would always win until I found out he was cheating with the way he was throwing the dice. I'd never been so mad at anyone before that day.

And then one day, his father left and Majid went away, and for a while Zeena wouldn't speak to me because she felt she had been abandoned for a mere boy when she was my sister.

We found out later that Majid's father had ties to the Hashashin— Order of Assassins. Stirring up trouble wherever they went, according to Baba.

I look over at Majid, but he's focused on the other patrons who are moving around the caravanserai, and I say nothing.

My boots crunch as we walk along through the courtyard to the stairs. On the second floor, the men inside do not look rougher than those I've encountered before. There are several empty rooms where we could stay and request food. It looks as though this caravanserai also has a little hammam in the back.

I'd murder someone for a bath, though I wouldn't dare risk it, disguised as we are right now. For a long moment, I think wistfully of hot steam and soft towels.

"You need a room?" asks a harried little man whose nasal voice snaps me back to the present. He's barely looking us over. He's overseeing so much that we four merchants are barely worth his notice.

I admit we are a shabby-looking and motley crew.

"No," I say. For we cannot afford a private room. And I begin to worry that we cannot even afford food for all of us. But then I think about Majid's charm with the gatekeeper; perhaps we don't need the last of our funds at all. Perhaps we can be clever again. "We're meeting someone."

"Suit yourself," he says, waving us away.

Zeena tugs on the sleeve of my robe. "What are you doing?"

"Improvising," I say.

"I was afraid she was going to say that," says Teni.

"Does she mean to intrude on someone else's private room?" Viva asks. I can't tell if she means that with judgment or admiration. Her tone is so unchanging.

"Probably," says a resigned Zeena.

I walk the whole length of the upper balcony overlooking the courtyard. The cooling night air is everything I need after a day of travel and bickering in the sun. I'm looking for someone who could welcome us, someone who would share our table. I can be just as charming as Majid when the situation calls for it.

And our situation calls for it. We cannot afford meals for all of us, much less a private room in which to sit and enjoy them.

I come to a door, which is cracked open. There's light and warmth spilling out of it. Perhaps this could be a room full of those who believe in community and hospitality, willing to help a few poor travelers along the road.

That hope is good enough for me. If the door is open, perhaps they're a merry party and they're more open to visitors. It's a gamble I'm willing to take.

I stride confidently into the room.

And I can see at once the horrible mistake I have made.

It's full of men. They're all Faranji and fair, and they all stare at me, frozen in the doorway. Where they had been loud and boisterous, they are now as silent as a tomb. I feel exactly how it must be to seek shelter in a cave, only to find that it has already been filled with a pride of lions. My heart stops for a moment as eight sets of gleaming, predatory eyes stare at me, waiting for an explanation.

I can see now why the rest of the patrons at this inn were giving this particular set of men a wide, wide berth. They've got giant red crosses on their tunics.

I can hear Teni behind me, though her voice is barely above a whisper. "Templars."

My God, have I picked the wrong room. They're the Templars from the gate who were harassing those who were seeking refuge in Haifa. Kicking that mother while she begged to be let into the city for safety.

Zeena groans, but she keeps her voice low as well when she says, "You had to pick the one place with Templars, didn't you?"

Majid whistles low; he knows we're in for it now.

For Templars are not just Faranji knights—they're the most powerful of them all. The bankers of this invasion, loaning the money that allows pilgrims to flood into all of their holy cities. They are righteous and filled with godly purpose. They hate foreigners and women in equal measure. They do not consider themselves strangers in a strange land; they are the owners of this space and *we* are the intruders, for we are those who dared to exist here before they ever arrived.

They came through and razed every crop to the ground. They slaughtered every animal on every farm—better to destroy all sources of food that they couldn't take with them than leave anything behind for the survivors. Those who they did not kill were enslaved and sold. The Templars have made a pretty profit off robbing and pillaging.

And now they make a profit off their pilgrims, off the lands they stole. Off the work of those they think are beneath them. Which is to say, in their minds, everyone.

To give them credit, they are also fearsome warriors. I saw them at Akko. They will never retreat from a battlefield. When their own standard falls, they'll join up with others. Even their rivals, the Hospitallers. They will fight until there are no flags left on the field.

Brutal, ruthless, and wealthy beyond measure.

What in God's name have I stumbled into?

Viva, for her part, laughs and slaps me across the back as though she's a fellow and a compatriot. "I can't tell yet if you've got the worst or the best of luck."

"I suppose you're about to find out," I say under my breath. I step farther into the room, walking right up to where the Templars sit and drink before Zeena can stop me or Teni can talk me out of it or Viva can make an observation about me going to my doom or Majid can whistle again.

These men are so comfortable, so secure in their position, that they leave their gold right on the table. They radiate wealth and privilege. And right now, unveiled annoyance at my presence. It is never good to be annoying to those so rich and powerful that they've never experienced a consequence a day in their life. You are but an ant to them, to be crushed under their weighty boots.

Still, I take a step closer.

Well, now that I'm closer, I can see the coins are silver, not gold. But currency is currency. And I no longer have just my own and my sister's mouths to feed. My new friends are counting on me, and I shall not let them down.

Besides, I've already walked into this room uninvited, and I shall not be outdone by Majid at the gate. I'll be lucky if we aren't all thrown out and don't have our horses taken as compensation for this ruckus.

But I've decided that I'm lucky.

The Templars are still staring, by the by.

I stumble as I reach the table in the center of the room. My hand goes to one of their coins. "Pardon me, sirs." I act as though I've had one tankard too many. "I seem to have lost my way."

But I don't steal the coin. Not yet. I lift my hand conspicuously. I leave each and every one of the coins behind. And I hold my palm face out, so they know that I've taken nothing.

The few sharper knights who were watching me relax visibly as I do so. A few of them believe I am as foolish as I look.

"I thought this was my room. I can see now." I pause. Hiccup. "I can see now I've made a terrible mistake."

That much is true, in any case.

"My apologies, my lords." It's probably not their actual title, but I don't think it matters. I speak Faranji well enough and I am showing I know enough of their customs to offer them respect. But I keep enough of an accent in my tone so that they realize that I perhaps could not have known better.

"Please." I hiccup strategically again. "Forgive my intrusion. I've embarrassed myself."

I look over my shoulder. Teni, Viva, and Zeena are all grimacing. Majid, however, is enjoying this. He's got that mischievous grin on his face that I have to struggle not to return.

"You're always embarrassing us," says Zeena. It's under her breath, but loud enough that a few Templars hear. They snicker.

"And my friends." I bow low, my hand practically scraping my boots. It takes all my pride to do it, but my folly got us into this and I must sacrifice my pride to get us out of it.

"How now, stranger!" says one of them. He seems friendly enough, but there's an edge to his voice; he's annoyed at having been interrupted. Templars are used to keeping to themselves. As an old and powerful organization, they are left to their own devices so much of the time. I've heard it goes from God to the Templars to their pope, in that order.

"How indeed," I say.

"You cannot intrude and then walk away, I think." The knight's posture is relaxed, but his eyes are alert and keen. He is not the biggest of them, but all eyes are watching him and all ears are listening to what he does. Their bodies, in one way or another, are all turned in his direction. A few of the other knights even directly mirror his body language. And I can tell, from this subtle deference that everyone else is paying him, that he is their leader. He has that kind of languid, easy control of the room that lets me know he's more ruthless than he wants anyone to imagine . . . until it's far too late.

No one else fills the silence. No one else would dare.

"You are right, my lord good sir, you are right," I say. I'm still bent over into a bow but I'm nodding. "I must make amends. I must buy you food. Drinks. Ale. What shall it be? No, no, no. I must. I insist."

Of course, none of these men need my assistance in buying food or drink. Their belongings are stashed around the room, dotting the otherwise plain chamber. Well-made armor. Good solid mail. Heavy broadswords. Not to mention the coin that's on the table, and probably some that's stashed in their travel bags and beneath their other worldly goods. They don't have gemstones or jewelry on—that would be impious, and the appearance of piety is central to a Templar's mystique.

There's one knight, younger than the rest, who looks miserable and practically run through. I catch sight of him as I am standing back up. His head is down like he's drunk more than anyone should in a lifetime. And beside him is a plate of food that's clearly made of the scraps of food from the rest of the crew. He looks like he's had a rough go of it—hungry and miserably drunk—and I wonder what he did to deserve such treatment.

I dare not ask. Not directly.

But his presence gives me an idea. I jerk my thumb in his direction. "He looks worse off than I am." And then I laugh one of those belly laughs that men are always letting out whenever they're in the presence of other men.

This does the trick. Even the sharp ones laugh alongside me.

I'm not sure why men are so charmed by the foolishness of their fellow man, but then again, who am I to question it when it has worked so well for me for so long?

"Sit," says the Templar leader. It's half invitation and half command—which is to say, my sitting is not optional. The others are already moving aside to make room. "And tell me how you came to came to be here, crashing our little party."

I bow, the way the Faranji bow, to show respect.

"I am with friends tonight." I flourish my arms in the direction of Zeena, Viva, and Teni. "I could not impose all of us on your hospitality."

"Then they may sit, too," says the head Templar, all magnanimity. "We are celebrating the addition of our new recruit."

He points in the direction of the miserable young man. No wonder he seems drunk beyond measure. They've made him suffer with indulgence, so that he might never do it again when he calls himself a Templar.

At least, that is my best guess. The games of perceived piety the Templars play have never made sense to me.

My companions all enter the room, looking as hesitant as I feel. But we've no other way forward. It was either this or starve for the night, or God knows what else these men might have in store for us if we refuse their hospitality.

I sit, and the others sit alongside my end of the table. Majid strides across the room and sits beside me.

We must drink with them. We must maintain the ruse of being men alongside them. As always, the only way out of the mess I have created is through.

On the bright side, at least we will have food and drink until we are discovered. We will not go hungry this night.

The man from the front of the caravanserai comes in. He scans the room and his eyes go sharp as he spots me, but he says nothing. He looks to the leader of the Templars. "May I bring you anything else?"

The Templar sneers. "Did we call for you?"

"I was worried about a disturbance." The man flickers his eyes toward me. It's a fair assumption, honestly.

"These are my friends," says the Templar. His tone is hard. Unyielding.

The man practically bends in two, just as I did earlier. "My apologies."

The lead Templar's face is coated in satisfaction; he takes great pleasure in the power he holds over others. The way they must bow and scrape to him in order to maintain their own safety. The expression turns my stomach.

The Templar orders more food and drink for us, as the rest nod in agreement. I do not object. Finally, the man comes close to me, bowing over. For a moment I think he is going to apologize again, but instead, he says in a voice so quiet I almost don't hear it, "And you?"

I laugh, hoping the sound doesn't come out strangled. "I shall have the same as the others. We all will."

The man dips further. "Very good." But he stays bowed, waiting for me.

I lean in close and whisper, "A bottle of your finest arak."

He bows lower for a moment and I know he's heard me above the din of the rest of the room. But he says nothing and exits.

My eyes catch Majid's. He's heard me ask well, but no other expression even flickers across his face.

We must cavort with these men if we have any chance to make it through the night alive and with all of our limbs and tongues intact.

I say a prayer, for it is to be a long night ahead.

CHAPTER FOURTEEN

Rahma, the Fox

THE LAUGHTER OF MEN IS DIFFICULT TO GET USED TO at first.

I can never tell if the laughter is a threat or not. It rumbles through your chest like a stampede of horses, low and jolting. In the animal world, to bare your teeth is not a sign of kinship; it is a sign of war. Even having been in the company of men for the last year, I'm still not quite used to it.

It reminds me of why Zeena learned to hunt snakes with her bare hands. It reminds me of the weight of the sword at my hip, the feel of the bow at my back, and the quiver of arrows I keep on the other side. The feel of the dagger in my left boot. My right-boot dagger, as well you know, is now up Viva's sleeve.

The laughter of men can turn to menace so quickly that even as I laugh alongside them, my own teeth are set on edge. I'm too tense to enjoy the meal before us.

The truth is I'm not sure how much longer I can spill my ale on others, or swap my drink with those of the men around me so that they look like they've not touched their grog while I've drunk mine down. We're all doing it. I know it's wearing on Zeena most of all.

Well, Teni's been drinking. But she doesn't seem too groggy from the stuff. She's definitely under-pacing the men. Viva is sniffing the ale like she's never smelled anything quite so disgusting. I'm half afraid at some point she's going to ask for wine and then we'll really be done for.

Majid seems at once both alert and at ease. A master spy if there ever was one.

And I—I have been pouring arak in all of their drinks. Slowly at first, but the more they've drunk and the less they can taste, the more that I've added.

I just hope that it's enough.

The men begin to pass out one by one. I cannot tell you how long this takes, for time is moving so slowly for me it is near torture. None of us can let our guard down. They laugh at their comrades as each of them loses consciousness.

Finally, there is only one man left. The man in charge. Of course it would be him.

As the last of his laughter dies out and the leader of this crew points a finger at me, I'm sure we're found out. He's finally spotted that we're not all men, that we're too mismatched to be local traders. That we haven't been drinking a drop and don't smell enough of sweat and ale. He's noticed that his drinks have been laced and that he's far more drunk than he should be.

For once, I thank God we've been unable to get a bath along the road—at least we reek of dust and the road and horses. It is an undeniably masculine smell, and I know it does more to confirm our disguise than anything. A scent can tip off a charade at once. It's so ingrained and so subtle, most would not pick up on why. They would simply know that there is something false.

In any case, I'm staring down the Templar's meaty finger. He opens his mouth. He says nothing at first.

I do not flinch. I watch. And I wait.

But I get a reprieve, for he drops his tankard and his face slams into the table. I pocket the remainder of the bottle of arak in my robes. Who knows when we might need this again.

"Thank the Great Tengri," says Teni. "I thought we were caught."

"We nearly were," says Viva. "If I had to slap one of these good-for-nothings on the back again, I was going to lose all feeling in my hand." As if to illustrate her point, she wipes her hand across her trouser leg.

Majid watches the gesture with laughter in his eyes.

"I think Zeena has already lost all her feelings," I say. It's not exactly on a laugh, but I must find humor, even in the darkest of situations. "She left them back in Akko."

"Oh no, she left them back in Amarah," says Majid.

For once I feel like I have an ally against my sister. I return Majid's grin.

Zeena is not amused. "Now what will we do with them?"

"Now," I say, "we rob them for everything they've got."

There is a long moment of silence as they all just stare at me.

"Have you begun to contemplate an existence, sister, where we do *not* rob everyone we encounter?" Zeena's expression is hard, her mouth a slash across her face and her eyebrows forming one furrowed line. "Or do you merely consider us thieves now?"

"Tell me, *sister*, how are we to get food?" I retort. "How are we to make it to Jerusalem? Or even, God willing, back home?"

Zeena doesn't look away but she does squirm ever so slightly in her seat. Viva scowls at me, for daring to criticize my sister in such a fashion.

"Truly, how would you feed five people and two horses?" I press on. "What honest means do we have? What labor would you say we are qualified to do?"

"We could fight," she says, holding fast to her dignity.

"Aye. Join up with the Faranji cause, would you? If they paid you enough?" I ask.

Zeena gets up abruptly from the table and does not answer me, stomping over to the corner farthest from me.

I look over to Teni and to Viva. "No one has to steal anything if they don't want to."

"Oh," says Viva, "I want to. These are djente de piron. And cruel ones at that."

Teni shrugs. "I'm not opposed. They have plenty to spare and we do not."

Majid watches me. "I'll help, but my cut will not be in the gold."

"And what will you have?" I ask.

"I'd like one of them as a prisoner, if you don't mind." He smiles a guileless smile. "I cannot return to the queen of Jerusalem empty-handed."

"You're immoral, the lot of you," says Zeena from the other side of the room. But she's suddenly got a smug smile on her face—like she might have lost the argument, but she's won on a technicality. "I'd love to know how you're going to accomplish such a feat. You've a room full of Templars. We're in the back corner and on the second floor. In a caravanserai full of people. We are five. They are eight. I wish you luck in your endeavor, *sister*."

The words *prove it* might as well be written across her face. But Zeena's always underestimating me. I look around at our makeshift crew.

Teni is watching, waiting. And there's a little bit of hope on her face, I can see it. She's only known me for a few days, but she believes I've got a plan, and she's ready to put her faith in it.

But her belief is unfounded. I've nothing to hang my hat on.

That's when I catch sight of Viva, her expression as detached and dispassionate as ever. Our time together has been brief, yet she has already established that she takes my sister's side in all things. But I know she is curious. I know she loves alchemy. And I think—I hope—that she might not be able to resist an interesting intellectual pursuit.

"How would you lift them?" I ask.

She blinks at me. "What?"

"I can see your mind. You're figuring it out. Solving the problem," I say.

"Perhaps," she hedges. She might be a great observer, but she does not seem too keen on being observed herself.

"You are among friends," I say. I mean it, too. Whatever she has seen and wherever she has been, here she is safe to show us the nature of how her mind works.

She must believe me, for she says, "If you can find rope and a small wheel, I think I know how to get them—and all of their worldly goods—out of here."

I look around the room. "Could a barrel work as a small wheel?"

Viva contemplates for a moment. "It's certainly worth experimenting."

And that's how we end up with four bound, unconscious knights dangling upside down by a rope that's been looped around a pair of barrels and hung out the second-story window.

Viva's on the ground floor, yelling up at us. "A little to the left!"

Teni and Majid and I are bearing the grunt of this work. As the tallest, we're in charge of the muscle.

Zeena is sitting in a corner laughing. "Yes, this is extremely inconspicuous."

"We are hiding in plain sight," I say to her.

She snorts, her disbelief evident. She doesn't make another comment.

The night air is cool. I've got the breeze of it from the open window. And while we all smell of stink and ale and the dirt of the road, I can still get that faint hint of the salt-sea air and the breeze running through the evergreen trees. I do my best to resist the urge to inhale, for that would be a strange sight right now, sighing with longing as I haul four large men out of a caravanserai window. My heart yearns to do it, though.

Down in the lane below, we've drawn an audience.

"Ten to one he shorts it," I hear a man saying.

"Are they taking bets?" grunts out Teni.

Before I can answer, I hear—"Seven to two, against."

Indeed, they *are* taking bets.

"I said *left*," shouts Viva from down below. In her frustration, her voice pitches upward.

The night air goes still. It feels like the only sound—despite the fact that we are in a bustling caravanserai and there are people down below taking bets as to whether we will drop these three Templars on their heads—is our huffed breathing and our footsteps against the dusty stone as we lower these enormous men away from the well-lit room and into a dark lane below.

The door swings open behind me. Teni and I both freeze. Majid nearly drops the rope.

I turn around.

It's the man from earlier—the one who must be managing this caravanserai. He looks around the room, at the ropes in our hands and the remaining four knights tied up and awaiting their fate through the window. One of them is snoring loudly.

You've got to have a strong disposition to run a caravanserai, particularly in these troubled times. So when he says "*Good God!*" I know he means it.

I don't blame him. I'd probably invoke God at this moment, too. But I'm more inclined to think Viva was right all along and we really have gone to the Devil.

"You've got to go," he says. "Take your friends with you."

"Sir—" I say.

"What's the holdup?" Viva shouts from outside.

"I'm taking sixteen to four now," says another voice. I believe it's the man who originally offered ten-to-one odds.

The manager of the caravanserai runs over to the window. He sees the ropes, takes in the dangling knights. The man crosses himself, then kisses his fingers, touches his head, aims for the sky. He's very thorough in his superstitions and blessings, this man. I suppose you'd have to be, when dealing with the sorts of people who come in and out of this inn all the time.

If there is one blessing, it's that we've loaded up all the knights with their own gear. So while we perhaps look reckless, we at least don't look like robbers. Even if that's exactly what we are.

"Sir," I start again.

"What," says the man, his voice low, "in the name of all that is holy *are you doing*?!"

Majid comes to the rescue with his affable charm. "Why, we're getting our friends down."

"You're *what*?" The caravanserai-keeper is so incredulous he looks like he's circled back around and is ready to believe *any* explanation.

"Aye," I say. "You don't think we'd leave and not take our friends with us, do you?"

"You make fast friends," he says, leaning farther out the window.

"Look," I say, taking a step toward him. But I've forgotten momentarily that I'm holding the rope. It slips from my hands, and the dangling Templars begin to take a quick drop toward the ground. The crowd below goes into a gambling fury.

It takes all of Teni's strength to right the men and stop them from crashing to the ground. We're all panting by the end, Majid included.

"Thank God you're strong," I say to Teni.

"Thank me, not the gods," huffs Teni. "The holy spirit of the sky is not the one holding all of these men."

The caravanserai-keeper is standing there, staring at us open-mouthed.

"If you help us, I'll make it worth your while." I take one of the whole silver pieces in my pocket—this time still keeping hold of the rope—and toss it to the man.

He catches the coin before it has a moment to fall and inspects it for a long moment. Then he looks up back at me. "Are you mad?"

"Just desperate, my friend," I say. And it's so much the absolute truth that even as an innkeeper, who deals with liars and vagrants and drunks all day, I can tell he believes me.

As the man considers the proposition, Teni and I finish lowering the first group of Templars to the ground. I peek my head out and watch as the crowd exchanges money in a flurry of activity.

"There's one more load, you degenerate lot," I call down. I give the gamblers a cheeky smile and they cheer.

"Double or nothing," a voice calls out from the crowd.

Viva is too delighted with her makeshift invention to worry

about it working a second time. "Spectacular! And with all of their mail on, too!"

I give Viva a little salute.

"Just make sure to keep the rope a little more to the left," she calls up. Then Viva's waving and tapping her fingers at nothing, doing some kind of calculation, using the air as though it were a bit of parchment or a piece of tablet to carve into.

I roll my eyes, but when I turn, I catch sight of Zeena in the corner watching Viva down below; she's smirking a little private smile to herself that I'm too puzzled to understand right now.

Teni and I haul the second group of tied-up men so that their ropes are wound around the barrels just as Viva showed us. The caravanserai-keeper must have come to a decision, for as soon as we have the ropes set up, he's behind Teni, helping her haul down the men.

With the three of us together, the work is quicker this round. It's not easy, but we're able to pull in unison. We get a few shouts from Viva about how we're still tracking to one side. Then too far to the other. Nothing seems to satisfy her. She's constantly checking, tinkering, telling us what to do next.

We've got them to about the height of a horse above the ground when one of the men groans.

We stop lowering them at once, holding our breath. Even the crowd below goes silent for a moment. Nobody wants to be anywhere nearby when a Templar wakes and finds himself hanging midair after being lowered out a second-story window.

But the knight does not rouse.

Viva motions for us to hurry along. "If he wakes, he wakes."

"That's easy enough for you to say," I call down in a huff.

"There's a crowd yelling down here," says Viva. "You lowering the men slower is not going to make a lick of difference."

Zeena just laughs in the corner. I glare at her.

It's the work of a moment and all the Templars—and all their worldly goods—are safely on the ground outside the caravanserai.

I can see from the window that more money passes hands across the crowd, and then they disperse, as though they had hardly been there at all.

"Come on," I say to no one in particular. "We should meet them outside."

Zeena, Teni, Majid, and the caravanserai-keeper all follow me out.

Once outside, however, the next problem becomes apparent at once: They are no less heavy than they were being lowered out of a window. Only now they're in the lane, and they need to be moved farther still.

"How are we going to get them home?" I stress the word *home* as I say it so that when four pairs of eyes turn to me, Teni, Zeena, and Viva all know that I mean *how are we going to keep them tied up and rob them* and the caravanserai-keeper can think I just mean *home*.

It's tricky business, keeping up all these pretenses.

I pull out another coin from the stash that I took off the Templars and offer it to the man. "Thank you for your help."

The caravanserai-keeper palms the silver. "Will that be all?"

"A barrow," I say. "And we need four of their horses."

The caravanserai-keeper doesn't question anything I say now. He's been paid good and well. Probably far more than the Templars would have given him, though they could easily afford it. And I haven't required him to bow and scrape at my feet, the way they have.

A boy from the stables comes out with the men's horses and a barrow, a large, flat conveyance with a wheel in the middle. Really, more of a cart. We tip the flat part of the wood down so that it touches the ground. Then we use the ropes and do our best to haul their armor-laden bodies up, up, up.

I'll be hungrier than when I started after all this hauling and lifting. I wipe the sweat from my brow.

Zeena is finally helping. She's lifting everything Viva attempts to pick up. I'm not sure if this is to annoy Viva or impress her, but I think Zeena is succeeding at both with equal measure.

Eventually, we've got the men on the barrow and one of the horses hitched to it. I toss one more coin to the boy. He looks at it with wonder as the silver gleams in the light. Then he pockets the coin and hurries back to the stables.

"You're overpaying everyone," comments Teni.

I ignore her. Considering what we've just done, we couldn't have paid those who helped enough. "Take the reins, Teni."

She does as I ask. We all follow her and the horse and cart, down the lane.

And that's how we end up winding through the streets of Haifa, trying to find a dark enough alley where we can rob our kidnapped Templars in peace.

CHAPTER FIFTEEN

The Gest of Rahma al-Hud

ROBBING EIGHT FULL-GROWN MEN WHO ARE TWICE our size is not as easy as it sounds, in case you were wondering.

We've got the men tied up and hidden. Well, one of them didn't fit in the corner of the alley; he's been tied up on the other side. And another Majid has loaded up on the wheelbarrow. *That* took some to-doing, I won't lie to you. But we've got all their silver and armor loaded up onto the horses. We left them their jupons with big red crosses on them. Zeena said that a Templar jupon is not worth the trouble it attracts. It's too specific. For once, I agreed with her.

We also leave them their boots, for though they would sell, I'm still not heartless enough to steal a man's shoes. Not even a Templar's.

"I'll take the horses to the stables by the gates," Majid says. "You can collect them on your way out of Haifa."

"They won't suspect you with him tied up?" I ask.

"The stables are just to the left of a bakery. They know me there. And I'll tell them that one of you will come for the horses."

"Are you sure the queen won't punish you for not bringing her the thief?"

Majid winks. "Don't worry about me. I'll land on my feet. You're not rid of me yet, Rahma al-Hud."

I manage to blink rapidly at him with absolutely no response. My kingdom for a witty response to Majid's winking. I hate that I've grown so tongue-tied around him.

And then he and the horses and the barrow are disappearing around the corner.

"Do you think we can trust him?" asks Teni.

I'm about to answer when I hear a noise at the other end of the alley.

Zeena sees where my attention has been drawn. "Leave it," she warns.

But I don't listen to her.

Truth be told, I rarely listen to Zeena. As the Nasranis would say, that's her cross to bear. And so I move toward the source of the sound. As I get closer, I see small shadows of movement.

When I get close enough, the movement and the noise stop all at once.

Whatever it was—whoever it was—they must have spotted me.

"Hello?" I ask, loud enough to be heard in this little corner, but not so loud that my crew on the other side can hear me.

No one answers. I know better than to call again. I look to the last source of the movement, and find two pairs of eyes peering out at me from the shadows. If the pale light from the moon hadn't been angled just so, I would have missed them entirely.

"Come out," I say. "I can see you."

It's two children. They look hungry. I'm no fool to think that the world hasn't hardened them as much as it's hardened the rest of us. But I will not treat them with such suspicion. "What are you doing here?"

"Looking for somewhere warm to stay," says one of them. Her accent is heavy, thick. She's not from Haifa.

125

"Where are you from?" I ask. I could guess from her accent, but it suddenly seems so important to know for sure.

"Akko," she says. "Originally."

"And what happened?" I ask.

"They took Baba," says the same one I've been speaking to. The other one, a boy perhaps around the age of four, doesn't say a word, just holds on to the elder. I cannot tell if they are kin by blood or kin by choice, but they're kin nonetheless. "And then Mama died. And then they said all the unbelievers must be sent from the city. So we were thrown out. Mama said that Jedati was here, in Haifa. But we cannot find her."

It's too specific to be a lie. But still, I have to be sure. "Where did you think you'd find Jedati?"

The girl leans in like she is telling me a great secret. "In the Latin quarter."

I startle. Not so rare for a Nasrani to marry a Muslim, but strange indeed for the invaders to mix with any of the locals. "The Latin quarter?"

The girl nods. "Yes. Before she married Baba, Mama was a Nasrani."

"And after?" I ask.

"Still a Christian, but they wouldn't have her at church anymore." The girl pauses for a moment. She looks at me and says, "It must be hard to worship without a masjid, do you not think?"

I'm not sure what to say to that question, so I settle on, "It must have been hard indeed."

The girl doesn't sniffle. I can tell she's holding on tight to her feelings, but she doesn't let it show. She's trying to be tougher, harder than she is. And this is what tugs at my heart more than any performance of woe ever could.

I know if I take her to the Latin quarter, we'll be putting ourselves in even more danger than is necessary. I also know that if I take her there, she'll lose the faith of her father's people. But I'm no good at theology. And as much as I believe in Allah and the Prophet, I know an orphan is to be cared for, no matter how they worship God.

I must give the girl her choice. "Do you want me to help you find Jedati? Or do you want to try your luck with us?"

"Who is *us*?" asks the girl, still holding fast to the younger child's hand.

Before I can speak, the others have joined me.

Teni looks at the girl. "And who is this?"

The girl sticks out her chin. "Farrah."

Teni bows her head slightly. "A pleasure, Farrah. I am Teni." She then points to me. "This is Rahma bint Ammar bin Ali that you have been speaking to. But we call her Rahma al-Hud."

"You do not," I say.

"We do now," replies Teni, grinning. "And this is her sister Zeena."

"Leave me well out of this," Zeena growls.

Viva steps forward and does a little bow. "And I am Viva al-Andalus. Adventuress of the known world and inventor of a trap that can carry eight men in the air."

Teni rolls her eyes. "Leave it to a poet to exaggerate."

"And a scientist," says Viva. She looks to the girl. "Are you looking for someone?"

"Jedati," she answers. "In the Latin quarter."

"This is not our purpose, Rahma," Zeena says.

"Perhaps," I reply. "But I gave the girl a choice. She can stay with us, or we can take her to Jedati."

Zeena snorts. "Why couldn't she find Jedati herself?"

"She's a *child*," I snap. "An orphan. Think of what the Prophet says and be still for once."

"Don't you *dare* remind me what the Prophet says." Zeena stabs her finger at me. "You who wouldn't listen to a cleric to save your life."

"I'll remind you as I see fit. I don't listen to stuffy men with their stuffy books. I know God, Zeena. And God wouldn't want us to leave this child in the road. It's not safe. She doesn't know where she's going, and she doesn't know whom to ask for help." I turn back to the girl and her brother. "What's it to be? Jedati or our lot?"

The girl considers this for a long moment. I respect her thoughtfulness.

"Jedati."

Her grandmother's house, it is.

CHAPTER SIXTEEN

The Green Hood

WE WALK THROUGH THE STREETS OF HAIFA AT NIGHT.
Everyone is tired. Everyone is grumpy.

But I want to make sure this little girl and her brother make it
to their grandmother's house. It almost sounds like a tale my own
grandmother would tell me, about a little girl trying to escape from
the jinn.

But I'm no jinn. And I know there are worse horrors that lurk on
the streets at night.

When we reach the Latin quarter, I look at the girl. "What was
your mother's name?"

"Baba called her Manoun," she says.

"And was she the oldest?" I ask.

The girl makes a look of tense concentration.

"Did she have a brother?" I ask.

"Yes," says the girl. "Mama said I have a khalu. Khalu Ibrahim."

I nod. It is an Arabic name and an Arabic convention. And this
girl's mother is from the Latin quarter. But I have no other leads.
"Then we shall look for Umm Ibrahim."

I am not in the mood to go knocking on doors all down the street at this hour of the night. But I know the quickest way to find the girl's grandmother.

"I need you to stay here," I say to her. She nods that she understands and pulls her little brother closer to her side.

"Stay back, all of you," I say to the rest of my companions.

"Where are you going?" asks Teni.

"The church," I say, pointing to the sacred steps ahead of me.

The church, blessedly, stays open at night. There is no one at the front. It's truly as silent as a tomb in there. I keep my steps light, for everything echoes against the wood and stone of a church. Around the back, behind the nave and beside a little private chapel, I spot an imposing-looking wooden door. Hopefully it leads to some kind of annex where the priest lives.

I knock. And wait.

And knock again.

Finally the door cracks open. "Who is it?"

I can only see an eye, but an eye is enough. "Father," I say in the Faranji tongue. "Is that you?"

"My child," says the priest. "Have you any idea the hour at which you call?"

"Aye," I say. "And I would not do so were it not a matter of urgency."

"Has someone need of their last sacrament?" he asks.

"No," I say. "But it is still of import."

"And what is that?" He sounds skeptical. "Do you come to confess?"

"No, Father, not at this hour. That I save for after mass," I say, though I've never confessed a day in my life and I don't plan on starting now. And I have no idea if confessing really is for mass or not. It's better for him to think we're on the same side, so to speak. I have a feeling he'll be resistant to my case otherwise. "I've found a child."

"A child?"

"She says her grandmother lives here, among the Latins. Says her uncle is Ibrahim. Which would make her grandmother Umm Ibrahim, whose daughter ran off with a Muslim."

"Infidel," says the priest.

"She's a child," I say. "Not yet seven."

It's a Muslim argument, I know. The age of reason is six or seven. The age where you decide you can understand your God and make a choice. But the priest understands: I'm offering this girl's soul to him. She's been Muslim in her childhood. But she's young enough to be taken in and taught the ways of the Nasrani. It's why Zeena is mad I'm here. But a life on the streets without kin seems worse to me than a life with a different kind of God. It's a price I'll pay to save a life.

"Bring her," he says.

"No," I say. "I've left her outside with my compatriots." I want him to know I'm not alone. And though he might feel he has God on his side, he doesn't have the power to take the girl from me. "I want to find her grandmother. Tell me which is her home. And do not lie to me, Father."

The implied threat must strike him, for he says, "Four houses down. Her door is orange."

"Thank you," I say, dropping a coin to the floor. He may pray to a God that he has decided is oh-so-different from my own, but money for parishioners is money for parishioners. I'm out of the church before I can find out if he's opened his door to take the money.

We find the house. Orange door, just as the man said. The rest of my traveling companions hang back with the girl and her brother. I knock, waiting yet again for an answer from inside.

"Who goes there?" asks a voice. It's gruff, old, and female. She's speaking the common tongue—Arabic. It's a relief to know she will understand the child.

"No one you would ever know," I say honestly.

"Then what brings you to darken my doorstep, soldier?"

She can see me well enough through the open latticework of wood at the top of her door to know that I am dangerous. Good. She's smart.

"I have something of yours," I say. "Two somethings."

"And what is that?"

"First, I must know," I say. "Are you Umm Ibrahim?"

"And why would I tell you my name if you don't tell me yours, stranger?"

"I've a child who says her mother is called Manoun, a Nasrani who married a Muslim. Says her mother was sent from home and they went to live in Akko."

"How do you know this?" asks the old woman on the other side of the door. Her voice is so strained, I know I have the right woman.

"The girl Farrah told me. And I asked the priest at the church where you live."

"And I suppose you want me to pay you for her?" The woman's disdain is evident.

"No," I say. "I've come to give her to you freely."

"I have no money," says the old woman. "I barely can feed myself. Take her back to her mother."

"Her mother is dead. Her father, too."

The door opens. The woman looks me right in the eyes. "You lie."

"See for yourself." I turn back toward the girl and her brother. "Come here, Farrah."

The girl comes to the door, holding her brother's hand. The woman takes one look at the children and she clutches her chest. That's how

I know that the girl must be the spitting image of one of her parents. There's no other way around it.

"I don't know how I'll feed them," says the woman. She's close to weeping, I can tell.

I've had enough heartache—not just for one night, but for one life. I fish out the bag of coins we stole from the knights. I pocket two coins but hand the rest of the bag over. "See to it you don't mismanage these. I'll know if you have."

I don't know if I actually will. But it's enough of a threat that the woman nods solemnly when the coins are passed into her hands. Perhaps she thinks I've got the jinn on my side.

I duck down to the girl. This next part is very important. "If you need me, you find me."

"How?" asks the girl.

"Ask for the Green Hood," I say, thinking of the reward on my head. It'll be news here soon enough, especially after those Templars that we've robbed awaken. "Can you remember that?"

The girl nods. "The Green Hood. Al-ghita akhdar."

"Good," I say.

The old woman is watching me; a curious expression crosses her face. "Who *are* you?"

And that's when a grin slips out, even though I meant to maintain my solemnity. "Why, haven't you heard? I'm Rahma al-Hud."

I give her a low, flourishing bow, and I disappear back into the darkness where my friends are waiting.

CHAPTER SEVENTEEN

The Nasrani

WE MAKE IT BACK TO THE ALLEY WHERE WE'VE STASHED the knights.

And unfortunately . . . the men are all gone. The odds that they have already gone to report that they were robbed, and by whom, are high. I can't tell if I'm feeling better or worse about having left them their shoes now.

Zeena was just recovering from her last fit—the one she had after I gave away the bulk of our money to the woman and her grandchildren—and now to say that she's furious would be an almost poetic level of understatement.

At least we still have the treasure we stole loaded up onto all those horses.

Unfortunately, we're about to find out if we're able to even reclaim those horses.

I told her as long as the goods were with those creatures, we could still sell the armor and weapons and continue on in our journey. As soon as we make it out of the city gates. It hadn't occurred to me that the Templars could be awake and away, that we'd have a tougher time escaping from this city than we had entering it.

"Not only have you been reckless with our traveling monies," she says, "but now we're wanted for how you got them. It's the worst of both worlds—to steal and then to give it away as though *we've* got nothing to pay for!"

"I honestly can't imagine how they escaped those knots," I muse, ignoring her.

"I told you to tie them up individually before tying them up together," says Viva. She seems—for reasons that are currently beyond me—to be trying to win Zeena over. And Zeena *is* won over. Every time. They have some little accord between them that I cannot make out. And I don't have time to understand right now, either.

"I did tie up one of them, but it was taking too long!" I say.

Teni simply shrugs. "We've got to get on the road. I'll go get the horses. Hopefully we can still retrieve them from the stable undetected. No one else would be able to handle the lot of them. And I'm the most believable as a horse dealer." She walks off before anyone can argue with her.

"I'm sorry," I say, turning back to Zeena.

She doesn't acknowledge me. Not even a sniff.

Viva seems to be holding in a laugh. Perhaps after you've trudged naked through the desert, giving away all the money that you risked life and limb and the ire of the Templars for—to a pair of orphans, no less—is quite amusing.

"They were children, Zeena," I say quietly.

"You're responsible to *me*," she retorts.

"I'm responsible to God, to myself, to Baba, and to you," I say. "In that order."

"Don't you dare bring God into this," hisses Zeena.

At least I've got her hissing at me again.

There's a noise at the other end of the alley, the faint sound of rustling against the ground. At first I think it's Teni, come back with the horses, though I cannot imagine how she would have been so quick about it. But when I look, there's no one at the opening of the lane. No Teni. No horses.

And then I hear a groan.

I look to Viva and Zeena. They've heard it, too. Viva's smirk has been wiped clean off her face and Zeena's eyes have gone wide.

They draw their daggers and I draw my bow and approach the other side of the lane.

There, still tied up, is the youngest knight. The one the men had been toasting, the one who had just joined the Templars. He's big and blond and dear God, he's still tied up and gagged.

He does still have his boots, though. So there is that.

"They left him," says Viva, in wonder. "The only one we tied up alone."

"I wonder if he remembers us," remarks Zeena. "He was so far gone by the time we met, I cannot imagine we are more than a hazy dream to him."

He looks right at us and starts thrashing. Whatever he's trying to say is muffled by the bit of fabric we've left in his mouth.

"I think he remembers us," I say.

"What should we do?" asks Viva. She's backed away, stepping behind Zeena.

"What do you mean what should we do?" says Zeena. She's puffed up a bit, though, and happy to be shielding Viva from this brute. "We leave him here. We have to. Or else he'll scream down the whole alley."

"I don't know," I say. I tilt my head, looking at him. Now that I can see him in the waxing dawn, he does have a kind face, especially for a Templar. Soft brown eyes and wavy golden hair. He's not quite angular like a man yet—his cheeks are still round and impish.

"Dear Lord in heaven above, we are *not* picking up any more strays. *Rahma al-Hud*—I forbid it." Zeena's trying to threaten me. But her words have the opposite effect. My name means something different today than it did even the day before.

Yesterday, Rahma al-Hud was a fighter from a big, loud family that held land in the Sawad, where the two rivers meet. She was not noble, but her father's name meant something to his community, and his father's before that. I know that this is what Zeena means to impress upon me.

But that was before I was the girl who followed my sister to the ends of the earth, just to keep her alive. Before I was the girl who had to steal from those with more, just to survive. Before I found two orphans who needed my help more than my sister did.

Just last night, Rahma al-Hud gave her name to a little girl who was lost and without family. She pretended to be Nasrani to help the little girl and her brother. She threatened the girl's grandmother. She stole money off a group of knights and then gave it away, for the care of a stranger. I was no longer merely the girl from where the two rivers meet.

I saved two orphans from the streets.

I robbed Templars in a caravanserai.

I stole a horse from the queen of Jerusalem.

Rahma al-Hud could be anyone now.

What a strange, fascinating thought.

I stash my bow and crouch down to where the boy is tied up. He's twice my size, but he can't be much older than me. More likely, he's a bit younger, if his cherubic cheeks are anything to go by. "If I remove your gag, will you scream?"

He stares at me for a long moment. He shakes his head.

"Of course he'll say that!" hisses Zeena.

He shakes his head again, wide-eyed and fearful.

Zeena and Viva move farther back from where I sit. I'm crouched close to him. I could pull down the gag easily. And I've still got an arrow in hand that I could use as a dagger in a pinch, though I don't particularly want to use it to threaten him.

"Let me tell you a story," I say to him. "Last night, we robbed you and your friends. We saw you as easy, drunken targets."

The boy strains against his bindings. He's clearly furious. Or perhaps he's just panicking from being constrained for so long. I don't think I'd take well to being tied up, either.

"We took your silver," I say. "And then your friends left you here."

He stops thrashing, his eyes suddenly full of anguish.

"And now we must decide what to do with you," I continue. "We could do what you expect. Leave you here to rot as your friends have. Or we could kill you, like heartless mercenaries."

He blinks at me.

"If you don't believe me," I say, "just look at the two behind me. They're furious enough with me already. They could take out all their ire on you."

The young knight looks over my shoulder. I'm sure that, for all their frustration, Zeena and Viva are nodding in agreement with this. Well, maybe just Viva. But Zeena's frustration is its own kind of tell.

"But we're not going to do that. We're going to try something else instead. Now, I am going to remove this gag, as a sign of good faith," I say. "And I'm hoping we can parley."

I reach down, slowly, and pull the gag out of his mouth.

He looks at me for a long moment. And I look back.

He spits the gag the rest of the way out of his mouth and says, "You have got to be the strangest thief I have ever met."

Behind me, Viva bursts out laughing.

CHAPTER EIGHTEEN

Stand by Me

ZEENA IMMEDIATELY STARTS TO PROTEST. "WE ARE not thieves—"

"Actually," I interrupt, "he is right. We are thieves. At this point, it's irrefutable."

"The worst thieves I've ever seen, too," the boy interjects, clearly not fearing for his life in any way whatsoever.

Viva goes cool and scientific. "How many thieves have you seen in your life?"

"That's not the point." He sits up a little, trying to make himself bigger and broader, despite the fact that his hands are tied behind his back. Viva's coolness, I think, gives him pause. The edge of his bravado deflates, but still he persists. "The point is, I'm a knight of the realm and—"

"You cannot be a knight of the realm," I say. "There *is* no realm. It's literally being divvied up and fought over. The borders are up for grabs."

"Then I am fighting to maintain the realm," he replies.

"You can't do that, either," Viva says. "If we were to maintain it, we'd have to go back to all those princes and qadis that were displaced a hundred years ago."

"That's not what I mean." He's quite frustrated now. But at least he's too distracted by the arguing to call for help.

"What are you a knight of, really?" I know the answer, but I want to make him say it.

"Honestly . . . I'm not a knight," he says.

"What?" we all say in unison.

"I'm just a chaplain. The Templars don't induct new members as knights. With them, you're either born a knight or you're not one at all. I wanted to be a knight, though."

"So you're a Knight Templar . . . but you're not a knight?" I ask. It's ridiculous to push this boy's buttons like this, but I can't help it. If I know anything about Templars, it's that they'll never surrender. Even if their whole company is dead on the battlefield, even if their flag has fallen, they'll keep on until the last man has been felled.

The boy shrugs.

"What are we to do with you?" asks Zeena.

"Let me join you."

We all stare for a moment, unable to comprehend what has just been uttered.

"You want to do *what*?" I ask.

"I want to join you," he repeats, quite patiently.

"But you're a knight," hisses Zeena.

"Chaplain," corrects Viva.

"Thank you," says the boy.

I wipe my hand across my face for a moment. "You do know that we are the opposite of whatever it was you just became a part of?"

"I do," he says.

I crouch down, close to him again. It's risky; his hands and feet are tied, but he could easily crack his skull into mine. Nevertheless, I have to understand him. I think he must be playing some hideous

140

trick on us, stalling us until his compatriots can return with reinforcements and have their revenge.

I look him dead in the eye. "What makes you think you want to
join us?"

"I saw you," he says.

"You were too drunk to see anything," I retort. "You should have
been too drunk to remember us at all." I tell myself this in order to calm
my nerves—I do not like being remembered or seen so thoroughly.

"I wasn't drinking," he says with a small shrug. "I was supposed
to be drinking. One last night of sin so that I might truly swear it all
off forever when I took my vows the next day. Today. I was meant to
take my vows today."

The admission nearly takes the wind out of me. But it makes me
realize he's been alert and attentive this entire time. From last night
all the way across through dawn. He's really seen it all.

"You were all drinking. You were drunk. You are all hypocrites and
you remember nothing." I'm commanding him to agree with me. I
know that he won't, but I do it anyway.

"I was doing as you were, spitting the drinks back out as I drank
them. Or swapping my tankard around. I touched nothing." There's
unmistakable pride in his voice.

"And now you want to join us?" I say incredulously. "After you
watched us get a bunch of knights drunk and rob them? What kind
of game are you playing at?"

"I saw you save those children. I heard you arguing about how
you gave the money away. I saw that you took a little girl of your own
faith and deposited her in the Latin quarter, that you would give up
one of your faithful to another God."

"God is God," I snap. "And a roof over your head means more
than how you pray. Especially for a young girl."

141

"Exactly," says the boy—the chaplain. "I want to join you. I want to be one of your company."

"For God's sake, *why*?" I ask.

"I joined the Templars because they're the fiercest order in these parts," he says.

Zeena snorts.

"They're the bravest," he continues. "Warriors for God. They never leave a battlefield. They never surrender." He pauses and looks at me pointedly.

"Indeed," I say. I cannot think what else to add, but he seems to need my acknowledgment.

"There are rules to being a Templar. Many of them. For one, no women. Not even meals with women in your family. Though I'm not sure they realized you were women last night."

"Alhamdulillah," I mutter with a smile, baiting him.

He doesn't seem bothered by the phrase, though. "And only so much meat and only so much ale and you sign over all your worldly goods to the order. Not that I, a chaplain, had many worldly goods to begin with."

"Will you please get on with it?" says Viva. She's no longer dispassionate. She's cross. Irritable. Ready to lunge at this boy, I think. "We understand. Chastity, poverty, a life of service. A life spent caring for others by murdering fields of unbelievers and heretics."

"But you saw them," he replies. "They don't care about any of those things. Taking pilgrims' money and getting them safely here sounds like a worthy goal, but they don't always pay attention to the vows of poverty. Or chastity. Or temperance with food and drink. They're just a bunch of men who take pleasure in gathering power and wielding it over those around them. And they've left me here,

I suppose, because I was dispensable. In the end, they're all out for themselves."

"I'm not sure if I should be impressed that you gathered all that so quickly, or disappointed that it took you joining the Templars to finally see it," I say. I'm watching him carefully now, looking for a tell. The sign of a lie, the half bit of truth he's leaving out.

I see nothing, though. Only an earnest, guileless face. He really believes what he's saying. Whether or not he's lying, well, that's another matter entirely. Those who lie to themselves are the most dangerous of all.

He's watching me, too. "I wanted to be a knight. I wanted to do good. And I think you're actually doing that."

"What's your name?" I ask.

"John," he says.

"Well, John," I say. "Welcome to our band of merry misfits."

"Are you *mad*?" shouts Zeena.

"Voices down, sister," I say lightly. "We don't want to wake the neighborhood."

Zeena is fuming but before she can say anything back, Teni has returned, Fouzia and Red in tow, along with three other horses from the Knights Templar.

"Who's this?" Teni asks, as if finding me speaking to a bound Templar is nothing unexpected.

"My sister has adopted another stray," Zeena growls.

Teni nods at him, hardly taking him in; her voice is shaking and she's out of breath. "Welcome aboard."

"But . . . this is not a ship," says John. He looks a little like he's been struck over the head when he catches sight of her. There's a dazed, dreamy look in his eye.

"Indeed," says Teni, still distracted and nervous. Then she turns to me, and there's a touch of panic in her usually steady voice. "We've got to get out, and quickly. That group of Templars we robbed were approaching the city guards at the gates and I think they saw me with their horses. They have to be right on my heels."

"I know another way out," John says.

We all turn to him for a moment. It's a big test of trust, to let him guide us out of this city. But right now, we've no other options.

Zeena stomps up to him and levels him with the most intimidating glare she can muster. "If you double-cross us, I will find the most creative of ways to kill you. Do you understand me?"

He nods. "I do."

So far Zeena's threatened everyone who's joined our little crew, so in a way it's nice that she's initiating John equally. "Then we've no choice. Lead the way."

We each mount a horse, and go dashing out of the alleyway as quickly as we can.

CHAPTER NINETEEN

I'm Good, I'm Gone

WE WIND OUR WAY THROUGH THE CITY AS IT SLOWLY starts to awaken. The real merchants with their carts are meandering around the lanes as the sun just touches the horizon. So far, John has been good to his word. We've barely been noticed by anyone, even in this early hour when everyone is noticeable.

"Just this way," John whispers.

The city is a maze, and, like all unfamiliar cities, dizzying with the ways the roads meander unexpectedly. We take two more rights, then a left.

"There's a small hole in the wall, just back here," John says. "They don't typically have a guard here this early in the morning."

Zeena is skeptical. "Why not?"

"They're usually changing over at this hour. We have to be quick about it."

The hole's got a tarp made of some kind of animal hide over it, but it's definitely a dent in the armor. I dismount my horse and the rest follow suit.

"Why wouldn't they fix this?" I ask.

John merely shrugs. "You have to know the city very well to know it's there."

"Someone who knows is always willing to tell," says Viva darkly.

We stare at her for a long moment. And then all heads turn to John. It's an awkward moment, to point out that he's betraying his fellow countrymen by showing us this vulnerability in the city's defenses.

"True enough," says John, taking the truth in stride with a bit of a smile. "Who's first?"

Zeena steps forward. "I'm the smallest. I'll go first and make sure the horses can fit through."

We all await with bated breath as she disappears behind the flap of animal hide. Then she returns, her face as stiff as stone.

"The way is blocked," she says.

John, to his credit, looks genuinely shocked. "That can't be."

"There's a large stone on the other side," Zeena replies.

John ducks underneath and is gone for a moment. Then he's back again, a startled look on his face. "She's right."

"Of course I'm right, I'm not a liar," hisses Zeena. She's staring at him like he's one, though.

John looks at us now, panic all over his features. "What are we to do now?"

"You're asking us?" says Teni. But she has none of Zeena's rage; she looks like she might start laughing.

"We can't climb the walls," he says, despondent. "You've horses."

"Aye," I say. "It looks like we'll have to go back the way we came in."

But before I can argue with Zeena—for she would surely try to argue with my plan—a city guard approaches us. We're cornered, backed into the wall. The guard is looking satisfied, like he's won some kind of prize.

"My, my, my. If it isn't the thieves that they've been looking for high and low," says the guard. "You'll fetch a good reward for me."

"If you've got another way out," I mutter to John, "now is the time to tell us."

But John is frozen. I'm not sure if he's overwhelmed that his plan went so off-kilter—a usual occurrence for me, honestly—or if he's realizing he's actually going to have to fight his way out of this. It's then that I see he has a gentle soul. He's no warrior.

"Right," I say. "Time for plan bab."

"I think we're well past plan bab," retorts Zeena. "I say we kill the Templar and then we deal with this guard."

John looks up, stricken.

"We're not going to kill him," I say.

"Honestly, it seems more like we're on plan thal," Viva says. "Or omega, if you prefer the Greek alphabet."

Teni snorts. I'm glad she finds us amusing. She takes laughing in the face of death to a kind of art, truly.

The guard, who has been holding his sword in our direction the entire time, has grown frustrated. He brandishes the blade in what he must think is an intimidating manner. "Enough. You're coming with me."

"Why should we?" I say.

He puffs out his chest. "Because I'm in charge."

"Don't be ridiculous," Zeena interjects. "There's five of us and one of you. Plus we've all the horses."

Then the guard looks over. I can watch him counting us in his mind. He registers Teni, who is a hair taller than he is, and then Red. His eyes dance across the group until he catches sight of Fouzia, then he whistles. "And you've the queen of Jerusalem's missing horse. This day just gets better and better. I shall fetch a mighty reward for capturing all of you."

He's made many errors. The first is assuming any of us will go quietly, or that he's got any authority over any of us. Perhaps it was John's Templar tunic that made the guard think we believe in his rule of law. The second mistake he's made is telling us what he's going to do before he does it.

But his biggest error is, of course, in reaching for the horse first.

Fouzia rears up with a piercing whinny and kicks the guard directly in the chest. As soon as he's on the ground, I pull her reins in and calm her.

I look over the guard. He's knocked out clean and cold. His chest still moves, so he must be breathing.

I stroke Fouzia's muzzle. "That's a good girl."

She snorts with no small amount of pleasure.

"There's a fool for you," says Teni.

"Aye," I agree. "And he's paid the price."

John is leaned over the man, feeling around his chest. "He's broken a rib, I think."

"Good for him," says Zeena.

"Does anyone have a bandage?" asks John. Not a warrior, then, but a healer. "A bit of cloth? I think I can bind him so he doesn't injure himself further."

Teni looks at John, really taking in the sight of him this time. "You have medical knowledge, do you?"

John blushes. "A bit."

"And how did you get that?" Zeena is suspiciously pointing her sword at him.

"I read Galen," he says, holding his hands up to remind Zeena that he's unarmed. "The great natural philosopher?"

Zeena glares in response.

Viva, meanwhile, is searching through a saddle pack on Red's back.

She pauses for a moment, looking startled at John's admission. But then she's back to work, digging through the pack. She pulls out a long strip of cloth and tosses it over to John. He seems to have decided that ignoring Zeena is his best course of action, and so he studiously wraps the man's chest so as to keep him from contorting himself in any one direction too far.

"Clever," I say, watching his handiwork. I also wonder where he's gotten such knowledge, for reading Galen is no small thing, but now is not the time. I look over at my sister. "Zeena, stow your weapons."

Zeena snorts. "He led us into a trap."

"He didn't know," I say.

"Says him," she growls.

"Enough," I say. "He's been spotted by a guard of the city riding with the thieves who stole from Templars and the queen of Jerusalem herself. They'll say he was in league with us if we leave him here. You know they will."

Zeena is waving her sword about in frustration. "I don't trust that he's not in league with *them*!"

Viva puts a hand on my sister's forearm until Zeena slowly lowers the weapon. The gesture is so tender and so intimate that I'm thrown off-kilter by how readily Zeena relents in such a moment. Perhaps it is Viva's dispassionate nature. And yet, nothing in Zeena's expression is lacking in passion or intensity. There is a new tether between them. That much I know.

Though I little understand it, I'm grateful that Viva has cooled the fight in Zeena. We cannot stand by arguing, or we'll be discovered again. I rifle through my bag, grab my jupon, and, throwing off my merchant's cloak, throw the jupon on haphazardly. I stuff my head into one of the knight's helmets that we stole last night.

"Ya Allah," cries Zeena. "Not that thing again!"

"I told you so," I say, and I cannot keep the smugness out of my voice.

Zeena crosses her arms over her chest. "Just because you happen to be using that jupon for whatever harebrained plan you've just thought of doesn't mean you were right to take it or even attack that knight in the first place."

"Her logic is sound," says Viva, still taking my sister's side in all things.

"Actually, that's exactly what it means," I say, making sure I can get the toggles tight and fixed across my chest. I cannot believe I have to argue now with two people instead of one. "And I am a creature of opportunity, not logic."

"This will never work," says Zeena.

"It doesn't need to work for long," I counter.

Once the toggles are in place—or enough of them are, anyway—I mount Fouzia. "All right. You're all my entourage. We're no longer merchants. Get on that horse, Teni, you're my squire. And Zeena and Viva are my two pages. And what was it you said you were, John? A chaplain? You're my chaplain. Now everyone hush, and if you don't speak Faranji, don't open your mouth. We're going back to the main gate."

The scare we just had with the guard means no one questions my plan. Even Zeena realizes to refuse to go along is tantamount to death at this point.

John is sullen. He's clearly upset that his way out didn't work.

"Buck up," says Teni cheerfully.

And for a moment he does, just from the sheer fact that she spoke directly to him.

We get going, but when we reach the main road, we find a checkpoint has been set up. It's manned by one of the Templars we robbed, and several of the guards of the citadel. If they remember any of us, we're doomed. And even if they don't remember us, we're still doomed. We've got John in tow and there's no way the knight wouldn't remember their newest recruit and chaplain.

"Damn it all," I say.

"This isn't good," says John.

"No kidding," says Teni.

"Let me guess," says Viva. "We now are going to pretend John has died of plague and carry his body out of here. You're the pallbearer. Zeena is a designated mourner. And Teni is his sister. I'm the other pallbearer."

"No." I sigh as we're funneled into a tighter space in the lane. If we don't move now, we'll be trapped by the other bodies waiting in line for the checkpoint. I look Viva dead in the eye. "Now we run for it."

"Wait."

All heads swivel to John.

"Do you have something you'd like to share?" I ask.

"There's another way," says John.

"Then why didn't you say so earlier?" Zeena hisses.

"Because I'd been hoping to never go that way again," he says.

"Into the lion's den?" asks Teni.

"Something like that." John sighs. He doesn't take his eyes off Teni. "Exactly like that."

Zeena's hand is twitching for her sword. Viva puts a hand on her shoulder, staying the motion. Damned if I know how she's working such soothing magic on my sister.

"And," he says, clearing his throat. He turns and looks me right in the eye, so I know he's not lying. "because we cannot take the horses that way."

"We must take the horses," Teni states flatly.

"Someone must stay behind, then," I say. "And take the horses out through the gate."

"The most likely to get through without being recognized should go," Viva remarks. "That leaves out Rahma."

The truth really does sting, my friends. I put my hand over my heart to convey the feeling to the rest of them. Viva laughs and Zeena ignores me. Teni just shakes her head.

"Not just that," says John, barreling ahead. "Whoever cannot handle closed spaces. If you cannot handle the dark and being confined, you must speak now."

Teni clears her throat. "I cannot."

We all look at her for a moment. It's a difficult thing to admit weaknesses to anyone. We all have them, but we all do our best to hide them. Or at least, I do. So the next thing I say, I know, must convey that I know she has been brave in telling us so, and that she has saved the mission in volunteering herself thus. "Then you must take the horses. It's dangerous work and we could not go on without you. Do you think you'll be able to make it through?"

"I'd rather risk it all in the fresh air with five horses by my side than in an enclosed space in the dark." Teni takes the reins and nods solemnly at us. Then she smiles, like it's going to be all right. "We will be as fast as takhi if we need to be."

It's difficult not to return her smile. I take off the helmet and stow it. Then I hand Fouzia's reins off to her. "May your gods be with you."

"And yours with you," replies Teni. She weaves into the crowd waiting by the south gate and eventually I lose sight of her in the rush of people.

I turn back to John and stretch out my hand with a sweeping invitation. "By all means, good sir chaplain—take us to our doom."

CHAPTER TWENTY

The Storm That Leaves No Trace

WE TURN DOWN A SMALL LANE. THEN ANOTHER. WE do our best to keep our heads down and keep moving. Without Teni amongst us, the mood is tense and less jovial. I didn't realize how quickly she had become our own ray of sunshine until she was gone.

Allah, I hope she makes it through. If anyone can seem unassuming, though, it's Teni and her horse. Red is the cleverest of all the horses. I pray Fouzia does not draw any undue attention and that the other horses follow Teni's and Red's lead.

We continue winding through the city until we come across a church.

"That's a Templar church," says Zeena, like it's an accusation.

"Now you see why I thought it best if we *didn't* try this way out of the city first," says John. He crosses his arms over his chest like he's finally scored a point with Zeena.

It's the wrong tactic to take, by the by, but I cannot fault him for it. There's something about Zeena that makes one feel you've got to prove yourself right. That you've got to tell her you told her so. It's not an admirable urge, but it's one I know well.

I start to move toward the front of the church when John grabs at my arm and pulls me back. "Not that way," he says cryptically.

We've no choice but to follow him. I hope my instincts are right, that we can trust him.

Around the side the masonry seems regular enough. But John takes us down another little alley. He walks straight up to a door that is so plain and unremarkable, I might not have noticed it was there at all had we not gone right for it.

"What is this?" I ask.

"The way the Templars move their gold," says John. "You must stay quiet. The walls will echo."

He says no more about it and the rest of us are left to decide if we follow him into the church or not. But I know I cannot show fear. I follow him through the door. Behind me is Viva. She's holding Zeena's hand and pulling her through. Whatever will befall us, it will befall us together.

The first chamber is dim but not dark. There are candles burning in sconces along the walls. Expensive candles made of beeswax leave a fragrant, sweet perfume in the otherwise dry air. The stones are big, heavy masonry, each bearing the small markings of a local mason. Crosses, triangles, stars. Little etchings in each piece. There are cubbyholes, some of them closed over, others open.

"It's a crypt," I whisper.

John nods. He then waves his hand, indicating we must keep going.

Deeper into the tomb we go, until the light really does go from dim to dark. John bends over. He pulls at something. A handle. And then . . . a hatch opens in the floor. And I see that there is a ladder.

Beneath the ladder is nothing—pitch black.

"Are you joking?" I ask.

John grins. "I told you. It will be dark and cramped. But it's the only way we'll all make it out. Unless you'd rather take your chances with the guards at the gate?"

None of us says anything for a moment. Not one of us wants to go back. It's bad enough that Teni is out there.

"We must take a light," says Zeena. It's as much an approval of his plan as any.

"We cannot," says John. "These tunnels are patrolled. Templars do not take kindly to anyone coming through and finding their gold."

"Then how are we to make it through?" Viva asks. "And out?"

"I was meant to be a chaplain, but I started by ferrying," he explains. "Through the tunnels, carrying all that gold and other worldly goods. I know these tunnels like the back of my hand."

"That's a large task to entrust to a novice," I remark.

John shrugs. "Nobody likes acting as a messenger or as an ox, ferrying things all day long. That's true whether you're a farmer or a merchant or a Templar."

I take a deep breath and say a small prayer. "Allahu Akbar. Into the belly of the beast."

And then I'm climbing down the ladder before I can think twice about it.

As soon as I'm down, I feel my heart kick up a notch. It takes everything in me to let go of the ladder and take a step away from it. I can hear the next person coming down and, as much as I want to hold on to the ladder like it is a lifeline, I know that I'll be kicked in the head if I stand in place.

With that one step I feel as though I'm drowning in an ocean of darkness.

A hand reaches out for mine. I take it.

"There you go, Rahma al-Hud," John says quietly. "You've made it to the tunnels of the Knights Templar. Not bad, huh?"

My heart will not calm. I fight to keep my breath long and steady, rather than the shallow, tight intakes that my body wants. "I'll feel more cunning once I've made it to the other side."

"Oof," says Viva. "Oh, thank you."

John must have grabbed her hand, too.

Next is Zeena. She simply hisses when she gets down. But that sound is cut short, I imagine, by Viva grabbing her hand.

I have no idea. I'm guessing at everything. It's all I can do to keep my body calm but stay alert at the same time.

John moves so that he's on the end and so that I'm now holding his hand, but also Viva's.

"One step at a time," he says. "And we must venture not to speak from here on out."

I'm surprised by how damp the air is. It's cool and a little dank down here. There's a musky smell of water and the stones that have been hollowed out beneath the ground.

I hear a shushing sound ahead. "What is that?"

"Water tanks," he whispers. "They collect rainwater and store it down here, too."

"How resourceful," I manage to get out. My heart goes flying like a hummingbird now. For everything that I fear in this cold and cramp and darkness, I didn't imagine that I could also potentially drown down here, too.

One step after another and somehow, I'm reminded of climbing down the walls of Akko. It's less brutal on my body, walking through this tunnel, but it's worse on my mind. I must tell myself to keep going. That now the only way out of this is through. But my body, by Allah, wants to freeze. Wants to stop. Wants to curl up until they find me in here. At least if they find me, they'll have a torch and a light.

But I take the next step, and the next. I hold fast to Viva's hand

and to John's. And still, I imagine that Viva holds fast to Zeena. I don't dare speak again, nor does anyone else.

We are the light crunch of our boots against the dusty stone floor. We are the sure and easy pace that John sets before us. We are my deep breaths and Viva's shallow ones and Zeena's occasional hisses of . . . I can't tell if they're of fear or frustration. I'm so used to being able to see her face that I didn't realize how much I was reading her expression and not her mere tone.

Eventually, I start to make out the edges of John before me. Perhaps my eyes have adjusted to the darkness, but I think it might mean that there is light ahead.

After a few more steps, I'm sure that there's light ahead when he grows clearer. John stops moving. I squeeze Viva's hand so she doesn't run into me, but I needn't have. Each of us is paying attention so closely that I think we have all noticed the light has grown from a faint hint to a real and glimmering presence.

John takes another step forward. We all step along with him. Then he swears under his breath, which, I won't lie, surprises me.

"What?" I whisper as quietly as I can.

"They're moving gold ahead of us." His tone is despondent.

Bad luck for us. "Is there only one exit?"

"No," he says. "There are three."

That gives me some hope.

But John squashes it immediately. "But they stand before the split in the tunnels that lead out. We cannot get to any of the exits from here."

"Can you lead them?" I ask.

"Are you out of your mind?" Zeena hisses.

I shush her. "John, can you lead them?"

"Yes," he says.

"Then tell me the shortest way out."

"Left, right, then right. And a final left. That last left is tricky to find. It looks like there are only two tunnels, but there's a third, all the way over. If you go to the middle one, that looks left, you'll double back and be done for."

"Good," I say. My courage has returned with the light, and I know what I must do to help everyone else out of this mess. "Get Viva and Zeena out. Take the safest route, the one they're least likely to be loading gold through, do you understand?"

"And what are you to do?" he asks.

I grin, though I feel dread in my heart. "I'm going to lead them on a merry chase."

CHAPTER TWENTY-ONE

Born to Run

I TAKE OFF LIKE A SHOT BEFORE ANYONE CAN ARGUE.

I'm hoping that I pull most of the notice, that all of the men will chase me and let everyone else get through in the confusion. I can't imagine why they wouldn't. I would certainly chase a madwoman running through my secret tunnels.

It's the least I can do, after getting everyone into the mess in the first place.

I never should have come to Haifa. I never should have hood-winked those knights from the tavern. Never should have stolen from them. Never should have given the goods away. Never should have befriended one of the knights—no, a chaplain—and let him guide us out of this city.

Never should have come to defend this part of the world from those infernal crusaders.

So I know that it's my job to take the heat for this. If I'm captured, then I'm captured. At least I kept Zeena from dying behind the walls of Akko. At least I've given her and Viva a chance to get out of these godforsaken tunnels.

My legacy. My claim to fame. Here races Rahma al-Hud, who

could only barely keep her sister alive, and did so by the skin of her teeth and at great personal cost to herself.

Not that anyone in this tunnel would afford me a tombstone, but it's the principle of the thing.

Ahead of me I can make out all of the men. They've got several torches and there's four of them, each taking one side of a coffer. Looks like they're carrying all the wealth of the sultanate of Rum, honestly, by the way they're lugging those chests.

I know I have but a moment. I run past them, creating my own kind of breeze with my movements. I look over my shoulder and I see this startles them. They don't drop their chests, but all eyes swivel toward me. At first their expressions carry alarm—surprise that I made it down here. But the faces quickly turn menacing.

"Hello, boys!" I cry out. My voice reverberates through the tunnels, echoing out like a beautiful taunt.

Hello, boys—

    Hello, boys

        —Hello

       Hello—

         Hello

  Boys

     —boys

       Boys—

I hear the sound of one chest dropping and I don't look behind me again. I pick up speed and I run like the Devil himself chases me.

"You stay behind," I hear a gruff voice call out to the others. "The rest of you follow me."

Then another coffer thumps onto the floor and footsteps echo behind me.

Most of the men are chasing me; I don't need to turn around to know it. My sense of hearing has been sharpened by the darkness. I can tell each footfall from the other. One is heavy and plodding. Another long and measured. And the final one, swift and smooth.

It's the final one I'm the most worried for. I'm quite sure I can outpace the other two. Ah, but the third. The third could catch me by.

Their advantage is knowing this underground labyrinth better than I ever could. My advantage is speed and a head start.

I try to keep track of the way that John gave me, for this is the only way I'll give the others a sporting chance. I pray that Viva and Zeena and John will be able to overpower the final guard. They at least have numbers on their side—plus Zeena's rage, which everyone manages to underestimate, particularly Faranji men.

God, the air is different down here. I'm heaving just to breathe. My lungs want to explode. Ah, there it is. The first split in the tunnels. What was it again? Left.

Left, right, then right. And a final left.

I plunge left. It's a bit darker in this tunnel, but I cannot let that slow me down. I cannot ease my stride. I run like God has given me wings beneath my feet.

"You there," calls out a new voice. It's the measured footsteps. His voice is as methodical as his gait, smooth and continuous. He's speaking Faranji at me. "Stop at once."

And then I remember, I'm dressed like a damned knight. I'd almost forgotten. The jupon. That source of great contention between Zeena and me.

I wonder if it's better or worse that my pursuers think of me as a Nasrani rather than as an infidel.

Of course they think I'm one of them. Well, not a Templar one of them. Perhaps the men chasing me think I'm a knight gone rogue.

I begin to sing the only Faranji song I know. It's an old tune I heard the men by the walls of Akko singing, about a girl with fair hair and lovely light eyes.

Men always sing about hair and eyes, no matter their language. It must be their great weakness in life, to go through the world only noticing a girl's hair and her eyes and never once thinking about the mind that such traits could conceal.

I try to sound off-key, and a little drunk.

There's the next turnoff. I go right.

This tunnel, mercifully, is a little less dank. I risk a look behind me and all the guards are still there, giving chase. Two of them have slowed, deciding that they are more put out than truly threatened.

I think my ploy is working.

Except, of course, there's the swiftest Templar. He quirks a smile and keeps on running. He's catching me up.

Now there's an incline to this tunnel. It's slight, but I can feel it. It's slowing me down. But it's slowing the men behind me, too; I can hear their footfalls grow heavier. Never a good sign, to run with heavy and flat feet.

But my momentary advantage in size is just momentary, for I'm to the next tunnel sooner than I realize.

Right, again. *Left, right, then right.* This is the final right.

I must use this gap to my advantage. I cannot turn around. I cannot tarry. I've built up just enough distance that, given that this next tunnel is sloping downward slightly, I have little time to take advantage of. I must get to the final set of tunnels before they can see that I know the way out.

I have to make them think I've gone the wrong way.

I'm running hard enough that I'm beyond out of breath. My legs are telling me they're done, that they cannot go any further. That if

I stop I will collapse and they will turn to jelly and I will be entirely done for. But I find a second strength I did not know I possessed.

I slow slightly, coming to a cavern chamber. The final turn. I see the first two tunnels immediately. And then, looking far to my left, I spot the third. It isn't obscured so much as hiding in plain sight.

I find two loose stones on the ground and throw them through the middle tunnel with all my might. Then I grab another pair and throw them a moment afterward. Then I creep toward the back tunnel, the one farthest to the left. I muffle my breathing with the jupon. I cannot make a noise. I have to slow my heart, my breathing, my lungs, my everything.

The rocks are still echoing down the middle tunnel when the Templars catch up. "Through there," calls out the Templar who had been closest.

His footsteps retreat. Then comes the next set of footfalls. These are the long ones, fast but a little heavy. I hear his panting breath as he calls out to the other, "Coming, coming."

And finally, I hear the slowest Templar. He's the most out of breath, his footfalls plodding and slow. I dare not look out, but I imagine that he's the most traditionally knightly. Big and long and muscled, but slow. Not built for a chase through tunnels underground. The Faranji have always had strength but rarely speed on their side.

As soon as he clears out, I begin to move through this final tunnel. I have no idea when the men will catch up with the rocks that I've thrown, or when the rocks will stop echoing. When they'll realize they're chasing a phantom.

I start to run again. My legs are slow. I try to keep my own gait from getting too heavy—I don't want them to hear me until they've discovered that their own chase is an illusion.

God, everything aches. Everything hurts. My lungs, my legs . . .

And to add further pain, the floor beneath me kicks up a bit. I know I should take comfort in this, that I'm headed up and out of these damned tunnels. But all I can think about is my legs. All I can hear is my own breath.

Ya Allah, of course, that's when I hear them in the tunnels. I don't know which of them cries out, for it's an echo—the beating of sound against wall until it's lost all markers of identity. "Damn! Not here!"

Not here

   Not here

      Not here

The sound ricochets and reverberates through the tunnels and I know I've got only moments before they're back in that central chamber and listening for my paces, listening for the sound of my footfalls to give me away again.

And then ahead of me—a door.

A door!

Tantalizingly close, but still nowhere near close enough for me to get through it in time, I fear. I keep running, though. I'd rather keep going and fail than quit before I even had a chance.

The footfalls of the Templars begin again.

I am racing.

The men are shouting.

The door is before me.

I have no time to stop. I've been going too fast.

And then a miracle happens: The door opens from the other side. I'm blinded by the light but I cannot stop. I'm going so fast that I'm practically in the air and over a boulder right by the door, and out of those tunnels as the door shuts behind me.

With nothing left, I crash down onto the ground hard. I would think I'd died, but the pain in my body is far too acute.

I hear the sound of feet scuffling. Of the door swinging shut. Of several grunts. Of a large mass moving. And then there are sighs of relief. But I see nothing and my face is down in the dirt.

I push my hands up, under my chest, and I lift myself just a little. Just enough to flop over onto my back and to not have my face pressed into desert sand and rock and ash. Just enough to not be eating the earth.

For a moment, I let the light of the aboveground world blind me. It takes several blinks to adjust to so much illumination.

Three faces are towering above me in an almost menacing way.

"Took you long enough," says Viva.

"We didn't think you'd make it," John remarks.

Teni's head pops over mine. So now there are four heads and five horses.

"You made it," I say, amazed and in a bit of a stupor.

"Aye," says Teni. "And so did you."

"By the skin of my teeth," I say. I look at John. "Thank you."

"For what?" he asks, a little astonished.

"You kept your word," I say simply. We trusted him with our lives and he got us out of the city, each of us in one piece somehow. I'm still not sure how Teni managed it, but I'll have to ask her later.

Zeena snorts. It's her way of showing concern. "We're not out of this yet."

"True enough," I say. And so I get up and look around me. They've shoved a boulder in front of the door I came through, so we don't have to worry about those men who were chasing me, not immediately at least. All around me are ridges and hills and desert brush. We're at the foothills of the mountains—Mount Carmel.

"The hermit caves," I say to John. The hermits who have gone to live in the mountain caves are infamous in these parts.

He nods. "We can take to the mountains if you want," he says. "Or we can try our luck in Al-Tira. The choice is yours."

I look to our little motley crew. We don't have long to decide, but we've made it through this together, and I think we ought to decide together. "What's it to be, then?"

Outside the
walls of Akko

In the tent of the
queen of Jerusalem

CHAPTER TWENTY-TWO

Shoot the Messenger

ISABELLA WANTED TO SCREAM.

Conrad had given away all of the prisoners. *All twenty-seven hundred of them.*

Simply because Richard had asked for them. And then he had fled to the safety of Tyre.

It was not too much to be believed of him, but it was too much to be borne.

Humphrey had never shown such disloyalty as a husband. Then again, Humphrey of Toron had been chosen as her first husband precisely because he had loyalty to Isabella and was not the sort of noble who threatened her brother-in-law Guy of Lusignan.

But her sister had died, and Guy was no longer allowed to sit on the throne of Jerusalem by proxy of his marriage.

That was when all those advisers—Balian and her mother and the Lord knew who else—decided that Isabella needed the kind of husband who *could* threaten Guy of Lusignan.

Her marriage had been annulled and she had been parceled off just like those damned prisoners. A bargaining chip given away with little thought to what it might cost to pay out so quickly.

Isabella hated them all in that moment. Her mother for separating her from her first husband. Balian for finding her such a domineering second one. And Conrad, for not having the stomach to stand up to Richard.

She would make sure there would be no peace for any of them until her throne was restored.

There would be no peace across this entire land if she could help it.

That was when the foreigner who Isabella had sent to hunt down the horse thief entered her tent.

"Did you find him?" she asked.

The spy shook his head. "Find? Yes. Capture? No, Your Highness."

Isabella had not thought she could grow even angrier, but she could and she did.

"I was prevented by this man," said the spy.

And that was when Isabella realized that he had another man—tied up and gagged—who he held by the collar.

"And who is this?" Isabella could barely keep the growl out of her voice.

"This is the man who kept me from getting my hands on the Green Hood," said the spy. His own tone was calm, but a sharp anger glittered in his eyes.

And that was when Isabella knew she had picked her envoy correctly. "Bring him here."

The spy pulled his prisoner up by the collar and deposited him in front of Isabella.

"Let him speak," she said, and he removed the gag.

"How did you come across the Green Hood?" asked Isabella, looking down her nose at the man before her.

"We were robbed," said the man. He was gasping and a little afraid. "I woke up and this man had me prisoner. And you—you look—" He was looking to the spy but Isabella did not let him finish.

"Did you see the Green Hood?" Isabella demanded.

"I saw one. With a green hood. He charmed us. Plied us with grog," said the man. His eyes darted between Isabella before him and the spy beside him.

"And what happened?" asked Isabella.

"I woke up. Tied to a cart," said the man.

He was useless. Just like all men were useless.

Isabella took out the stiletto knife she kept hidden in her chatelaine belt and held it to the man's throat. She'd gladly spill a man's blood on this day.

A cough sounded.

Isabella looked up.

"If I might, Your Royal Highness," said the spy. "Kill him if you see fit, but perhaps he might be of further use. From what I have gathered, the Green Hood is a master of disguise. We now, at least, have an eyewitness."

The spy waited a long moment, then bowed. "But if you feel you must kill him . . ."

Isabella sighed. It was sound logic. And he did make sure to understand that she was in charge of this man's life. "Spare him. Keep him in a hold somewhere. Make sure Conrad's remaining men cannot find him."

The spy bowed. "At your command, Your Highness."

And then the spy and his prisoner were gone, and Isabella was left alone to plot her revenge against Conrad.

She didn't have long to think, though.

One of her ladies-in-waiting, Marie, walked through the tent flap and curtsied. "Your Highness. I have news."

"Good news, I hope," said Isabella.

Marie smiled, all daggers. "The best."

Isabella leaned in and waited.

Marie pulled a scroll from the sleeves of her robes. "We intercepted your husband's messenger. He was on his way to treat with Saladin."

Ah, so Conrad thought to cut out Richard. That was his move, to play the docile vassal to Richard's face and to plot against his liege in secret. No small wonder that Conrad had made it as far as he had in this life. "Is this the message?"

Marie shook her head. "*That* died with the messenger. This is the initial treaty for peace that Conrad drew up with his advisers."

"And what has been done with the remains of the messenger?" asked Isabella.

"No one will find him where he rests," said Marie.

Isabella could hardly believe her luck. The messenger disposed of and the treaty in her hands? She could write her own history, on her own terms.

She took the scroll from Marie. "Who knows of this?"

"Just myself, Your Majesty. And one of your guards, who helped dispose of the body."

"Good," said Isabella. "You will speak of this to no one. Reward the guard with gold. Give him a better position and remind him of what he stands to lose should he speak of this to anyone."

Marie nodded and backed out of the tent.

Isabella examined the scroll in her hand, Conrad's seal perfectly securing the document. She would have to do the work herself. She could trust no scribe with this matter. But she would scrape off a layer of the vellum and remake this treaty in her own image.

The queen of Jerusalem would reign in truth. And no man could stop her this time.

Meanwhile, inside
the walls of Akko . . .

In Richard of England's
Tower of Victory

CHAPTER TWENTY-THREE

The Lionheart

IT IS NOT SEEMLY FOR KINGS TO MAKE WAR UPON EACH other.

That's what the message had said. It was a lecture on kingship. The insolence of the words had made his blood boil.

But still, he had sent word back. He'd *had* to; there was no other way forward. The kings must parley. But Saladin refused to parley, king to king. He instead sent messages via messengers and lectured on the nature of kingship.

As though he knew anything of being a true king.

And now Richard paced the length of the room. He was impatient to hear back from his enemy, Saladin. Conrad had relented and handed over his most valuable prisoners to Richard, giving up his leverage in this war to keep all the monies that Philip had given him. It was as much as Richard expected of the man who already had two living wives and had made himself king by a hasty third marriage to a young princess. Though, Richard supposed, she was a young queen now.

So, Richard had sent word to the sultan to discuss the terms of exchanging prisoners. The Christians now held Akko. They had dominion again over what had once belonged to the false king. But nothing had come back yet.

He'd already sent word that they should meet, of course. That was when Saladin had responded with his patronizing message.

Richard stopped pacing. He stood in the turret that they'd captured—himself, Philip, and Leopold. It was a tall, imposing structure in the city. He could see all the way across the Mediterranean, from whence he'd come. He could see to Jerusalem, to where he wanted to charge forward.

But Richard was waiting. Waiting to hear back about the exchange of prisoners, the ransom of his men. Not all his men—some of the captured soldiers belonged to Philip, others to Leopold. But good fighting men were worth their weight in gold, as far as Richard was concerned.

He stopped looking out over the expansion before him and resumed pacing back and forth in the small room. This had to be a trick. A trap. Cunning Saladin, out to outfox him.

Richard would not be outfoxed. He would strike before his enemy had a chance to even consider double-crossing him.

The problem was, of course, that protocols had to be followed. You would speak with your opponent; you would exchange your prisoners. That way, the nobles would not all be lost in a single battle. That way, your fighting men and your loyal men could be returned to you. That way, your men knew that if they were captured in good faith, they would be returned to safe harbor.

But of course, Saladin refused to parley. Refused to talk, king to king or man to man.

Instead, he stayed in his camp and hid while Richard took the initiative. While Richard bore the brunt of the decision-making. While Richard had to keep the peace between the French forces and the emperor's men, and the Normans who he commanded.

He was playing into Saladin's hand by waiting. Let the enemy eat itself, like an ouroboros, rather than fight the enemy directly.

Richard was tired of waiting, tired of the protocols. He felt like a caged lion, pacing around in his little room in a tower, waiting for his enemy to deign to respond to him.

Richard was king of all England and leader of this Crusade for the Lord Almighty. He was accustomed to wait for no man. He answered only to God himself.

He knew that Saladin was cunning and clever and had a stronghold in these parts. He knew that his enemy held some of Richard's most trusted men. And Richard knew that if he did not wait, did not follow the order of precedence after a battle, that his men might not charge forward again.

They would call him rash. Hotspur. Unguarded.

Unkingly.

No, this would not do.

What kind of king would sacrifice his own men just to settle a petty vengeance with his opponent?

It is not seemly for kings to make war upon each other. How that phrase taunted him.

But damned if Richard didn't want to take action. And damned if he did not want to make war upon Saladin. For he wanted to best Saladin on the field of battle, like true kings. And to parley, face-to-face, as true kings ought.

What kind of king would let his own men wallow while he awaited a trap?

Leopold of Austria had promised the queen of Jerusalem to help free Akko, and he had done so. Now he was already back in his ship and on his way home to safety.

An opportunist if ever there was one.

Richard had no time for opportunists. Leopold had wanted to be on equal footing with Richard, king of England, and with Philip of Alsace. It was unconscionable impertinence. While sorry to lose those extra fighting men, Richard had been glad to see the back of him.

Richard was a true believer and he would tolerate true believers only. He knew that he would lose men in this endeavor. He also knew that he did not want Jerusalem to fall out of Christian hands again. He was here to save the soul of a city. God's Heavenly Kingdom, here on Earth.

He wanted the Holy Land open to all Christian pilgrims. He wanted the Church of the Holy Sepulchre—the site where Christ had been crucified and the site of Christ's empty tomb, the site of *the resurrection*—open to Christian pilgrims again. He wanted the Holy Land open to himself, and himself alone.

Richard, the savior of Christendom.

And yet there he sat, waiting for the messenger from the sultan of the Ayyubids. Waiting for a messenger to deign to give him a response on how many of his prisoners would be traded for how many of Saladin's.

This interminable waiting.

Like playing a game of chess.

Richard did not like chess.

A knock sounded at the door of the turret.

"Enter," said Richard.

"My lord." It was Bertram of Verdun, one of Richard's loyal followers. A good Norman and a good Christian.

"Speak," said Richard.

"I see that the crown weighs heavily today," Bertram replied.

"Aye," said Richard. "But what news have you?"

"The sultan has brought his first payment. To free his men." Bertram pointed his way out of the room.

Richard's gaze followed where Bertram indicated. He saw the money, stacked in chests, as it was brought in. And then he saw the line of prisoners. All good soldiers and fighting men. But. Richard felt the reins he held on his ire loosen. "Not a single nobleman in these ranks?"

"No, my lord," said Bertram. "I'm sure he means to send them back last."

"No," said Richard. "This won't do. This won't do at all."

"Sire?" asked Bertram, a touch of concern in his voice.

Richard couldn't believe this insult. He couldn't believe all of this stalling. Saladin meant to have his victory, by any means necessary.

Two could play at that game.

"Round up the prisoners," said Richard. "All of them. Soldiers. Men. Women. Children."

"Yes, Your Highness," said Bertram.

Richard looked Bertram dead in the eye. "Kill them all."

Outside the
walls of Akko

The defender's
remaining siege

CHAPTER TWENTY-FOUR

The Righteous of the Faith

YUSUF WAS NOT ACCUSTOMED TO WAITING SO LONG for a response from his opponent.

He knew in his bones that something was wrong.

He knew it the way he knew many things. The way he could tell that the tide of a battle was changing. The way that he could sense that a city was on his side or not. The way he knew which were the weak points—in a person's mind or in a city's defenses.

There were some things that Yusuf simply knew. And he knew that something had gone very wrong.

What that was, he couldn't say.

He had sent over the prisoners earlier in the day. The nobles had not been sent first. But then, what would the incentive be to send any further soldiers? The nobles always went last. The most valued prisoners would always have to be guarded and kept the longest. That was their leverage. That was the point in keeping them in the first place.

Yusuf needed to know what was causing the delay, what had shifted in the air. He didn't like to wait to discover that his instincts were correct. He went looking for the truth—the things he could not yet see but could sense. So he'd asked his men to bring a prisoner before him: one of Richard's most loyal followers. He didn't care who it was, really, but he needed one who was more hotheaded than the others. Easy to rise to the bait of anger. That he had specified. Patient men were always harder to outwit than clever ones. Patience guarded a man's temper, his honor, and even his deepest secrets.

A clever, hotheaded man? Well. Yusuf could break him without trying. They broke themselves, usually.

And so a man was brought before him. He was chained and bowed low, but the man's spirit was still intact. Yusuf could see that. The man was dirty and worn from the battle, covered in mud and blood. The blood, Yusuf doubted, was the man's own.

"Tell me," said Yusuf. "What does your king do, waiting like this?"

The man spat on the floor.

"That," said Yusuf, "was very rude."

The man laughed.

"I know you understand me," said Yusuf. "I know you speak this tongue as well as I do. I know you know the language of the poets and the Qur'an. The holy language."

"There is *nothing* holy about your speech," said the man, in Arabic. He spat again.

"You know, I'd really advise against the spitting," said Yusuf.

"I'll take no orders from you," snarled the man. "I take orders from my king and my king alone. I owe you no allegiance and I've sworn you no service."

Yusuf nodded. "That is fair and true."

The man watched Yusuf. He sensed a trap, a trick of some sort.

"Tell me," pressed Yusuf again. "Why does your king delay?"

"You'll get no answers from these lips," said the man. "They say you're a sorcerer. A wicked infidel. That you'll trick me into betraying my king. But you won't. I won't let you work your magic on me."

"Let us play a game," said Yusuf.

The man's face twitched but he said nothing.

"If you win," said Yusuf, "then you get to keep your life."

This had the man's attention. He turned and stared for a moment. He was a warrior, and Yusuf assumed he had been hardened by the prospect of death. But the idea of making your fate a game—that was always unsettling.

"*If* I win?" asked the man.

"Yes, if you win. You are free to go," said Yusuf. "No harm will befall you, and you will be able to walk out of here a free man."

"If I lose?"

Yusuf shrugged. "Your life is forfeit."

"And what is your game?" asked the man.

Yusuf could spot the soul of a gambler. This man was not one of the patient ones. "The game is this: If your king stands by you, stands by his men, then you shall be amongst the first to leave. But if I am right and your king plays a trick, then you shall be the first to die."

"I do not play games with heathen kings," growled the man.

"Ah, but you already have. When you signed up to come to this faraway place and fight a war on land that was not your own. You decided you *did* play games with all manner of kings and princes and qadis. You decided you were here to play an elaborate game of who sits upon the throne of Jerusalem, though the city has never been, by any rights, your own."

"Jesus was the king of Jerusalem, in his own right," said the man.

"And do you call him kin?" asked Yusuf.

This silenced the man at once.

"So, do you want to wager with your life?" Yusuf asked. He was testing the man. He wanted to know if the man had faith in his king.

181

He wanted to know if this wait was normal. He had no other means of knowing.

But before the man could answer, there was a sound outside Yusuf's tent.

"Enter," said Yusuf.

A messenger stepped inside and bowed low, trembling. He spoke in Yusuf's ear, then bowed out.

It was the news Yusuf had been waiting for. Not the news he had hoped for, though.

Yusuf moved toward the flap of the tent.

"Do you not want my answer?" asked the man.

"No," said Yusuf. He had no time to tarry. He had to step outside and see the hill of Ayyadieh himself.

"Why not?" asked the man, confused.

"It no longer matters," said Yusuf.

"How so?" There was the lightest of tremors in the man's voice.

"Your king has abandoned honor and reason," said Yusuf. "He slaughters all his captives. Their heads are now rolling off the walls of Akko and down the hill of Ayyadieh. So that every man in my camp sees what death and carnage your king can reap from this land."

"Surely not all," said the man, aghast.

"To the last child," said Yusuf.

The man did break now. He crumpled to the floor, knowing his death would come soon.

And Yusuf?

He'd give his life for his cause now. He swore revenge.

The kind that shakes the earth and shatters cities.

The village of Al-Tira

Near the foothills of the
Carmelite mountains, along
the coast of the Middle Sea

CHAPTER TWENTY-FIVE

Credit in the Real World

I FEEL A SENSE OF DREAD THAT I CANNOT SHAKE.

The village of Al-Tira is an old Nasrani village. There cannot be more than fifty or sixty families dwelling here. The land would not accommodate much more.

It has three claims to fame. The first is that it is called Al-Tirat al-Lawz, because there is already another Al-Tira to the east. I've always wondered if it's called that because they grow almonds, or simply because the shore nearby is the color of an almond that's been washed and blanched. Both Al-Tiras claim they were the first. Neither is probably correct. Cities always have memories, and to me, these cities must both hearken back to a place that no longer exists. A place that was once between the two. But perhaps that is too metaphysical for us now.

This leads me to the second claim—that the village is built up against the shore. The waves come crashing in as we enter. The little village looks both smaller and more magnificent at once next to the curling waves of the great expanse of that perfectly jewel-like sea. We call it the White Sea—Al-Bahr al-Abyad. But to me, the white curling waves dance along a deep, spectacular, and glittering azure, like lapis lazuli or some other precious stone. Al-Muttawasit. The

Middle Sea. Bahr al-Rumi. The Roman Sea. Sometimes it feels as though the sea has as many names as ships that traverse its waters.

I wonder if the sea is why the air is cooler, or if the seasons are changing before me.

For the third claim—the reason we are here in this village—is that Al-Tira is nestled just at the foothills of the mountains. And in the mountains dwell the monks—the hermits—in the Carmelite caves.

In the caves, of course, there is the safety of being hidden and obscured by the shadows. I think of the Prophet when I look at those cavernous mountains above us, about his hiding from pursuers as he fled the holy city of Mecca. It's a tempting vision of safety. A beautiful illusion. Hide in the caves, where the Templars will never find you.

But there are also the hermits in these Carmelite mountains, and the hermits are fanatics.

I hope I do not need to tell you what it might be like to encounter a hermit in a lonely mountain cave. It is only a thing I will risk because I know the sort of powerful people who are on our heels.

But first we must pass through Al-Tira. We cannot go around. The best way to find a good horse track is by speaking to the villagers. Even Teni has suggested this, though she's the best guide I've met in my life.

The townspeople of Al-Tira are not of my faith, that is true. They are a village-bound people, which means they are likely suspicious of outsiders. They are probably half Faranji and half locals, even if we're very lucky. But I pray they're reasonable people, that they do not carry the kind of suspicion in their hearts and the sort of disdain for the world at large that a hermit does.

I have one other hope: that the Templars who chased me through the tunnels are no longer behind us. They would have had to double back, and John says the other entrances are a good league away from where I came out.

But it's their job to catch up to us, eventually.

Perhaps for a moment they thought I was drunk and lost in their deep, secret caves. But by now, the Templars have to know we're the thieves they've been looking for. The ones who robbed their fellow warrior monks. They have to know that a random drunk soldier could not have doubled back like that on them, could not have made such a quick and clever escape.

I wonder if they think we've kidnapped John or if he joined us willingly.

But the truth is, even if those men are not directly behind us, I'm sure they've gone back for reinforcements and that my—*our*—reprieve is a temporary one.

By God do I need a reprieve, though. We all do.

Of course, there's the other risk. The chance that word has been sent ahead of us—that there were thieves operating in Haifa and that they would seek refuge in a nearby village.

Tricky, always tricky, deciding which danger is worse than the other.

I slow my pace. "What's it to be, do you think? Shall we risk it as ourselves?"

Teni laughs. "I say we do."

"I agree," says John, looking sidelong at Teni.

Zeena, of course, gives an answer that is entirely unrelated to my original query. "How can you trust him again? He's the one who led us astray the first time."

"He got us out in the end," I say, taking off my jupon and stuffing it back into my saddle pack. Honest village folk deserve an honest self from me. No tricks, no games. "He was trying to help."

"You don't know that!" says Zeena.

"Then what would you have me do, sister?" I ask. "Throw him back to the wolves? Send him to his compatriots who left him tied up and essentially for dead?"

"Perhaps it was a ploy," says Zeena, but she's got no heart in it.

"Perhaps," I say. "And perhaps we are all far from home and trying to do our best. Perhaps he's just as lost as the rest of us."

I get out my green cloak and throw it over my shoulders, for if I'm to enter the village as myself, then I shall be fully myself. When I'm not in disguise, I decide here and now that I shall be Rahma al-Hud, the bandit with the green hood. The girl who stole a horse from the queen of Jerusalem and, so far, has lived to tell the tale.

"I am not lost," says Zeena, miffed. She'd cross her arms over her chest, but she's got to hold on to her horse's reins to stay upright. "And you should keep that cloak well out of sight. It's conspicuous enough. We're not likely to run into anyone as kind and friendly as Viva if they mark it again."

"I was not lost, nor was I being particularly kind," says Viva. "I simply decided that I'd rather not betray you, having seen the effects of such betrayal in my own life. But I say we trust him. I think he means well. And his shock at finding the wall blocked was genuine."

John looks at her like he might fall to his knees into a rakat and touch his forehead to the ground in thanks. Viva rolls her eyes at his desperation but she doesn't change her position on the matter.

"Only a fool would still be with us otherwise," Viva adds.

"Then he's a fool," says Zeena.

"No," says Teni. "I don't think he is. And I believe Viva is right. He should have deserted us for his compatriots a long time ago."

"Thank you," says John.

"I still don't trust him," says Zeena.

"You don't trust anyone," I point out.

John, however, doesn't seem to mind. "I thank you for your faith, though I've done little to deserve it."

We're to the heart of the village now, so there's no turning back. We all stop, though, looking over the quiet little houses by the sea.

"What are the odds the Templars sent a messenger ahead?" Viva asks no one in particular.

John shrugs. "Your guess is as good as mine. These things are always changing. And the commanders don't tell us what they're doing, for fear that any one of us could be a spy for the other side."

"To be fair," says Viva, "you did turn out to be a spy for the other side."

For a moment we all go dead silent. We're so nervous as to how John will take this assessment.

But instead he throws back his head and starts laughing. "You're absolutely right. I did turn spy. Or at least, traitor."

Teni laughs in return. "Better than I. I left all of my fellow fighters to join up with these two."

"Why is that?" asks John.

Teni shrugs. "Seemed like the right thing to do at the time."

"How so?" asks John, as though he might be infinitely curious about everything.

"Akko had fallen," she says.

But as I watch Teni, I can sense a hesitation on her part. Something she wishes to say but has not.

"You were at Akko?" John asks. "Why?"

But before any of us can answer, we all hear footsteps. There's a man leading his donkey toward us, and he's taking in the sight of us the way he might take in the sight of a cart full of plague victims.

I was right about villagers not being trusting.

I cannot blame him, much as I do not desire to be the object of such a gaze. These people have seen so much war and they've borne the brunt of so much destruction. Every time a conqueror comes through, they burn the farms to the ground. Or at least, that was what the Faranji would do. Sometimes, in a fit of retribution, our own princes and qadis would follow suit. Once the win-at-all-costs kind of warfare was introduced, it was difficult to reverse it.

I do not know how to put this man at ease. John still looks like a Templar, with his red-crossed tunic and his broadsword. We're riding five warhorses between us. I've got a bow strapped to my back and all of us have swords and knives. And that's just the weapons that are visible to this man.

We look perhaps like an unlikely group of companions, but we also look like what we are: soldiers.

The man with the donkey walks on, and a village woman comes out of her home. She spies us and hurries by, her eyes trained carefully on the ground.

We are not welcome here. "We should leave," I mutter.

"Too late now," says Teni.

A man is approaching us, his pace quick and direct. He's simply dressed, but there's an air of assurance about him. I cannot tell if he is in charge, but he seems important. He also seems like he was sent to deal with us.

We all stop. I dismount Fouzia, though I do not indicate that anyone else should get off their horses. If they need to flee, best to stay on them. I put my hand to my heart and bow. My compatriots follow suit. John does this, however, a bit more awkwardly than the rest of us, as the gesture is not natural to him.

"As-salamu alaykum," I say to the man. No matter the religion, the idea of peace upon any of us feels like the blessing we all need right now.

"Alaykum-asalam," he says in return. I'm relieved to learn that he agrees with me.

But still, he's watching me. Watching all of us.

"What brings you to our humble village?" he asks.

I bow further. "We are simply travelers along the way and happened to pass by your village. We hoped to stop, perhaps, and rest our horses."

"On the way to where?"

I dare not say Jerusalem. But my other option is just as bad, I think. I say it anyway. "Jaffa."

"Ah," he says. "The citadel by the sea."

I nod. "Indeed. I can understand you have seen much hardship, being so close to the coast. We are happy to leave you and continue on through."

But the man is rubbing his beard thoughtfully. "You are a motley crew."

I put out a hand to stay whatever it was Zeena was about to do next. I don't need eyes on her to know aggression would be her first tactic. "Aye."

"You are a Muslim, as is the girl you hold back. But then you have a Christian boy with you. A Templar, by the looks of him. Then there's the fierce rider and her horse—she's from the land of the horse lords." He turns, looking to Viva last. "And I'm not sure what *that* girl's faith might be, but she's not from here."

"Al-Andalus," says Viva. She bows beautifully from atop her horse. "Though I'm not from there. Just my people."

"But you are like us, then. We have long memories here."

190

Viva nods, understanding. "Very long memories, indeed."

I'm watching the interaction between them. Something curious is going on. "Would you have us go then, sheikh?" Perhaps he is not a sheikh, but I know no other word to offer respect.

A smile plays about his lips. "That is not my honor to bear such a title. But I see you are from farther east to call me so."

"The land between the rivers," I say proudly, my chest puffing up a bit. Home fills me with that feeling. That sense of knowledge of who I am and where my roots truly belong. Zeena does not have the same reaction to home, and I've never known why.

The man continues to tug on his beard. "And you wear a green cloak."

We all freeze.

"I do," I say. My hand is itching to reach for my bow. But something—I do not know if it is reason or instinct—stays the impulse.

"With a green hood," he says.

"And what does that mean to you?" asks Teni. She's got her hand on the edge of her bow, but she's not drawn it yet.

"Peace," I say to her. To all of them.

The man laughs, not unfriendly. "Your friend is right to worry. There's a prize on your head that's worth more than all the land of this village."

The moment that passes between us is long and silent, but still. I do not draw a weapon, and no one behind me draws theirs, though I can feel the urge to fight or flee pulsing through all of them. Instead, I'm watching this man and he's watching me.

"And now that the choice is before you, what shall you do?" I ask calmly.

The man smiles. It's a wise, old smile, and I can see now why he's been sent to deal with us. He does not seem to be a man who easily softens, but I see in his eyes that he has a capacity for joy that is important, too. To laugh at the difficulties of life is no mean feat.

"I am here," he says thoughtfully, "to welcome you to our village. And to ask if you would stay the night."

"You offer us hospitality?" I ask. It's honor among all of us, to offer hospitality. To violate that is not impossible, but it would take a hard man indeed to do so.

"I do," he says.

"Why?" asks Zeena from behind me.

The man's lips quirk into a smile again. "I have heard of the bandit with the green hood. A thief so cunning he has stolen a horse from the queen of Jerusalem herself."

The man pauses, taking a good, long look at Fouzia. She seems to know she's being discussed, for she stamps her feet.

Viva rolls her eyes. "Honestly, if your hood doesn't give us away, the horse nearly always will."

"Hush," says Teni, still watching the man carefully. "Let him finish."

"Then I heard that a group of Templars were robbed," he continues. "They were drugged, so they say."

"They were not!" Zeena shouts indignantly.

The man's lips twitch again. "Indeed. We have had enough dealings with them to know their ilk. They profess piety and take money. They resent women and rob power from us all."

Viva dismounts and steps forward. "We do understand one another, don't we?"

The man bows, all courtesy.

"Revenge," says Viva. She does not bow. And suddenly I can see her long, ancient lineage. I can see that she was not royal, but she has the bearings of nobility about her. It's not in her blood, but it's that sense of spirit within her. She knows exactly who she is and where she's from, and what it means to be her.

Zeena is looking at her like the sun just came out from behind the clouds. Like she's been blinded. Or blindsided. I cannot tell which, truth be told.

"Yes," says the man. "Perhaps it would be a little bit of revenge. But mostly we believe in honor. And hospitality. And the old ways which have long gone. We keep to them, despite this." He looks me in the eye. "You strike me as one who remembers the old ways and honors them."

I bow, hand over my heart. "I do my best."

The man nods. It's good enough for him. "Stay. Rest your feet. Feed your horses. And take what little we have to give."

Zeena and Teni and John all dismount now.

"That we can do," I say, accepting his gracious offer. "But you must do me a favor in return."

This startles him slightly. "Oh?"

"Aye," I say. I reach into Fouzia's pack and pull out some of the goods we stole from the knights in Haifa. Well-made coats of mail and knives and a couple of swords. It's some of the most beautiful metalwork I've seen—made for battle, yes, but also intricate and crafted with great care. But they're about to be made more beautiful. "Melt this down and use it to feed and clothe and shelter whoever in your village needs it."

The man's twitching smile grows into a full-blown grin. "It really is you, al-ghita akhdar."

Zeena just rolls her eyes. "Ya Allah, don't start giving her nicknames. The rest of us will never hear the end of it."

The man just laughs and leads us into the heart of the village.

CHAPTER TWENTY-SIX

The Girl All the Bad Guys Want

WE ARE TAKEN INTO A HOME THAT IS MUCH LIKE ALL the other homes around it. I would not have marked it as particularly special or notable. There's a lack of hierarchy in the architecture in this village that means finding my footing—in terms of where we are going and who else we might be meeting—is a little difficult. But the man who met us holds open the door and we all duck into the modest structure.

Inside nearly stops me in my tracks.

The room is like a little jewel box. There is one large, plush carpet along the floor, and smaller mats of equally fine weaving placed upon it. There's a little tea tray with glasses and a teapot. Along the walls are beautiful hangings.

And at the center of it all is a woman, sitting cross-legged and sipping on her tea. She sets the demitasse in its saucer and looks over my crew.

"Ah, I see we have the Green Hood in our midst," she says with a smile. It's a wry expression, though not unkind. More thoughtful than anything else.

"Rahma al-Hud, at your service." I give her a courteous bow. "I thank you for your hospitality."

She smiles again. "Whether you will thank me, that remains to be seen."

I can sense everyone behind me tense.

"Leave us," she says. She's looking directly at me so that I cannot be mistaken. "I have things to discuss with you and you alone."

I hold my arms up, holding back Zeena and, to my surprise, Teni. "Can I have your word as our host that my companions will not be harmed?"

She nods. "My word as sheikh and my promise as your host."

She could have ordered us struck down the second that we entered this little village. She could have us killed now, in closed quarters, and sent back all our bodies to the queen of Jerusalem for a pretty price. Well, as the queen wants to kill me personally, perhaps all our bodies but mine. But she has not . . . not yet, at least.

"All right," I say.

"Rahma," says Zeena, her voice a worried, throaty warning.

"Stand guard outside," I say. "Keep your knives out and sharp if you like."

"Aye," says Teni. She takes Viva and John out alongside her. Zeena hesitates, but she follows, with a quick look over her shoulder. The old man leaves behind her.

The woman and I are alone in the little jewel-box room.

"Sit," she says. She gestures to the carpet, across the tea tray from her.

I approach and take my seat. "Shall I call you sheikh or sheikha?"

"Either," says the sheikh. "The power is the same to me."

Up close I can see that her face is weathered and aged. She's got deep lines around her eyes, and the kohl settles into the wrinkles there. She's got an alert but neutral expression as she watches me.

"Tea?" she offers.

I accept and she pours. It feels a bit like a game of cat and mouse, this. Like we are dancing around what she will not yet say.

"You knew who we were?" I venture to say, accepting the glass of tea from her.

"From the moment a boy in the village spotted you on the ridge," she replies.

"Ah," I say. "We were so worried about those who followed us, we did not think of those who could be ahead of us."

"You did not take to the mountains," she says.

"No."

"You risked this little village. Why?"

I look at her. "Would you risk the mountains without provisions?"

"Not if I did not have to," she acquiesces.

I raise an eyebrow in her direction and take a sip of tea. I don't think I need to say anything further.

"Of course, this gave me time to decide what to do with you," she says.

"And what have you decided?" I ask as though she's to tell me when the next rain is predicted to be. A question of casual interest, but of no direct import to me, a stranger and a soldier in this village. "Shall you take the reward, I wonder?"

She shakes her head. "It is not in my nature to sell out my fellow man without good reason."

"Is not that I am a thief reason enough?" I wonder out loud.

The woman takes a long drink of her tea; then she sets the cup and saucer down on the tray. "How came you to be a thief, Rahma al-Hud? You're dressed as the strangest thief I have ever seen."

"I came by way of Akko," I say. "I was in the siege, the one inside the city. I was sent away from my troops alongside my sister, and we were told to make our own way back to Jerusalem."

An expression flashes across the sheikh's face, but it's gone so quickly I'm unable to read it. "And so you stole a horse to make some coin?"

"No, the horse was an accident."

A smile tugs at the sheik's lips, but she says nothing. "I have never heard of such a thing."

"We stumbled upon the horse. She was being mistreated." I think about how Fouzia was when we found her—tightly reined in with no room to run. Pulled at and penned in and painfully spurred on with metal. "I had plans to set her free. But she stayed with us."

"A clever horse, to be sure."

I shrug. "Perhaps."

"So, you accidentally stole a horse from the queen of Jerusalem. And then you accidentally stole from the Knights Templar?" She's watching me carefully now.

"No," I say. "We needed the money. We could not have stabled the horses or fed ourselves otherwise."

"And where is your plunder, I wonder?"

I laugh again. "I admit, ya sheikh, that I might be the worst thief that ever lived. For a reputation that I have built so quickly, I have very little to show for it."

"A soldier turned thief," says the sheikh. "With a loyal band of followers. Who gives away her plunder to the village man who greets her. And who gives away her coin to orphans in the street."

"How could you—" I ask.

"Word travels faster than you might realize, girl."

On this point I am silent.

"You are worth one hundred bezants alive," she says. "Though I'm sure the queen will triple that when she hears what you have done in Haifa."

"At least," I admit.

"I plan to feed you," she says. "Clothe you. Let you stay for a night."

I'm bewildered by this. "I thank you, though I am at a loss to understand why."

"I'm sure you are," she says.

"You risk your entire village to harbor fugitives and outlaws so."

"That is my risk to take," she says. "And they need hope. We all need it right now. I cannot promise them safety, but I can give them hope."

It takes all my will to not flinch away from her gaze. I feel like a fool who has been rambling along, barely keeping my motley grew together and alive. For before me is a woman who knows how to out-last an endless war. An endless war that I have contributed to. Shame flushes my face.

But if she notices this, she says nothing on the topic. "And now I have the unhappy task before me. I must give you news of Akko. You must decide for yourself how to tell the rest of your companions."

A knot tightens in my stomach. "What is it? What news?"

"Richard refused Saladin's exchange."

"What?"

"The prisoners. They're all dead," she says. "Every last soldier and, if the rumors are to be believed, down to the last child."

The saucer rattles in my hand as I set down the tea. I think of the men we fought with who are now gone. Of the children who were not so lucky, like Farrah was, to escape the city before the siege was over. I think of Omar, who protected us. I close my eyes for a moment. When I reopen them, the sheikh looks directly at me.

198

"I do not doubt that you will know best how to break this news to your traveling companions. Particularly to your sister."

I swallow my nausea, my grief. I blink back the tears in my eyes. I rein in all feeling until I am calm again. Now is not the time to grieve. Not my time, at least. "Yes. I thank you, yes."

She allows me to compose myself. Then I stand, bowing again. "I thank you again, ya sheikh."

She waves this away, as though what she has done is nothing, is unimportant.

"I might request," I say, still in my bow, "that we are able to grieve tonight. A proper memorial."

She nods. "Consider it done."

I am about to back out of her room when I stop, look up. "How did you know she's my sister?"

"The eyes," says the sheikh, with another thoughtful smile. She looks as though she's come to a decision about something. "I have one other piece of news for you. And I wonder now what you will do with this information. A soldier turned thief is a dangerous creature indeed."

"Then do not tell it to me," I say. "I do not trust myself with any more knowledge in this state."

"And yet," says the sheikh, "I think this is precisely why the news should be yours."

I look up.

She stares right at me. "The queen of Jerusalem is to pass by the mountains two days from now. On her way to reclaim the throne of Jerusalem."

I return her gaze steadily. "And what would you have me do with such news?"

The sheikh returns to her tea for a long moment. "I would not have you do anything. Not for the world. But what you would do—what the girl who accidentally stole a horse from the queen of Jerusalem would do. What the Green Hood would do. Well. That, I imagine, is up to you, is it not?"

CHAPTER TWENTY-SEVEN

No Dawn, No Day

ZEENA SCREAMS WHEN I TELL HER.

I lock my arms around her, so that she struggles to hit and kick at me, but she can get at no one else. Her wail pierces my heart. But I hold her fast. She must feel it, this grief and this rage. She must release such feelings back into the wild, where they belong.

Teni stands still and stoic. Her mouth forms a grim straight line across her face. She was in no danger, being party to the second, outer siege. But she understands war, and she understands what it is to fight alongside your men for a year.

Worry coats Viva's features. She seems to know grief well and she is affected by the sight of it on Zeena.

John sits down, as though his heart is heavy, when he hears. He hangs his head in his hands, as though he cannot believe that such a thing would happen. As though he had still held on to hope of the honor of battle, of the duty of a king to parley with his enemy. He looks ashamed. As though perhaps not a person has died, but a whole way of life that he believed in.

And still, I hold fast to Zeena as she screams and rages. I will not release her until she changes back from this feral creature. I do not hush her. I do not lull her. I let her spend all her sorrow in one go.

She will not know peace until she does.

I hate to be this messenger. The one we all fear to be in war—the bringer of news of death.

Zeena's movements slow; she has exhausted her body. She begins to weep. Here, I hand her over to Viva, who holds my sister tight as she sobs.

I take a deep breath. "Tonight, we will mourn."

Teni nods. "Yes."

John looks up. "What do you do on such an occasion?"

I look at him. "We tell stories."

CHAPTER TWENTY-EIGHT

The Only Living Girls in Akko

WE SIT NOW IN THE SHEIKH'S HOME. TEA IS PASSED around the circle of people sitting on a worn but still fine carpet. I know I should start, but I have never been a poet. Never been good at mourning. I have always left that to Zeena.

She knows this, intuitively, and so she begins to speak. She looks at Viva as though the poetry were for her and her alone. "In the stories of the days of old, there was once a prince among men."

Zeena has a sense of rhythm, of grandiosity, that I lack. I can charm—but Zeena? She can enrapture. She just rarely sees the point of it. She'd rather fight all her problems in this world.

Her voice is lighter, airier than my own, but there is gravity there, too. "His name was Omar, and he led his men through valor and conquest. Through campaigns in the muck and the blood and the filth. And still, he kept his hands clean. Still he kept his purpose. He could be buried in a pit of tar, and still he would come out clean."

Across the circle, Viva is looking back at Zeena as if she's never seen her before. No one has until they've seen her recite.

Her soft soprano carries across the circle. "They called him captain, as though that were fitting enough. But while other men would be gifted command and be satisfied, Omar would not rest until he gave his soldiers victory in return. His soldiers would have followed him into the great Middle Sea, had he led them there. Such was their faith in him."

The other villagers hum around the circle. Zeena's voice is clear and true. Hypnotic at times. Soothing when she wants it to be. "I will recite tales of my captain long after his death. And long after my own, my words will put you to shame. They will tell you of a man who did not run from his fate. Who stood fast, as though he were a mountain and not a man. My words will find you and will strike your heart, so that you might beat your breast and howl, that you never had such courage in you as Omar did within him."

I don't notice until tears fall onto my robe that I'm crying.

For Omar, the man who saved us by commanding that we go. For the men who fought alongside us for a year and a half in this god-forsaken land. They're all dead, at the hands of the king of Faranji, who would rather break all bonds of honor than trade his prisoners.

There's a hole in my heart that I know will never be filled. I've learned this from the death of our mother. That people you let in will make room in your heart. And when they leave and go to meet their maker, the hole remains. I've gotten used to the gaping hole where our mother used to be. And I suppose at some point, I will be used to the hole shaped so distinctly like Omar that it's nearly impossible to see beyond it right now. The other men, too. Their low laughter and their campfire stories. It is not that we had never lost fighting men before. But never so many, all at once. And never like this.

There's a lull in Zeena's recitation; it's my turn.

"I am not a poet like my sister," I say. "But I know many men would not fight alongside us. Would not take us into their company. Omar did. He did not turn away good swords just because women held them. He saw my skill with my bow. Said he needed as many good archers and as many good fighters as God would give him. He made sure the men accepted us as fellow soldiers, as compatriots of their own."

I see Teni and she nods. She understands why this is important. Not everyone does.

"He valued courage. Honor. A good fighter. Loyalty." I feel my throat catch. I don't want to cry. Not when I speak. I don't mind weeping silently along to Zeena's poetry, but I must finish what I have to say. "I shall ever endeavor to be like him."

"And I," says Zeena, "shall ever endeavor to avenge him."

I'm not sure why the statement startles me so much—I should have known this was Zeena's feeling all along.

A hush falls over the entire crowd. I take Zeena by the arm and pull her out of the circle. It's one thing to be identified as an outlaw who might be wanted for stealing the queen of Jerusalem's horse. It's another to openly plot treason against the occupiers here.

I tow Zeena outside the house, into an open courtyard. The night air is cool and the breeze out to sea carries the scent of the dust and the desert and the cypress trees. It's a delicate smell. There's also the smell of cardamom and tea wafting out from inside the house.

"And you call me reckless," I say.

Zeena wrests her arm from my grip. "You *are* reckless."

"You speak aloud of treason," I press.

"None of them are my king."

She's not wrong to say it. I agree with her. But I have to ask: "Why must you spoil for fights that are not your own?"

"You wouldn't understand," she says.

But I refuse to let up. "And how am I to understand when you never tell me? How do you propose we get revenge?" I ask. "We cannot go back through Haifa again. We'd be lucky if we never ran into the camp of the queen of Jerusalem. We cannot go back to Akko. Do you propose we go to Jerusalem, to the Sacred City, and have our revenge there? Take it out on unsuspecting Nasrani the way that their kings take out their disdain on any and all of us that they meet along the way? Feasting on our flesh because we do not believe in their one true God?"

"You know nothing!" shouts Zeena.

"I know everything," I say to counter.

"Enough." It's Teni who speaks.

Zeena and I pause. Neither of us knew that Teni had such a big, resonant voice.

"You two have been fighting since I met you," she says. Her voice is not unfriendly, but stays level, just short of an order. I can see now why she was sent out to fight. She's been so jovial, I hadn't noticed her quiet air of command.

"You've only recently met us," says Zeena.

"I've seen enough," Teni replies.

Viva stands behind Teni, and beside her is John. They're all looking to us, worry and grief across all their faces. Viva's expression is subtler. John's is wholehearted. And Teni's is solid and persistent, just as she is.

"What would you have us do?" I ask my sister.

"Kill the king of Faranji," says Zeena, with no hesitation.

"You would have us kill the king of Faranji—and what then?" I ask.

"Then he would be dead," she counters.

"Yes," I say. "He would be dead. And then they would send twenty more like him—no, a hundred. Do you not see that, sister?"

Zeena says nothing for a long beat.

Viva steps forward. "If you want revenge, we're with you."

Zeena raises an eyebrow. I stare at Viva.

"We're with you, as far as you want to go." Viva is not one to come to a decision lightly. She's a great observer and contemplator, so I know she means this—has thought through every angle—before she says this aloud. She knows what she's agreeing to.

"You cannot mean that," I say, because I don't want her to mean it.

"We trust you," says Teni. "Both of you."

"You shouldn't," I say. "You hardly know us."

John gives me a weak smile. "We have seen enough."

"You have not seen anything! These are *your* people!" I'm shouting again, I'm not sure why. I don't know who I'm trying to convince. I'm tired of being cautious, of being the voice of reason. "We cannot go down this path. Not of revenge. It's dark and it's not what Omar would have wanted. It's not why he let us go."

"We came here to fight," says Zeena. "And he ordered us to Jerusalem because he knew we would keep on fighting."

"We cannot fight every single Nasrani from here to Jerusalem," I say. My voice has gone quiet. I feel like giving up, like surrendering. I'm not sure how much more of Zeena and her bloodthirst I can take anymore.

"Perhaps we don't have to," John murmurs.

All heads swivel toward him.

"The queen of Jerusalem marches on the Holy City," he explains. "She's anticipating that King Richard will march down the coast himself. It's well known she wishes him to change his mind and aid *her* in the reclaiming of the throne. She wants to force his hand."

Zeena just snorts.

"I know. The sheikh told me she'd be passing the mountains in two days. And what good does that do us?" I ask.

This time Viva interrupts. "Don't you see?" She's vibrating with unusual excitement. "She's the richest of all Faranji women. And she

207

marches, slowly, with her entire court down the coast and to Jerusalem. Without her husband, who has fled to Tyre. You already stole a horse from her without even trying."

My heart kicks up a notch. "And just what are you implying?"

"Well," says Viva. "What if we *were* trying?"

The question hovers in the air for a long moment. It's tantalizing. Tempting.

Steal from the queen of Jerusalem, one of the richest of the Nasrani invaders. Daughter of Faranji and Rum. Possessor of the keys to the city itself.

"She has more money than God," Viva continues. "And her bargaining power is her riches and her ties to Rum. From what I've heard, she's got to convince King Richard that the throne is rightly hers and not Guy of Lusignan's. Apparently, her husband, Conrad of Montferrat, was the one who gave up all of his prisoners to Richard. Her money is her last bargaining chip."

A smile tugs at my lips. I know if anyone can best the queen of Jerusalem, it is I. I know if anyone can take the things she cares for, it is I. For I am Rahma al-Hud—the Green Hood—and there's a king's—no, a queen's—ransom on my own head.

"Let's go steal her kingdom, then."

CHAPTER TWENTY-NINE

How to Disappear Completely

WE SET UP SHOP IN THE HOME OF THE SHEIKH THE next day.

We try to work out the most likely route that the queen will take through these parts. We passed her once, on our way to Haifa. She'll have to pass us again in order to get to Jerusalem, at least until she turns from Jaffa. We try to work out the best vantage point we will have from each. The sheikh gives us news of the scouting reports coming out of Haifa.

I've also sent word home, via letter, that Zeena and I have survived the siege at Akko. I don't know if it will arrive before the word of the massacre reaches our homeland. I don't know if the missive will arrive there at all. But I must try, and let my sisters and Baba know that we're still alive.

The letter is sent along with a merchant who stops to feed his horse in Al-Tira. The rest of us hide while he's here—he thinks someone in the village has a family member who is a merchant and traveling his own route. He said he would see to the letter personally.

It's the best I can hope for, given the circumstances.

Zeena is sharpening all the weapons in the back. Beside her is Viva, who is working out her own little recipe for Greek fire. I tell her she can't use it, but she says we should have some anyway. She says she can also make a little concoction in the same small clay vessels they use to lob and launch the Greek fire, to make a simple smoke screen.

"Are you *sure* you're not a wizard of some sort, Viva?" I ask.

Viva does not laugh. "No."

"Then how would you even know how to go about such a thing?" I say.

"I studied my brothers' alchemy books when they weren't looking."

Zeena, who is sharpening a knife, stops. She sets the blade down and gives Viva her full focus. "You must be very determined and very clever. They never let girls learn anything."

"And yet," says Viva, with a particular kind of smile on her face, "we manage to do so anyway."

"I'm glad you're in our camp, rather than the enemy's," I say. Though, I confess, I feel as though I'm interrupting a conversation I'm no longer a part of.

"Sí." Viva winks. She's still looking at my sister. "I am a dangerous enemy to make."

I move toward the front of the house. John—who has been given a change of clothes so that he is no longer a conspicuous Templar—is there ripping and rolling cloth to make bandages. I ask him if he needs any help, but he waves me away.

I take a tray of tea and sit on the rug. I look over the plans and maps that Teni has made, trying to figure out the routes that the queen could take and the best spots where we might lay our trap. It's the job that requires the least physical effort, but at the end of the day I find myself aching and tired and ready to fall fast asleep.

It's been so long since I've slept without the need for a ready guard that I find I am grateful for even that, though.

210

And in the morning, we start again.

Teni is out of the house, meanwhile, acting as our own scout. She's learning all the footpaths and horse trails along the village edges. A village boy has shown her some of the routes, but mostly she's been finding her own. She's watching the mountains, too, to see if there are ways some of the hermits take that she can catch sight of. I'm sure she wants to know the quickest ways up the mountain as much as she wants to avoid someone else's route.

She says she's found six good paths so far, and five difficult ones that would work in a pinch. It's so many more than I dared hope for.

If we are to pull this off, we need to be able to get in and out without being caught and without being chased. Ideally, if all goes according to plan, no one in the queen's entourage will know that we have robbed them until it is far too late.

But you've got to plan on everything not going to plan. You've got to have backups to the backups, so that there is always a way out. This is what I learned on that race through the tunnels and our exit through Haifa. You cannot have one exit plan; you must have several.

This is why I'm poring over maps, why I'm sending Teni out to learn each and every trail, why I'm having her mark all the trails she finds on our maps. Even if we do not go with her, we must all be able to share in the same knowledge.

With each plan comes more possibilities. With each possibility comes more things that could go wrong.

The simplest plan is the best plan. But it's difficult to keep your plan simple when your enemy outnumbers you at least a thousand to one. And while I have a solid plan for getting the best and weightiest chests out of the caravan, I have no idea how we are to gain entrance in the first place. I have already seen the security that the queen of

Jerusalem employs around the perimeters of her camp. And that was before she'd lost a horse.

If only we could be invisible. Appear just where we need to be, and disappear just as quickly.

"Viva," I ask, calling back to the other side of the house, "have you any magic for invisibility?"

She snorts, sounding frighteningly like my sister. "I told you, Rahma, I'm an alchemist and a great lover of poetry. Not a magician."

"Says the girl with her own recipe for Greek fire," I counter.

"That is not magic," she states simply.

"Leave her alone to her work," shouts Zeena.

"I did not know you were her keeper," I shout back, spoiling for a fight. For anything that will make these maps and these plans make sense. Anything that will keep us alive in such a foolish quest as ours.

I look up and see that my tea has been refreshed while I wasn't paying attention. I'd been holding my own little cup the entire time.

And that's when the idea strikes, like a flash of lightning in a storm: There are people you notice in this world and people you do not.

There are people who have a right to look the queen of Jerusalem in the eye.

And then there are the rest of us.

I cry out in delight. I cannot wait until Teni returns from her scouting mission.

I've just worked out how to be invisible.

CHAPTER THIRTY

When She Comes Around

FOR A MOMENT, I WONDER WHAT I'VE DONE IN MY life to bring me to this place.

"This is a bad idea," says Zeena, echoing my own thoughts.

"It's a better idea than killing the Faranji king."

"No, it's not. Then he'd be dead," she says. "And Omar would be avenged."

"Don't argue with me." I watch the valley below. There's the faintest hint of the dust that accompanies such a large traveling entourage. The queen and her caravan should be here soon.

Soon.

Teni is closer to the road. Viva is farther down, on a path that leads to the caves in the mountains.

"Would you rather be a soldier of fortune?" I ask.

Zeena hisses. "And need I remind you, sister, that *you* are the reason we're here at all?"

"You need not," I say, "but no doubt you will."

It's been so long since it was just the two of us that for a moment, I forget that we aren't really close to home and bickering about climbing date palms the fastest or running the best way around the heart of the village. I forget that we are about to steal from the richest woman in the land and use the plunder to get back home.

Well, Zeena believes we will use the plunder to fuel further revenge.

But this is it for me. We will not go on to Jerusalem. We will not keep to this foolhardy quest. We will get the funds we need to go home. I will give away the rest—to Al-Tira and to the orphans we encounter along the way. In my mind, I pretend that Teni comes along, too. That she sees the Tigris and the Euphrates. That Viva marvels at the science and learning in Baghdad on our way down to the south. That John would love the great bimaristan built by Harun al-Rashid.

My imaginings always stop short before I can get to Majid. For I know he was sent from our land and told on no uncertain terms to never return—the son to also pay for the sins of the father. And that is when my heart reminds me that each of my friends has their own home to get to. Their own story that they live.

Their own life, in which I am possibly a passing player. A mere line in an otherwise long and epic verse.

But I do not let myself dwell on such thoughts. For we have a plan today.

We will keep the queen from buying back her throne. And we will hopefully create enough chaos that al-Nasir can take advantage of it.

Sometimes, all you need is one stroke of luck for things to go your way.

Zeena taps my arm, but she needn't have.

I see it. "She's here."

Zeena's eyes light up. For all that she resisted this way of revenge,

I can see that she's ready. The thrill of the chase, of besting her opponents, is one she cannot resist. "Give the signal."

I take out my dagger, let it glint the right direction in the sun. It's a signal to the others to get into their agreed-upon positions.

Here goes nothing.

CHAPTER THIRTY-ONE

The Highwomen

ZEENA AND I ARE AT THE SIDE OF THE ROAD BY THE time the caravan has made it through the canyon pass. I'm holding several demitasse glasses in my hand. Zeena holds the teapot.

"Refreshments along your journey," I call out.

"Tea, thé, chai, tea, shai," calls out Zeena. She's using a mixture of dialects of Arabic and a few times she's calling out the word in Faranji. So that she's really just shouting *tea tea tea tea* in any language that anyone could possibly understand. She sounds like such a peddler of goods that for a moment I can't help but admire her single-focus tenacity of purpose.

We're back to our earlier disguises from Haifa. A little modified, so we look less like well-off merchants, but the overall effect is the same—we've our turbans and our loose trousers and we're covered; hopefully, no one would able to make out our faces too closely.

I hope that no one would bother looking us in the eye.

The caravan slows before us and I think the man at the helm is going to use his crop on us to get us out of the way. I shuffle back slowly, using my best effort to convey the posture of one who has never fought a day in their life, much less for a living.

But before he can crack his whip or shout at us, Zeena trills in that voice of hers, "Chai! Ash-shai! Tea! Tea! Chai! Shai! Thé!" She is using singsong tones so that her voice sounds less feminine and much more playful. She could be anyone selling anything at a marketplace, such is the way she shifts her tone.

But it seems to get the point across—rather than yelling at us, the man looks down at the inviting teapot in her hands. He looks across the way and he must spot Teni, who is tending to the small fire and a pot of water. And then Viva, who is ferrying a kettle between the fire and Zeena and me.

John is too big and too blond to hide amongst us in this way. I pray that he got my signal, because otherwise he would have no way to know that we've proceeded with the plan. But if all has gone right so far, he should already be within the caravan—in his new clothes given to him by the village of Al-Tira. We didn't think it was right for him to be a Templar, not when the queen of Jerusalem rides mostly with the Hospitallers.

In any case, I'm pouring tea for the man at the front of the caravan and offering the rest of his traveling companions a glass. They take them and drink, throwing us a few coins.

But the best part is that we have stopped the entire caravan.

Which is the opportunity we need.

Viva keeps ferrying the hot water back and forth. We've made a big pot of tea, but each time she brings the smaller kettle over, she's rolling one of her little clay pots filled with smoke and acid under the most heavily protected wagon. That has to be the one with the coffers of jewels and valuables.

Viva says that the acid will release a corrosive smoke that will drift upward and melt through the wood of the caravan cart. Once the wood melts, the coffer will drop down. When I asked earlier how she knew it would only go through the caravan floor and not the coffers—and also would not alert the guards or destroy the wheels—her answer was not confidence inspiring.

"It might," she said with a shrug. "But this is the only way to lift the coffers out from under them, short of digging our own trapdoor into the desert floor, which would take actual magic. This should not harm any living soul."

I tried not to focus on the *should* and hope she was right in her assumptions.

We scurry back and forth and back and forth and "chai chai and tea tea and a-shai" all the way down the front of the caravan. It's tedious work. We rinse out the glasses as best we can. Some of the men share their drinks with one another, regardless. Zeena and I do not pull any faces of disgust, for we must be chai-chees, accustomed to all manners and undisturbed by any of our customers.

Out of the corner of my eye I see John, and I know that the time for the swap is nearly done. I wait until I am all out of tea and I head back toward Viva.

"Eh! You!" I cry out, as though she is going too slowly for my liking. "Come and do your work!"

As I'm shouting and gesticulating for her to move faster, I trip myself. I go flying, but more important, all the glasses in my hand go flying. And they crash all around me in spectacular fashion. Just as I mean for them to do.

I've fallen and landed beside the cart with the most guards, the one that Viva has been throwing her little bits of clay beneath. I hope to distract the guards.

It's worked well enough that a few of the guards jump out of the way—out of the path of the broken glass. That was John's opportunity, and I can only imagine he took it. A couple of the men help me up, dusting me off.

"Thank you, thank you," I say most obsequiously, my head bowed.

And then I lay into Viva for all I'm worth. "How could you be so foolish?! How could you move so slow?! Now we have no glasses and no more ways to serve! What will we do now, eh?!"

Viva keeps her head down. I know her well enough now to know she's trying not to laugh. But it doesn't matter—our scene is believable enough.

And suddenly there's smoke everywhere.

John has done his job well—he's used one of Viva's other little clay pots to create a smoke screen.

A loud *THUNK* sounds. The coffer is out of the wagon as planned.

And then one of the little clay pots explodes with a *BANG*.

That . . . was not supposed to happen.

But hopefully, before the smoke clears, the coffer is onto a handcart that John will take, and, inshallah, get the money away before anyone knows where it's gone.

The men around us are all coughing and shouting.

For my part, I'm shouting as well. "Get to the meeting point!"

"Aye, captain." This is Teni. I can't see her, but her voice is unmistakable.

My eyes sting, but luckily my mouth is covered from my disguise. That, however, I must shed now, if I'm to do my part. I pull out my cloak from a bag at my hip, doing my best to hold my breath and not inhale the smoke.

Then I take advantage of the chaos to climb atop the nearest wagon.

When the smoke clears, I'm standing on top, looking down at all the guards and all the men.

"It's him," one cries, pointing right at me.

"The Green Hood," shouts another.

I look out of the corner of my eye. I spy John behind the rows of guards, holding a handcart. The barrow is covered and it looks like it could hold anything at all.

We've got it.

Which is why I say, "Good evening, gentlemen." I give a little bow. "I'm al-ghita akhdar, and I'm here to rob you blind."

Then I take off, running across the tops of the wagons and wagon covers.

An arrow goes whizzing by; I duck just in time. I do a roll off the top of the cart, then land on the ground and keep running. I'm bobbing and weaving until I can duck into the nearest wagon.

I am everyone else's safe exit strategy. I am the bait. Again.

Chapter Thirty-Two

Electric Feel

I THROW OFF MY CLOAK AND STUFF IT BACK INTO MY hip bag. I'm sure they'll search me if they find me, but if I change my disguise correctly, they won't have the opportunity to. I'm half-way out of the tea seller's robes when—

"I wouldn't do that if I were you."

I stop my movements at once. I know that voice.

I spin around, looking for him. And there, sitting right behind me, is Majid. His posture is that same lazy, unaffected one I saw all those days ago at a campfire outside Akko. He's in a different costume this time, something that would blend in with the coterie of the queen of Jerusalem. But his voice I'd know anywhere now, no matter how he tried to disguise it with languages or accents.

"Majid." I'm so relieved to see him I reach out and pull him into an embrace.

Too late do I realize that this was not the thing to do at all. Neither of us are children anymore.

I step back and release him at once. "I didn't know if you'd made it."

He laughs, his posture still relaxed. "You know us Mirza boys, we have nine lives. Like cats."

Outside, the scene around us goes on—the men shouting *in there,*

I saw him go in there, the clank of metal and wood, the jostling of people as they search for the Green Hood—but I feel untethered from everything in this moment. The two of us, eyes locked. Like when we were children and we grasped hands and spun so fast we couldn't breathe, falling to the ground in a fit of laughter.

None of this seems funny now.

I need someone to shake me from my senses, because all I want to do is lean in and see if he still smells of the dirt beneath his fingernails and the heat of the sun on his skin, even here in the cover of darkness.

I suspect that he does. I also suspect that the smell will not bring forth comforting childhood memories, but instead stir something long forgotten, or perhaps something never known before. Is there a word for a memory that's been reshaped? A name for a person so firmly rooted in one part of your mind that all it takes is one look and suddenly you've been entirely unmoored?

I don't know. I feel as though I don't know anything anymore.

The men-at-arms have reached this wagon. Majid hears this the same moment I do. "You really are trouble, you know. Quick," he says. "You've got to hide."

He takes me under his arm and stuffs me behind a wooden chest. Then he throws his cloak casually over me and part of the chest for good measure. By the time the men enter, he's back sitting in that lazy position I found him in.

My heart is pounding, and the smell of earth and sandalwood wafting off his cloak feels like it's under my skin and in my hair and in places I couldn't even name.

"Where is he?" calls out one of the guards.

Majid answers in perfect Faranji. "Where is who?"

"Answer me! They said he went in here!"

"You'd do well to change your tone." That lazy arrogance he's cultivated so well in his voice comes through.

"You'd do well to answer the question, boy."

One foot lands, then another. Majid is standing now, from the sound of it. "Search all you like. I know not of what you speak. I came in for a break from the sun. No one has been in here but you and your thugs."

"You lazy ass," says the guard.

Majid tsks. "Is that any way to treat your special guest? All the way from the courts of Byzantium?"

"Damn Byzantium for all that I care." The man-at-arms takes a step closer.

"Shall I go and tell your queen that?" Majid asks mildly.

This stays the guard's movement.

There's a long, tense moment. I'm sure that I'm going to die with the scent of sandalwood all over me. I'd always thought it a pleasant smell before now.

Another set of footsteps approaches, and a new voice speaks. "Anything in here?"

"No," says the first guard. "Must have gone elsewhere. Keep searching."

Two sets of footsteps retreat from the wagon. I hear them jump off the back and land in the dirt.

Majid pulls his cloak off me. "Quick. Off with you. That won't work a second time and I'm sure you want to get going before they double back again."

I nod at him. I thank God I was clever enough to wear my second costume under my first. When I disrobe, there's nothing but a soldier's plainclothes. Then I grab that old, worn jupon out of my bag and throw it on. The toggles are always the slowest part.

"Who do they think you are?" I ask.

He smiles, and the expression is familiar and foreign all at once. "Does it really matter?"

"I suppose not." I duck toward the front of the wagon, in case the men await me at the back. I turn over my shoulder before jumping down. "I hope we meet again."

Majid smiles. "You know, I think we just might."

As for me, I'm out of the wagon as fast as I can be without drawing notice. Then I dip up a little footpath that is all but invisible to anyone who is not looking for it. Behind the bend, Fouzia waits for me.

She stamps her feet, impatient that I have taken so long.

"I know, girl," I say to her. "Time to ride like the armies of hell are at our backs."

CHAPTER THIRTY-THREE

Such Great Heights

THE PLAN IS TO MEET FARTHER SOUTH, IN THE FOOT-
hills on the other side of the mountains. Everyone's horses were hidden along the first ridgeline so that we might escape quickly. We've each taken one of the many roads that Teni tracked out for us. It will take us most of the day to arrive at the meet up point, but that is why we started so early in our endeavors.

I try not to think about whether Zeena has made it through the wilderness. Whether Viva got lost. If John has still got the barrow in hand. Whether Teni ran into hermit monks along her own path through the foothills. I try not to think about Majid in that caravan wagon and how he went from a boy at my father's diwan to a spy, traipsing all over this land getting into who knows what sort of danger.

I try and fail, but I do not stop trying, for this effort is the only thing that calms my nerves as I ride along the barely trodden path.

It's a pretty forest in these hills. There's pine and oak and all these beautiful, swaying laurel trees. The trail itself is dusty, but the landscape is still green enough for my liking. Fouzia keeps her footing. And we wind along.

We round a bend in the road and I'm into a little valley, beyond the mountains themselves. At once I feel that my position is precarious; anyone just a little higher up could see me, and I would have no idea where they are.

The hair on my arms stands on end; I'm being watched.

Perhaps the smart fighter would take off running. Perhaps they would ready their weapons. But I have learned enough of war. I understand that what people want most is to know they have control—over another, over a situation, over the land, and over themselves. So I dismount Fouzia, moving slowly. As I walk a little farther, I pull off my bow and remove the knife from my boot, then the sword at my hip and the arrows at my other hip. Fouzia trails beside me. She is calm because I am calm.

I disarm myself and hold my hands high enough that whoever is out there can see.

For I know, deep in my bones, that someone is out there. I can feel eyes on me, the way anyone can feel that they are suddenly prey.

I come to a halt, but I do not call out. I wait.

And I wait.

It has probably only been a moment. One breath. Two. Now three.

An eternity in each inhale. To not rush. To know if I am right. To be patient when my body screams to react, to attack.

And then, like some kind of miracle, a figure appears out of the brush.

"Rahma, you really do surrender too easily," says Teni. She's cracked the most enormous grin. "My emee would tell you to hold your course, as she told me and my mother before me."

I run over to her, leaving Fouzia to stand amidst my weapons, and throw my arms around her. "You made it," I say with such relief. "And my father said something similar. But my own grandmother, my Bibi, she taught me about strategic surrender."

"I can see now where you get your wild ideas," she replies. She winces a little as I pull away. But she keeps speaking before I can remark on that. "And I worried. I thought for sure you would be caught and killed."

"Not this time," I say.

"Is that my sister?" Zeena has come out of the brush holding hands with Viva. One hand, at least. The other has a sword out and it's pointed in my direction.

"Do you really have to threaten all of us before the day is out?" I ask.

"It's in my nature," she says. "I like to be thorough. Make sure you are who you say you are—as the master of disguise, you could be anyone."

I look over all of them for a moment. "Where's John?"

I know just from looking at their faces that he has not arrived yet. Zeena's face is scrunched up in frustration—she still doesn't believe John is on our side. And Viva is watching Zeena, her concern taking on the edge of worry.

And then there is Teni, who looks over my shoulder, on to the many paths behind me. "He had the most work." She says this simply and without judgment.

"And you gave him the easiest path because of it," Zeena points out.

"We wait," I say. "He should be here by nightfall. We can worry after the sun has set."

Zeena snorts. Viva squeezes her hand. Teni keeps tracking behind me, looking far off into the distance.

"Come," she says finally. "Get your weapons out of the road. The sun will set soon and we'll need to make sure we have a fire."

"Is it safe?" I ask.

"Safer than being caught in the cooling air at night without one," she replies.

We set to gathering the kindling, and as much as this is an active task, it feels like waiting, like biding our time. I believe John will come. I *know* he will. But as we build the fire, Zeena grows more irritable and Viva grows more worried.

"I wonder if I did not make the right mixture," she says. "I wonder if I should have added more sulfur, but then, it would have smelled more and drawn more notice."

"The fault is not in your alchemy," says Zeena darkly.

"Enough!" I say. "It's bad enough we have to sit here and wait to see if he made it through. We do not need to add betrayal to our worries." I turn to Viva. "And I saw the barrow pulled out from the cart. Your trick worked beautifully. Though I'll still think of you as a magician."

Viva blushes. Zeena growls in the back of her throat.

"Go brush out the horses," I order, pointing at Red and Fouzia. I cannot handle her moods any longer.

She opens her mouth to protest.

"Just go," I say. "Or I'll wind up killing you myself."

Zeena makes so many death threats that hers have no weight. But mine? Well . . . mine do. She stalks off to the horses, pouting as she does so.

"That was badly done," says Teni, working with flint over the kindling so as to spark a flame.

"After you spend a year with her in a besieged city, I'll listen to any advice you have to offer. But as it is, I'll say that I let my temper go when I need to with her."

Teni shrugs. "She's your sister."

I sigh. "That she is."

And then, like some kind of Qur'anic miracle, I hear the sound of footsteps. That in and of itself, perhaps, is not a miracle. But they're accompanied by the trundle of wood on dirt—wheels turning in the dust.

I take off running toward the noise before anyone can stop me.

And there, standing in the lane, is John.

He's exhausted, sweat all over his brow and I imagine everywhere else. His horse trots alongside him. His breaths come in tired huffs. And in his hands is the cart filled with a queen's ransom.

CHAPTER THIRTY-FOUR

When the Levee Breaks

WE ALL GATHER AROUND THE BARROW.

John, in a flair for the dramatic that I did not know he had, pulls back the cover with a flourish to reveal the chest.

On the outside is a lock. But Viva merely says, "Give me a minute," and ducks beside it. She's got some kind of metal pin inserted into the mechanism, working it from within. *Click, click, click.* And then—

It's open.

The lock falls to the ground. Viva turns and looks at all of us.

"Go ahead," I say, impatient to see if we've done as we set out.

She pushes open the lid.

I gasp, and I am not alone in it.

For there inside, in the waning light, is such a glittering amount of gold that it nearly looks liquid.

"Rahma could give nearly all of this away and we'd still have enough to be the richest in the land," says Viva with a laugh.

"I confess, I would do not know what to do with this much wealth," Teni remarks. She looks a little pale at the sight, sweat forming at her brow.

"Nor I," I say. "But I'm sure we can find those who need it."

Zeena cuts in here. "Before you give away all of our hard-earned and ignoble plunder, let us figure out how much we need to make it to the Site of Holiness in one piece and without further theft."

Ah, ever practical Zeena. But I have one thing to say on that score, too. "We have enough to go home, Zeena. All the way home."

"We must stay and fight this fight, sister," she says.

"The war is almost over," I tell her. "One way or another."

"How can you say such a thing?"

"Easily," I say. "The invaders took Akko, and now they march on Jerusalem. The queen herself is on her way to reclaim her throne before Guy of Lusignan can get there. We are at the end of this war. It is inevitable."

"Nothing is inevitable," says Zeena.

"I shall use my bit of the money to buy books and the proper tools for alchemy," Viva says, clapping her hands in delight. "Oh! I could make proper equipment with this money. We do get to keep a bit, do we not?"

Zeena smiles at Viva as she speaks. The expression is a little silly on her and I hardly know what to make of it.

"Aye," I say. "Though the bulk should go to those that need it more."

I look back at the gold. It's enough to save so many orphans from this war. It's enough to send us all home. It's enough to reunite families that might have been separated from one another across this land. It's so much, and to think it was all in the hands of one woman, all because she wanted to buy back her kingdom from a fellow invader. Well, that makes me angrier that I could possibly say.

"And where will you go?" Zeena asks Viva.

"Wherever you choose," she replies, as though that were an obvious fact.

Zeena blushes a deep crimson, and I feel as though I have surely missed an important conversation between the two, but I do not ask now. "And you, Teni? Will you go home?"

Teni shrugs stiffly. "I would perhaps like a new deel. But I cannot fathom much more than that. I was made for an active life. If I return, I will be expected to guard the home front and to not travel again."

I nod. "And marry."

"And marry." She returns the nod. "Though I am not against the idea on principle. It just seems quite strange to me in practice."

"Why is that?" asks John.

"Why is it strange?" Teni asks in return.

"No, why must you go home and marry?"

Teni pauses. "I confess, I have not been honest with you all."

We all look at her.

"I am not a true warrior," she says, her voice growing faint. "In my land, I am something akin to a princess. I could have a court and reign over my own piece of the clan. But I have a wanderer's heart. I did not want to move only with the seasons. I wanted to see the world."

"Heaven help us," says Zeena. "We've now got to add harboring a fugitive princess to our list of crimes."

"I thought if I went with you, I'd have a little while longer with my freedom," says Teni. She does that shrug of hers and then winces again. "I cannot avoid my duty. But I thought I might delay it for a time."

We are all running from something, and we all found in one another what we needed. So I do not hesitate when I say, "Then stay as long as you need. And go home when you feel you must."

Teni nods, and I smile.

John sighs his own relief. "With my portion, I will buy books. I never had my own copy of Galen. Or Al-Hawi. Or Algorismus. Avicenna."

Viva gives John a curious look.

I turn to my sister. "And what shall you do with your portion, Zeena?"

"I shall save it—I know I will need it after you have given all your money away."

I know she means to jab, but I cannot help it. I start to laugh.

But then I look over at the treasure. And I catch sight of a bit of— is that brass?

I fish for it and I find two keys. Two large, impressive keys. And they're attached to a scroll.

"What is it?" asks Teni.

I do not know. But I feel the weight of the keys. And then I see the seal on the scroll. I take my knife, heat the tip in our campfire, and then used it to try to lift the seal. It's tedious work, but no one interrupts me as I do it.

Finally the seal is loose, in such a way as we can reattach it.

I open the scroll carefully.

Ya Allah.

"We are in so much trouble," I whisper.

"What is it?" asks Viva.

I look up at the faces of my crew, my little band of misfits. "We have stolen the peace treaty."

Teni puts her hand over her mouth. "Tengri forbid."

"And," I say, "if I am reading this correctly, the keys to the Holy Sepulchre."

We are silent for a long moment.

We have accidentally stolen the peace from this land.

Teni opens her mouth to speak . . . then falls over in a dead faint.

It's then that I spot what I was missing before.

Seeping through her garment, at the shoulder . . .

Blood.

＋

CHAPTER THIRTY-FIVE

The Princess, She Sleeps

WE'VE MOVED TENI TO A NEARBY CAVE. WE CAN SEE
our original fire from the mouth, so there's still some light to see by,
and at least she's sheltered here rather than exposed to any of the
wind that whips through the mountains at night.

John is ducked over Teni. "She's still breathing."

The rest of us are standing around her, tense and afraid.

"Humdulillah," I say, but I'm not thanking God for saving her—
I'm thanking God that the worst has not happened yet. "What can
we do?"

John's calm surprises me. He doesn't panic. He's gone so cool and
so clinical. I've seen others in battle do so: focus on the task at hand
so they have no room for fear, no space for panic.

"Have you any vinegar? Or distilled spirits?" he asks.

I pause for a moment and then rush over to one of Fouzia's saddle
packs. I stored the arak from the caravanserai there. I hand it to John.
"Here. What do you mean to do with it?"

"I need you to remove the robe so I can clean her wound with
this," he says. An accompanying tinge of embarrassment is the first
emotion that seems to register on his face.

Viva and I move at the same moment to help get Teni out of her deel.

"How do you know that will work?" asks Viva.

"I read it in al-Razi. That a clean wound is necessary. But we've got to have clean bandages, too. We need to boil the linens before we use them."

And Zeena—Zeena is already in motion, gathering up more wood to make another fire in the cave.

"You read al-Razi?" says Viva. She removes Teni's deel from her arm and then uses her dagger to cut away her undershirt. "I thought the Templars took great pride in not knowing how to read?"

John frowns. "The knights do. But the chaplains and the servants have to know how. You cannot manage so much money across an empire, nor can you manage prayers and rites, without someone being literate, no matter what pride you take in ignorance."

He pours the arak on Teni's wound. The pain must be great, for she awakens, gasping about fire and burning.

John places a gentle hand on her forehead. "She's not feverish yet. That's good. That's what we must hope for. Keep her humors in balance. Like the great philosopher Galen says we must. She hasn't lost too much blood. Not yet." He crouches closer, examining the wound. "Some bit of the clay pot is in here. She must have been too close to the explosion."

"Damn it all," whispers Viva.

I put my hand on her shoulder. "She knew the risks. We all did."

Viva looks up at me—the pain in her face is unmistakable. "Perhaps the villagers were right to call me a witch."

"No," I say. "They will never be right about that. And John can fix this."

I look to our young chaplain. I know I have said with certainty what no one can guarantee. But he looks back at me and nods, knowing what he's agreed to. Knowing what I've asked of him.

"I cannot remove the clay piece until we've clean bandages," he says.

"We need water," I say. And if we are near any, I cannot tell. The only person who could find a stream easily is the one who is currently whimpering in pain and in need of a surgeon.

I look to Zeena. She looks back at me. She shakes her head slightly, but I know what I must do.

"I've got to find one of the hermits. We need water for the bandages."

And then, before anyone can argue, I grab a clay pot off one of the horses' saddles and a piece of wood that Zeena has yet to throw on the fire. I rip a bit of cloth off my own undershirt and soak it in the arak.

Then I light my makeshift torch and take off back down the trail, in search of one of the fanatical monks.

CHAPTER THIRTY-SIX

The Mendicant

I'M TRACKING MY WAY UP THE FOOTPATH AS QUICKLY as I can—given that it's dark and I'm sure my torch will run out eventually. Alcohol burns faster than oil.

But I get lucky: I spot tracks leading up into the mountains, away from where I have just come. I follow the footprints.

The forest around me grows denser, wilder. There are wild olive trees up here. I have seen battle and learned to fear fewer things than I would have imagined in this life. But the wildness of these mountains, of this forest, speaks to some primal urge inside me. *Run. Flee. And never come back.*

Instead, I hold my course, and the trail grows more and more narrow. As though the mountains themselves have punished me for not listening to that instinct.

But at the end of the trail—and at the end of the footprints—is a little clearing.

And then, a cave.

I have to marvel at the ancient simplicity of such a dwelling. To live in the mountains the way our ancestors must have, before, perhaps, we even knew a name for God.

I hear a noise, echoing out from the cave's mouth, and I take a gamble that the source of that noise is human.

"Hello," I call out. "I know someone is in there. I do not mean you harm. I am Rahma bint Ammar bin Ali al-Hud. I have an injured friend. I need to know where there is water."

A man appears at the mouth of the cave. His robes are brown; his hair is tonsured. "Have you come begging from a beggar?"

"I have." He's different than I imagined a fanatic to look, but perhaps that was my own judgment clouding my expectations. I cannot tell if there is a wildness in him the way there is a wildness in these mountains. Perhaps he simply finds peace where I cannot. "I know not what form of payment you might accept, but if I do not find water or a stream, my friend could die."

"Then your friend would go to the Lord Almighty and be at peace," says the monk.

I rein in my frustration. "Perhaps. Or perhaps the Lord God sent me to find you, so that she might live a little longer."

The monk defies my expectations here by smiling. "Ah, a canny warrior."

There is a long pause where neither of us says anything. I look at him and he looks back. I do not know what he sees. But I refuse to flinch under the scrutiny of his gaze.

Finally, he says, "I shall show you where to find the stream." And then he steps out of his cave and leads the way back down the narrow mountain path.

We reach most of the way down, back toward where my friends are, when he turns up another little path I had missed. We do not speak. I hold my slowly dimming torch as the only source of light, aside from the slim moon. There is the sound of the forest at night—the scurrying of little creatures, and perhaps some not-so-little creatures—and the crunch of our feet in the dirt.

I hear the water before I see it. That slow, rushing sound that, at times, can almost sound like the ringing of a bell. It must be a very small stream to have such a pitch.

The monk turns to me then. His face is covered in shadow, though I know mine is lit by the torch. "Ah, I see you can hear it, too. Not everyone can. Not everyone listens."

I am not sure what to say to that, so I say nothing. I merely nod.

When we reach the edge of the stream, I put the clay pot into the water. "Is it clean?"

The monk nods. "It is here, at this point."

We walk back to the fork in the road, again in silence.

"Will you not accept anything in return?" I ask. "Even my torch to take you safely back?"

The monk shakes his head. "I have provided for you as I hope the Lord God will provide for me. I know my way back. I shall pray for your friend."

I bow as best I can with a torch in one hand and a pot of water in the other. "I thank you. I pray God keeps you as well."

And then the monk is gone, into the darkness, and I'm left to make my way back to my friends.

CHAPTER THIRTY-SEVEN

To Watch and to Wait

"This is what you get for playing with kings and queens and sultans," says Zeena.

"That is hardly helpful, sister," I reply.

Teni's wound has been cleaned and bandaged. She's sleeping now and she has no fever. We must wait. And hope.

John has tended to her well.

"You should all sleep," says John. "I can watch over her for the night."

But if John thinks any of us can sleep, he's guilty of wishful thinking. I sit down by the fire. "I think I shall stay up a little while longer."

Viva sits beside me. "Yes, so will I."

Then Zeena sits beside her, and pokes the fire with a stick.

"Do you really think she's a princess?" asks Viva.

"For my part," I say, "I do."

"Aye," says John, staring into the flames.

Zeena looks to Viva. "It would be a strange thing to lie about, no?"

"It would," agrees Viva. Her head tilts, as though she is thinking. "I wanted revenge so badly. For what was done to my people."

"In Al-Andalus?" I ask.

"Yes," says Viva. "Well, no. We came here because of that. But

I lost my mother and father and my brothers to the rest of these damned wars. I wanted to send fear into the hearts of those who had put such feeling in my own. For a moment I forgot that there could be another cost."

"It is war," I say. "There is always another cost."

"And this time Teni paid it," whispers Viva.

"Would you blame me, I wonder?" I look at Viva as I say it. "It was my plan, after all."

"No," she says.

"Then do not blame yourself. We could follow this chain of blame all the way back to the Faranji, for invading these shores a hundred years ago," I say.

John looks at me now. "Why did you come?"

I'm startled by the question. Between my faith and my sister, nobody has ever bothered to ask me. I look at Zeena, but she's still staring into the campfire, still prodding the smoldering wood with her little stick.

"I could not let Zeena ride to war alone," I say.

Zeena's attention snaps to me. "That is not what you said. Not when we left."

And perhaps it is this night. For the next thing I say is, "I lied."

John nods, as though he has understood this all along, but needed confirmation. "I just wanted to make a difference. I did not know what the Templars truly were."

"And if you had not had your learning, you might not have been able to help Teni now," I say.

Zeena nods, then looks to Viva. "You should not regret what you made. I wish you had seen the looks on those soldiers' faces when the smoke began to pour out of those clay pots."

"I did," says Viva. And she cracks a grin.

That one little expression is all we needed, for we all start to laugh, thinking about the sight of all the queen's men, scrambling about as they tried to figure out how there was suddenly smoke in the air and where the wealth of the Kingdom of Jerusalem had run off to.

Eventually I nod off to sleep. I'm not sure whether we all do eventually.

I hope Teni awakes in the morning, so she can join in our laughter.

CHAPTER THIRTY-EIGHT

I Heard It through the Grapevine

I AM THE LAST ONE TO AWAKEN IN THE MORNING. Zeena tends to the fire, still, to keep Teni warm. And Viva sits beside Zeena. Teni is already sitting up, drinking some broth that John has made. I'm baffled as to how he made it, given our limited resources, but I've stopped questioning his methods. John is as capable as the rest of us, albeit in his own, different way.

Teni is pale but there is light in her eyes. Enough to give me hope.

"You gave us quite the scare yesterday," I say.

"Aye," says Teni, wincing through a grin. "I scared myself."

"Still no fever," says John, his voice heavy with relief. "I think we're through the worst of it."

"Mashallah," I say. "How long before we can move again?"

"I'm not sure. A week, perhaps? More?" says John. "She'll have pain, but that should ease eventually. Luckily we have provisions in the horses that the sheikh sent us on with. We should wait until she has recovered her strength. Thank God for these caves."

Thank heaven for mercies, large and small. That's one problem down. But then there's the other. "What are we to do with the peace treaty and the keys to the Holy Sepulchre?"

No one answers for a long while.

"What are the keys to the Holy Sepulchre?" asks a weary Teni.

I realize then that she passed out before she saw what had been hidden in our treasure. "The chest contained not only the coffers of the false queen of Jerusalem; it also held a treaty for peace, which we have stolen. And the keys to the holiest of churches for the Nasrani. The Holy Sepulchre."

John crosses himself. "Where Christ was crucified, and then where He was risen."

"And what is the trouble there?" asks Teni.

"If we give these back to her, we give the queen power," I say. "These keys are what Richard has been searching for. He believes that al-Nasir has them. Everyone does. He cares deeply about opening up Jerusalem to Nasrani pilgrims again."

"We cannot give the key to Richard," Zeena says, then spits.

"Sister," I say. "These are not the keys to our own masjid. Not the keys to the Dome of the Rock. We cannot hand such a thing over to al-Nasir, either. I would not use the brutality of the Faranji against themselves. I would not become them to defeat them."

"Well, perhaps you should," says Zeena. "Their brutal tactics gave them dominion over this land."

"Then you can kill and eat a Faranji and tell me how you feel afterward," I snap.

Zeena looks mutinous.

"But if we do not give back the keys," I continue, looking at Teni. "If we do not return the treaty. Then we have stolen the peace. And God knows how much longer this war will go on."

Teni nods. The grim look on her face tells me she understands all, now.

Viva is drinking her broth, her face contemplative. "If there is a way to use the Greek fire—"

I hold up my hand. "No Greek fire. Not when we could burn down the wilderness and the villages. That's a last resort. And really, to be saved for a battle at sea."

"Then I shall pray to the Lord God for a sea battle," Viva says with absolute finality.

John scratches his head thoughtfully. "I shall have to pray for the opposite, I'm afraid. I have no idea how to swim."

"If any of you think that we will live long enough to see a sea battle, you've lost your minds," says Zeena.

"You've all lost your minds, if you don't mind my saying," a new—but very familiar—voice says from behind me. "Sitting here in the cedar forests, speaking of sea battles while the queen of Jerusalem searches high and low to put your heads on pikes. Again."

I jolt and spin around to find him standing at the edge of our camp. "Majid!"

He looks at me and simply says, "Hello, Trouble."

"How did you find us?" I ask.

Majid shrugs. "Easily enough. I followed your trail through the woods."

"That's not good," remarks Teni. She's got a little frown on her face.

"It's hard to cover your tracks in the dark when you're worried about finding clean water, you know," I say defensively.

Zeena gets up and walks directly to where he's standing. "I might have known you'd show up, yet again."

Majid puts his hand over his heart and bows low. "Still the sovereign even in retreat, I see, Zeena."

She sniffs. "Ever the charmer, Majid Mirza."

He laughs, then says, "I have news."

"What is it?" I ask, a little bit breathless. Mostly because he's

246

mentioned news and not because seeing him again has gone to my head. In any way.

"Did you know he was here, Rahma?" asks Zeena before Majid can answer.

"Well, yes," I admit. "He was in the wagon. He helped me escape from the caravan."

"I provided a little bit of cover, that is all," says Majid.

I smile at him and he smiles back.

"You were impossible as a boy and now you're impossible as a man," says Zeena. "How did you come to be riding with the queen of Jerusalem?"

"You've never missed a thing, have you, Zeena?" he says with a grin that Zeena does not return.

"I have not."

John, who has been watching the exchange in silence until this point, speaks. "And what news have you?"

"The queen of Jerusalem wants your capture," he says.

"We already know that," snaps Zeena.

Majid is unbothered by this, though. "And do you also know that she means to offer five hundred bezants to pay for the recovery of the treaty? She says the very peace of the land is at stake. She begs the thieves to reconsider."

"Ya Allah," is all I can manage to say.

John whistles. Teni nods in agreement.

"She means to *pay* us for our theft?" asks Viva.

"No," says Majid, his tone somber for the first time in the conversation. "She means to lure you into Jaffa, where she will be camped, and to take you all as prisoners back to Kerak Castle. Undoubtedly, she will kill you there, after she's had her fun torturing you at her own pleasure."

"How can you know this?" I ask.

"I heard it outside her tent," says Majid.

John steps forward. He takes one look at Majid and says, "You're an Assassin."

It's never the most flattering accusation to lead with, as a rule, but Majid takes it in stride. "And why say you that?"

"You're either an Assassin, or you're here to betray us," John says. "If you ride with Queen Isabella, your being placed so high and in such a position to have information and then give it to us freely could only mean one thing."

I hold my breath. The Assassins are even more notorious than the Templars. If the Templars make kings, then Assassins destroy them.

Majid nods, a concession. "I am not an Assassin, no, though my father's sympathies lie with Nur ad-Din Muhammad. I am gathering information at his behest."

"Stirring discord, more like," spits Zeena.

But Majid does not back down. He steps toward my sister. He does not threaten her. Does not tower over her. But he means to show her that he will not be cowed by her. "You still speak in absolutes. In right and wrong and black and white. It's a pretty picture you paint. To say my loyalty to my father means nothing, and your loyalty to a sultan who is not even your own means everything. It's easy to say I stir discord and you plant the seeds of righteousness. But you have always been amongst those who believe your God is right. You do not have to convert to save your own skin, as many of my brethren have."

John looks over, confused. "I thought they all believed in the same God—Allah."

But he's looked to Teni—as he's always looking to Teni—and she just shrugs. "Don't ask me. I worship the Eternal Blue Sky and Mother Earth and the gods of old."

Viva leans in to clarify. "Actually, we all believe in Allah, which is just God. The one true God."

"I do not call Him that," remarks John.

"Perhaps not, but the Nasrani here do," Viva says. "And the Muslims, they split long ago. Much like the Christians of Rome from the Christians of the East. You have a pope and they have a patriarch. You would not worship with icons as they do. But to the rest of us, you are all Nasrani."

"That's blasphemy," says John.

"To you," says a smiling Majid.

I wave my hands in the air. "Enough theology. I tire of it."

"You always have," says Zeena under her breath.

"Are you truly an Assassin?" I stare unflinchingly at Majid.

"I am not. Not truly," he says. "I am not a righteous enough believer for any cause, as well you may remember. And I've never had to kill another in service of getting the information I seek. But I'm sure with the information I have given . . . there is blood on my hands."

I nod. "There's blood on all our hands."

But Zeena has not lost focus. "Do you know how they mean to trap us? The queen and her cohort?"

"No," confesses Majid, looking away from me. "I heard footsteps and then they called for us to hunt you down and bring you back to the queen. I had to stop listening at the tent before she said how she means to trap you. But I volunteered when Balian asked for those to send out the message. I followed your tracks here and had to warn you off before you heard from another source."

"Thank you," I say, my mind whirring.

"No," says Zeena, staring right at me. "Absolutely not."

"You haven't even heard what I'm going to say!"

"I don't need to. I can see your mind at work." Zeena shakes her head. "It's all over your face. You mean to get the treaty *and* the reward. But she knows it's you. No one else could have the treaty but *you*. Do not play the fool."

"We stole from her twice," I say. "We could outfox her a third time."

Majid's expression grows quite serious. "It's a trap."

"And now we know it," I say. "Thanks to you."

"You cannot be serious," he says.

Zeena just snorts.

"I am," I say. "I cannot risk the peace simply for my own safety. We must find a way to get this treaty into the right hands. Though I am still unsure whose hands those are." I reach out and grab his hands. That feeling—of the familiar and the brand-new—washes over me again. "I thank you for the news you have brought. But I must do what needs to be done."

"Here we go again," says Teni.

I look over to her. "I do not ask any of you to go further down this road. If you wish, you can take your part from the chest and go."

Teni nods. "You've taken us this far."

Viva steps forward. "We're with you as far as you will go."

"I would not leave you to do this thing alone," says John.

I look to Zeena.

"You're a fool," she says. "But of course I'm coming with you."

I look over at Majid. "To Jaffa?"

He nods. "I must return to the camp so that they do not suspect me. But I will meet you there."

"Then when Teni has recovered some of her strength," I say, "we shall march our merry band on Jaffa. And we will decide how to return the peace we have stolen."

Near Arsuf,
just north of Jaffa

In the queen of
Jerusalem's camp

CHAPTER THIRTY-NINE

Every Step You Take

ISABELLA LIKED TO THINK HERSELF A REASONABLE queen.

Perhaps not merciful. Or just. Not kind or warlike. Neither a she-wolf nor, even, in her nineteenth year, a blushing bride.

But reasonable? That was something she could do.

So it was a struggle to not do the *reasonable* thing and execute every last man who had allowed for her most precious coffer to be taken by a thief.

The same thief who had taken her horse.

It was too much to be borne, this kind of insult.

"You called for me, Your Highness?" The spy had reentered the tent. *Good.* She'd at least have someone to take out her frustrations on.

"Yes," she said, then snapped her fingers. The men-at-arms who stood guard outside her tent came in and seized the spy on either side.

He fought against their iron grip, his usual mask of poise nearly slipping from his face. "What is going on?"

"You've failed me," she said. "I told you to find the Green Hood. Not only did you not complete this very simple task, but that thief came and stole from my caravan *again*."

The spy struggled against the two men who held him, but he had not lost his wits. "You need me to negotiate a peace with Byzantium. At least to call for reinforcements."

He was right, of course. But Isabella was tired of men who were right and forced their will upon her. "That is true. But I think you are like every man who came before you. You underestimate me. I cannot imagine one so canny as you could have let him slip through their fingers so many times. You are in league with the Green Hood. Perhaps it is what the other councillors shall dismiss as feminine intuition. As Eve's witchery and cunning. But I know what my instincts are telling me."

The spy said nothing as he looked at Isabella. His eyes were not filled with fear, but alertness. He was trying to *read* her.

How dare he.

Isabella smiled. "I have something *special* in mind for you. I thought I would lure the Green Hood with a mere reward. But I see now, that would never work as I hope. He is clever with treasure. No, I have a new plan. *You* are to draw out the Green Hood, whether you mean to or not. I suspect the reward is not enough. Not for what I have in mind."

Then she snapped her fingers again and the guards hauled the spy away. She would hold him as her prisoner for the time being. Until she could make his death useful to her.

Right now, Isabella had to *think*.

She had taken the treaty so that she might parley directly with Saladin. Altered the terms so that they benefited her and her alone. The sultan might be a dog, but at least she could keep him away from her borders. She had planned to use that charming young fool from Byzantium to gather her own allies from her mother's side of the family. She had planned to end the war and buy back her kingdom.

Now she had no money. No way of tricking Saladin into agreeing to her terms, under the guise of them being Conrad's. Now she had to find a new plan.

Richard of England had defeated Saladin at Arsuf. This gave Richard an edge, and weight among the nobles. If he were to call a council to determine who would rule Jerusalem, Richard could sway the votes against her and in favor of that rat, Guy.

If there was but a way to keep the fighting going . . . to delay a little while, until Richard's army was weary of being here in the Holy Land, and was ready to retreat back home. Then time would be on Isabella's side and not Richard's or Guy's.

What Isabella needed was, perhaps, then *not* to treat for her own peace.

Perhaps what she needed was to keep this war going *indefinitely*.

Until everyone's coffers were empty. And they had no choice but to give her back her throne so that they might finally be allowed to limp back to their own kingdoms.

If she could use Richard to wear out Saladin and Saladin to wear out Richard, then Isabella didn't *need* an army of her own. She didn't even need her treaty. And she could keep the keys of the Holy Sepulchre, to use when she saw best. She could wait until Richard was at his weakest before she brought those keys back into play.

Isabella would have her crown back.

But she had to be clever. First, she needed her treasury back. And now, more than ever, she wanted that thief's head on a pike. The Green Hood would pay for what he had done. For the embarrassment he had caused her.

And then the rest of them would pay.

She called for Balian of Ibelin. When he entered, he bowed. "My queen, I understand you are upset—"

"Oh, Balian," said Isabella. "I am long past upset."

This silenced him, for he was an old campaigner and a survivor. One did not get to be such an age as he without the right instinct for when to shut up.

"I would like to lay a new trap for our little friend," said Isabella. "I do not think the reward enough, anymore."

"And what do you propose? A royal tournament to tempt his hubris?"

Isabella laughed. "This thief is no fool. He will not simply come because I have offered the chance to play childish games."

Balian tilted his head. "He might. Men are foolish when it comes to pride."

Isabella nodded. "Indeed they are. But I doubt very much it's pride that marks this thief's downfall. Too clever and too bold by half, this Green Hood."

Balian nodded. "You are right, of course, Your Majesty."

"He has had the advantage of me twice. He has taken from my camp and I never saw him coming, despite my guards and my security and all the loyalty of the men I travel with."

Balian must have heard the dryness in her tone, for he said, "My queen, we are all loyal to you and to the crown."

"*You* are," said Isabella. "But as for the rest, they are more loyal to the crown than to myself. If a strong enough contender came along, they would abandon their posts and side with whomever they thought likeliest to win."

Isabella had no illusions about this. Power was all that mattered in this world. Honor had very little to do with any man's choices in battle. It was useful, that personal interest. But Isabella never mistook it for loyalty. Not really.

"The thief took something of mine," said Isabella. She need not tell Balian of the keys to the holy church that she had held and lost.

She would recover them soon enough. She need only let him think she cared for her gold and her gold alone. "Something of great import."

"Yes," said Balian.

"So we shall play a little game with our thief."

Balian looked at her. "And what game is that, Your Highness?"

"We shall test our thief's own loyalties. We shall march to Jaffa. And there I will stage a public execution of a spy that I have found in our midst. The envoy sent from the fringes of Byzantium."

Balian's words had abandoned him; for a moment he could only stare at the queen in shock. "You mean to start a war with Byzantium over this thief?"

"I believe the Green Hood shall be lured by the siren call of saving one of his men," said Isabella. "And I believe our friend has been in league with this Green Hood from the start. If I risk war in executing a spy, so be it."

Balian, proving himself a true survivor, did not counter her. "Consider it done. I shall send out word directly. There is to be a public execution in Jaffa of the traitorous spy found in our midst. Is there anything else I might do for my queen?"

Isabella smiled. She was going to tear down Conrad's court from the inside. And then she would make sure that no one in this land knew peace ever again. Not until she sat on the throne of Jerusalem.

"That will be all, Balian."

In the caves of the
Carmelite Mountains

CHAPTER FORTY

Return of the Mack

THERE IS MUCH WORK TO BE DONE FIRST. I'M SORRY to say it, but you cannot just ride into battle without your strategy, though I wish it were so. Actually, Zeena is the one who wishes it were so.

Everyone is growing restless with all this waiting and planning, though.

"Teni," I say. "You must find a local smithy."

She is much recovered from her injury and claims she can ride without pain. I have to believe her, for her sense of direction is best, and I would entrust this errand to no one else. I hand her a sack of coin and the keys to the holy site. She is my most trusted companion, next to Zeena, and I know that she will see this task through. "Get them to make two copies of this. Pay them whatever they need for both expediency and silence."

Teni grins that jolly grin of hers and takes the keys in hand. "Ah, you do have a plan, don't you?"

"Always," I say. "And several more plans besides for when it all inevitably falls apart. But perhaps we can make enough keys so that everyone feels they are in charge and everyone accepts the peace."

Teni laughs and mounts Red. She rides off south, toward a nearby town.

I task John next. "Have you a steady hand?" I say. "I know that all monks, do. Though you're a chaplain and not a monk."

"I can do it," says John.

I know he is a Templar and a Faranji, but he's learned enough to know more than one script if he's read al-Razi. "I assume you can you imitate the Faranji style in your writing. But can you also do a naskh script?"

John's smile extends across his whole face. "I can do that. What do you need written? A copy of this scroll?"

"No," I say. "Leave this original scroll intact. I will tell you what to write. But I will need both a Faranji and an Arabic scroll as well."

John shrugs, but doesn't question it. "Give me two days to get the inks and the parchments and you'll have your treaty as long as my hand can stay steady."

"A good forgery," I say. "It must look as though it came from the court of al-Nasir—Salah-a-Din himself. And the other, like it came from Jerusalem."

He nods. "A good forgery." He stops, though, as he's examining the document. "This treaty has already been altered."

"What?" I ask.

He points to a spot on the vellum. "It's been scraped away, just here with a knife, and rewritten."

It's the faintest hint of ink below the current script. But now that John has pointed it out, I see the alteration at once. "I see."

"Does this change your plan?" he asks.

I shake my head. "Not yet. It's a problem, but I must consider all the pieces again. Perhaps it's something we can use to our advantage.

The false queen of Jerusalem must have altered this treaty for some reason. If we can figure out why, then it could be her problem and not ours. But get the inks. And the vellum for a proper Faranji parchment. And paper for the Arabic one."

John nods and sets himself to his tasks.

Viva is standing nearby. "It'll never fool them. Not without the right seal."

"Oh," I say. "I know."

"Then what do you mean to do?" she asks.

"I mean to get close enough to get the right seal. You'll see." I grin. "And you, I give the two most important jobs of all."

Viva leans in, alert. She's hated this waiting most of all. More so than even Zeena.

I pull off my mantle. "You must copy this green exactly. Can you get the color right? Green is such a difficult dye. And we will need much of it to dye enough cloth."

Viva nods. "I can do that. I'll need more time than the others, though."

"Just do it as quickly as you can. And make some more of those smoking clay pots."

Viva's eyes go wary. "Are you sure?"

"Very," I say.

She pauses, and then the light of joy returns to her eyes. "And what about the Greek fire?"

I think for a moment. "All right, you can make those, too."

Viva hurries off before I can change my mind. She's already drawing with her finger in the air and talking to herself as she walks.

I expect Zeena to yell at me now, but she's just watching Viva with a silly sort of grin on her face.

"Sister," I say. "You look lost in thought."

Zeena's eyes snap to mine and her expression grows sharp. "You've got a foolish plan, don't you?"

"It's my best one yet; would you like to hear it?" I worry a little bit, that Majid has not returned to us in all this time. But he did say he would meet us in Jaffa, so I will hold him to that. I hope he is safe.

Zeena crosses her arms over her chest like she is deeply uninterested. But she doesn't speak and she doesn't move away, so I know that really, she's dying to know. "Not costumes again. You live to dress up as another."

"Ah, but this time I will not be dressed as another." I've a harebrained scheme. And it won't just take cunning. It will also take all the nerve that I possess. We are going to steal back the peace from this land. From Richard, from Salah-a-Din, from the queen of Jerusalem.

We are going to end this war. Because Zeena was right: Nothing is inevitable.

I must make it so. I must steal back a peace long forgotten in this land.

But before I can tell Zeena all, Teni rides back from town and she is out of breath.

"What is the matter?" I ask. I still worry about her injury flaring up again. "Are you ill?"

"I am fine," she says, panting.

"Were they unwilling to copy the key?" I ask.

"No, the keys I have," says Teni, her breathing slowly steadying. "News. I have news. I have just heard, though, from the villagers."

"What?" I ask.

The expression in Teni's eyes looks haunted. "The queen of Jerusalem has arrested Majid. She means to execute him in Jaffa. Three days' time."

Allah above. Not that.

Words fail me entirely.

"It's a trap," says Zeena.

"Of course it is," I snap.

"We will be outnumbered if we attempt a rescue," says John.

"Then what shall we do?" asks Viva.

"Now," I say, "we must steal two things—the peace and Majid."

Meanwhile, just
outside Jerusalem
In the camp of Richard
of England

CHAPTER FORTY-ONE

Seven Nation Army

RICHARD COULD SEE HER. THE HOLY CITY. GOD'S kingdom here on Earth.

He had brought his army from the north, and he meant to recapture the Holy Sepulchre and reclaim the city from heathen invaders. Meant to take the keys to the holy church back from the hands of Saladin himself. Meant to take back what ought to be in Christian possession.

But how to do it . . . that was the trick.

Jerusalem was Richard's for the taking. But he had angered many of his fighting men when he had refused to parley with Saladin. Saladin had lost Akko. But Richard had, himself, lost the spirit of his own fighting men. They had lost their faith in him the moment that Richard had executed his prisoners.

And then the weather had turned. It was going to ice and sleet and, God forbid, snow. Richard could not lose his head again. He could little afford it. Not when victory was so close at hand.

True, Saladin had lost in Akko. But he had lost because Akko had her port and could be defended and replenished by sea. There was no such relief that could come for Jerusalem.

So, Richard ordered his men to make camp. They would sit here, and he would think what best be done.

"Shall we attack in the morning, sire?" asked Bertram of Verdun.

"No," said Richard.

"Do we await reenforcements?" he asked.

"No," said Richard. "We must see which way the sultan turns."

"But by then it will be too late! Our advantage is that we are ahead and we have superior numbers. We bested him at Arsuf, let us best him here and be done with it. The emirs have forced Saladin to disband a good portion of his army. They fear him so that they take his power from him. Now is our moment to strike. Cleanse our Holy Land of the unbelievers and those who doubt the One True God once and for all!"

It was a sentiment that Richard agreed with wholeheartedly, but he held up his hand to stay Bertram's speech. Something unsettled him. Richard had come all this way in order to defeat the great Saladin. And defeat him, Richard had.

And yet the disquiet in his heart had not gone away.

If anything, it had increased.

"And I have seen this sultan fox at work," Richard said. "He will use our advantages against us. He will twist and turn everything we do like clay in his hands. Do not question me again."

Bertram nodded, bowed with real fealty. "My apologies, Your Majesty."

Richard did not care for apologies. He was a man of action. But where would Saladin strike next? Would he defend the holy city at all costs? Would he double back to Akko with her strategic port?

Richard could not say. And that he could not say, gave him pause.

Richard had conquered Sicily and Cyprus. He knew how best to lie in wait for his enemy, how to make the most of his chances. It was cold and icy now. The rain would laden them all down and make conditions in a siege miserable. Perhaps the city would fall quickly. Perhaps morale was already very low. But then again, perhaps not. Perhaps he would end up besieged himself: with a hostile city on one side and hostile forces on another, with no chance of relief.

Richard had written to Conrad, who had refused to send aid unless Richard ratified his treaty—explicitly stating that he, and not Guy, was king of Jerusalem. But Richard had not received such a treaty from Conrad. He received no further word from Conrad at all.

And then there was the rumor that Conrad was suing for peace with Saladin himself. Richard did not know who was his ally and who his enemy in this land.

It was an unholy mess. But then war always was.

"We wait," said Richard. "We wait."

Outside the gates
of Jaffa

CHAPTER FORTY-TWO

Gives You Hell

THE FIRST THING THAT YOU MUST KNOW ABOUT JAFFA is this: The city has passed back and forth between hands so many times, it's impossible to say to whom she belongs. The problem with being the last port city before you get to Jerusalem is that you are strategic. And while strategic cities are ideal in times of peace, you never want to live in one in a time of war.

Jaffa sits atop a sloping coastline, so that—even though it is one of the most ancient cities around—it looks nearly constantly in danger of sliding back into the sea. It has none of the easy relaxation of Haifa. It's precarious, this city.

I love it immediately.

The sheikh had sent us on with enough provisions to get here, even after we had to wait in the mountain caves; we're still laden with dates and bread and geymar and sour yogurt. We made good time and were lucky to run into no one along the road.

It's probably the last bit of luck we'll have. You can only get lucky for so long before your luck runs out. Or, at least, I have always felt so.

But I don't give in to this feeling of foreboding. Instead I push ahead.

I've got the real key to the Holy Sepulchre and the original treaty deep inside one of my robe pockets. I've stuffed one of those clay pots of Greek fire beneath all the arrows in my quiver. None of it can be discovered at the wrong moment. Teni has the cart strapped to a barrow behind Red as her own sort of disguise. We're going slow, trying not to overtax Red or any of the other horses. Fouzia, for her part, refuses to pull a cart.

Former mount of the queen of Jerusalem, indeed.

In any case, we have plans here in Jaffa. We're here to meet the false queen, and it's an appointment we mean to keep.

John wears the costume of a local Nasrani. Teni is dressed as herself, as are Viva and Zeena. We draw no notice, not in Jaffa, which is a city so filled with foreigners that nobody knows who is supposed to be here anymore and who is not. It helps, too, when you've enough coin to bribe the guards.

Isabella, queen of Jerusalem, has set up court in the fortified tower of the city. She has called one and all to come forth to the tower's courtyard, to watch a spy, a traitor to the crown, be hanged.

She has decided that her prisoner is not a true nobleman, that Majid is not of Faranji or Norman blood. Therefore, he will have a thief's death.

She has set her trap well, this queen. She knows exactly how to bait me into her territory.

I hope I can keep my cool long enough to save Majid. And the sacred city from her clutches.

We gain entry to the courtyard area without much fuss, as the execution is open to the public. It's a big stone building, meant for keeping out threats. But, by the same token, I doubt we will be able to make it out of here if we are caught.

There is no going back, not once we are inside this fortress.

We have left the horses outside the city, in a caravanserai. It will be easier to walk amongst the people and blend in than ride about. It's not like we had to worry about paying to stable the horses.

We follow the line of traffic, deeper into the tower courtyard.

At the center is a platform. On one side of the platform is the gallows. There stands the executioner, readying the noose. On the other side of the platform is the royal audience. It makes me sick to look at.

For there, on a throne, sits the so-called queen of Jerusalem.

There she awaits her entertainment, and seated all around her are her men—guards and councilmembers. She is in all her royal trappings—deep brocaded velvet and bell sleeves trimmed in fur, a nod to the cooling weather. She wears a gold circlet on her head.

One of those seated alongside her is another woman. She's older—and given her own regalia and her own circlet on her head, that woman must be the dowager queen, Isabella's own mother. The false queen's husband, Conrad, is noticeably absent. They say he's stayed in Tyre, sending out messengers to parley directly with Saladin.

So the queen's presence here is notable. She is playing at what she is often labeled as—a spoiled and petulant girl-queen. But I can see the calm and the fire in her eyes. She's in charge, whether any of the other men realize it or not.

And most of them don't. I can tell by the smug look on their faces. They think they've got the girl well in hand. But far off to the side is one man who seems to know differently. He's dressed as a resplendent nobleman, same as the others, but he's got an air of attention that is unique. He's older, much older; his hair has gone white. And his sense of deference is subtle. He seems to sense the queen is in command in a way the others do not—that she has a mind of her own. He's tense, standing there. They all turn their bodies toward that man. But he—his head is tilted in the queen's direction.

And from such a small thing I know he's a kingmaker. The kind of man who sees the potential for power, not just what is visible and present in the moment. He has the look of a man who sees the future, then makes it so.

"That's Balian of Ibelin," says John, who is standing beside me.

I scan the crowd. "Majid should be here. Why have they not brought him out yet?"

"Stick to the plan," says John.

"Do you think this will work?" I ask.

Teni answers me. I can hear the grin in her voice. "Knowing you, even if it doesn't, you'll find a way to make it work."

I resist the urge to turn to face her. We cannot seem to know one another, not yet. "That one there. He's smarter than the rest of them by half."

"More than that," says John. "He's preternatural. If he were a woman, they'd probably call him a witch."

"But as he is not?"

Out of the corner of my eye, I see John nod. "He's been adviser to the king, her father. The king, her brother. And the queen, her sister. He has never picked wrong, not for nearly thirty years."

"A true survivor," I say.

"Indeed." This is Zeena, who stands behind me.

The drumroll starts from the platform. And there, surrounded by guards, is Majid. He's been stripped down to his kaftan and his hair has been shaved close to his head. He's still got the scruff of his beard left, but they must have shaved that at some point, too, for he cannot have more than a day or two of growth there.

He looks tired and underfed. But, God love him, he walks with his head high. A bubble of a laugh forms in my throat that I have to suppress—for the grim nature of all of this, Majid has kept his pride intact.

Which means I do not have to worry about him not knowing what to do in the event that we actually pull off this rescue.

Teni clears her throat. "Shall we?"

I glance at her; she's got her green mantle on. She's holding a stack of green cloaks in one hand. So, too, are John and Viva and Zeena.

I throw my own mantle on. "Let the game begin."

CHAPTER FORTY-THREE

The Shadow in the Background

BACKGAMMON IS A GAME OF LUCK, BUT YOU MUST PLAY it as though it were a game of skill. That is what I learned from Majid all those years ago.

I tell you this so that you might understand what comes next.

Majid is directed to the center of the platform. The noose is tied around his neck.

I move to a spot along the courtyard with stairs so I can climb to higher ground.

I will, after all, only have one shot at this.

The sound of the drum rattles on.

Queen Isabella does not watch as they tighten the noose around Majid's neck. She does not watch as they position him above the drop in the floor.

She watches the crowd. And this is how I am sure that this is a trap.

But I refuse to cower to this queen.

The executioner reads the chargers. That Majid stands accused of treason against the crown. Spying. Thievery. Threatening the peace and the Kingdom of Jerusalem. He is to hang by his neck until he is dead.

Not if I have anything to do with it.

The executioner strings him up. And in that moment, I get out my bow.

I watch as Majid closes his eyes and says a prayer.

I nock an arrow and pull it back.

The executioner yanks the lever. Majid drops.

But of course, I have already loosed the arrow.

And my aim is true.

The arrow slices through the rope and thunks into a wall, just above Balian of Ibelin's head.

And Majid has fallen through the trapdoor, disappearing under the scaffolding.

"There!" shouts Queen Isabella, pointing in my direction. "The Green Hood. Arrest him!"

But here is my trick.

While I was climbing the stairs and setting up my shot, my friends were all handing out cloaks to many in the crowd and had people wear them for a coin or two.

We are no longer alone in wearing green hoods now.

I stash my bow and jump back down into the crowd as quickly as I can, knowing the guards are on my heels.

I hope that John has gotten to Majid under the scaffolding. It is his job to get them both out of here alive.

It is time for the next phase of the plan.

From her vantage point, Viva lobs her clay pots filled with smoke.

As the air blackens, the gathered crowd goes into a panic.

The queen is screaming, "Stay where you are, you fools! We're meant to be dispersed by this! Find the one with the green hood!"

Ah, I was correct. I smile—I knew I was right to not underestimate the queen. I knew she would see through at least two levels of subterfuge. Hopefully not three, but she is cleverer than any of the men around her give her credit for.

John and Majid should be out of danger by now.

The guards go sifting through the smoke and roiling crowd. They grab at someone in a green cloak—even I cannot tell if it is a random member of the crowd or one of my comrades—but they miss and whoever it was runs free.

I pull out my bow, regardless. I do not want innocents being trapped on my account.

"Got him!" shouts one guard, who has someone in a hold. He pulls back the hood and it is no one I recognize.

I fire an arrow at that guard's shoulder and he releases his quarry at once.

"No, I've captured him," says another. The hood is pulled back, but again, it's a stranger that they've nabbed.

I fire again, and while the guard ducks, the stranger runs free.

Everyone is in green hoods, and the guards have realized that they have been outwitted.

At least, that is the hope.

"There's too many of them!" shouts another guard.

"Then round them all up for execution!" the queen of Jerusalem screams, a violent, harsh sound. "It matters not to me."

The crowd really begins to panic now. The smoke has cleared and everyone is running for their life, green hood or no.

But I feel my stomach all the way in my throat when I hear a cry and then a guard shouting, "I've got someone!"

A guard holds Zeena by the back of her mantle; I can tell it is her by her boots. He's smart enough to have put a knife to her throat and shifted her body in front of his like a shield. A tricky shot.

Damn it all. I hop back up onto the stairs to get a better angle for my shot.

In an instant I've got an arrow nocked, but before I can fire, the queen of Jerusalem walks over to the guard. She towers over Zeena, reaching out to pull back her hood. "What have we here?"

"I would not, if I were you," I call out.

The queen smirks and looks up. "I see I was right. The thief is in our midst. And I must have captured a favorite of his."

"Aye," I say. "And I've got an arrow aimed right for your heart."

Despite my threat, the queen flutters her hand to keep her guards back. "Why would you send a boy in to do a man's work?"

"Release your captive," I say, keeping my voice as steady as possible.

"And why would I do that?" she asks.

"Release your captive," I call down. "And you may have me."

The queen is looking right at me. "And how might I trust the word of a thief?"

"How might I trust the word of a queen such as yourself?" I retort.

She smirks. "I will kill your companion."

"I don't doubt it," I say. "Send them along and I'll surrender."

There is a long stretch of silence.

"Or," I say, swallowing the fear in my throat so that I might appear calm and collected. "Kill my friend down there and never know who I am. The choice, dear queen, is yours."

Ah, there, I've piqued her interest. If she thought to lure me with my loyalty, then I will lure her with her own pride. She needs to know who has bested her twice, almost thrice now. I can see it in her. She's not one to forget an enemy or take such attacks lightly.

It's all too personal for her.

The queen snaps her fingers, and Zeena is dropped to the ground. Before my sister can pull any tricks of her own, Teni pulls her into the thick of the crowd, and they both disappear into it. She's done the job I asked of her. If there's one thing I know about Zeena, it's that she would never back away from a fight. So, I made sure she would have no choice. I'm sure she's kicking at Teni the whole way out of the courtyard.

I stand from my vantage at the far corner of the hall and give a long bow. "Greetings, Queen Isabella."

She stares at me, not believing I would turn myself in so quickly and with so little fuss.

A path manages to clear before me and I step up to the queen's little stage. "As promised."

She approaches and pulls the hood back. She smiles like a satisfied cat. "A girl."

"As are you," I say.

We stare at each other, each sizing the other up. I wonder if I've played my gambit too well, if she will decide to execute me here on the spot. If I really did sacrifice my own life for Zeena's. It's possible, I know, that the queen will have her revenge here and now.

And if that is what is to come, I'd make the same choice again.

But I had hoped for at least a chance of escape.

The queen waves her hand in the direction of her men. "Take her to Kerak Castle. I've questions for her there. And if any of you lays a hand on her before We are able to question her, then your life is forfeit. She will know no end of pain from Ourself, and from Ourself alone." And then the queen leaves behind her royal *we*, looking each of her soldiers in the eye. "Am I understood?"

They all accept her command with disgruntled obeisance.

And then I'm bound with rope and trundled off, carried away to the big stone fortress in the desert, where I am to await death by the hands of the queen of Jerusalem herself.

Outside Arsuf

In the camp of al-Nasir

CHAPTER FORTY-FOUR

Take Me Out

YUSUF COULD NOT BELIEVE THAT RICHARD HAD NOT taken Jerusalem. He'd had an age to do so, and yet, he had stayed, as though frozen outside Jerusalem. That was the report from his scouts.

Still, Yusuf could not believe it, not when his own forces were so demoralized by their defeat at Arsuf. The great al-Nasir, victorious no longer.

It had been a heavy blow to the men and their morale. And then the emirs had taken advantage, forcing Yusuf to give up half his troops. For though Yusuf had protected all those emirs and qadis from the great barbarian invaders, local politics were still as they were, and each man would scramble to protect his own little kingdom at the cost of the whole.

It had always been this way. It was these very divisions that Yusuf had taken advantage of himself, all those years ago, when he had first started his conquest and taken Al-Qahirah.

But given how badly all of this was turning out, Yusuf had not expected this stroke of luck—to have Richard, king of the Faranji, the Qour de Lion, wait outside Jerusalem and refuse to attack the city. *Where had the king's famous courage gone?*

And yet, Yusuf had been blessed with such an occurrence.

From what Yusuf knew from inside those walls, the city would have capitulated in an instant. But then the Faranji began to in-fight amongst themselves. Richard supported Guy of Lusignan for the throne of Jerusalem. And Conrad of Montferrat, who had married the Queen of the Bloodline, had retreated back to the safety of the north, back to Tyre.

So, instead of falling into enemy hands, Jerusalem held steady, and Yusuf had time to regroup.

He would march back on Jaffa. He was going to take the city by the sea back. He was going to unleash his forces in an attack so heavy, the invaders would not know what had hit them.

Perhaps he did not have the numbers that he once held, but his men still had rage in their hearts. They still remembered the massacre outside Akko. They still knew what it was to win, though they most recently had been stung by defeat.

So Yusuf called forth his troops to rally and to attack one last time. And they were going to deliver a death knell to these invading troops, the likes of which these men had never seen.

The Faranji would long not for home, but for death, once his troops were through with Jaffa.

Meanwhile, at Kerak Castle, nestled in the desert to the east of the Sea of the Dead . . .

CHAPTER FORTY-FIVE

There's a She-Wolf in the Closet

TIME HAS NOT EVER BEEN ON MY SIDE, NOT SINCE THE beginning of this quest. And I certainly have little of it left now. But wait I must, for the queen of Jerusalem has other business to attend to, rather than torture a simple thief.

Affairs of state, no doubt.

But something must be happening, for I'm being taken out of my cell. I figured I would be brought to the queen and questioned. And then if I were lucky, immediately killed.

Luckily, my plan revolves around no luck at all.

As we wind farther down into Kerak Castle, which is one of those proud stone buildings that jut out of the desert like the invaders had no sense of geography, I'm struck by how strange it is here in our own landscape. When I entered, I saw that the invaders have even surrounded the fortress with a little moat, so that only those who are allowed through the drawbridge might enter. How they sourced such water, in a land where water is as good as gold, I'll never guess. It seems a great waste to me. But then again, I am not one of them and I will never be able to guess any of their motives.

Perhaps if I make it back alive, I can get John to explain it to me. The thought grips me for a moment. That fear that I might not make it out of this alive. That I might never fight with Zeena again. That I might never sing off-kilter with Teni or watch Viva's mind begin to calculate and whir or listen to John list his favorite natural philosophers. That I might never see Majid and his cheeky grin again.

But I do not allow any of these thoughts more than that fleeting moment to pass through my mind. I've a job to do here, and I mean to make it back to all of them in one piece.

Though how I'll make it through the desert again is anyone's guess. Makes me long for Fouzia something fierce.

We take a turn, and they have tunnels beneath this building, too. I should have figured that. That they source their water from down below, just as the Templars did beneath Haifa.

We wind our way through the tunnels. One of my captors kicks me from behind, and I stumble. I'm sure they just wanted an excuse to beat me up before the adventure is through, so that they can say I fell and not that they hurt me. As though the queen would not see through their tricks.

But bullies must have their fun, I suppose.

I'm thrown into a new room—practically a closet in the back of another cell. This one is darker and danker than the cell before. The men pick me up from the floor, nearly pulling my shoulders out as they do so, and tie me roughly to a chair. I've only just the presence of mind to make sure to hold my hands taut as they do so, to create some slack for later.

Then the door to the cell closet grates open, and in swans the queen of Jerusalem herself.

She's so pale she glows like the moon. It's an uncanny look, and I feel like I will be haunted by the sight of her in this cell for the rest of my days.

"Leave us," she commands. "And if you hear screams, it is just my prisoner meeting her untimely end."

"Your Majesty, it is not safe," protests one brave guard. Or perhaps just a foolish one.

The queen gives him such an icy stare that he bows and backs out of the room. The door shuts behind us.

"Here she is," says the queen. "The girl-thief who has brought me such grief."

"Yes," I say. "And here *she* is, the girl-queen who has brought *me* such grief."

She's to my side in three strides. "You *dare*—"

"Aye, I dare. I've no fear of you."

She reaches out, grabbing my face in her hands. Her nails scrape against my cheek; I can feel the moment she draws blood.

"That is your choice then, to be a fool." She releases her grip but does not wipe the blood from her hands. She admires the red tint there, taking a step back.

I refuse to flinch at the stinging pain in my right cheek. "And yours as well."

She grins. "How have I been a fool? I've captured the great al-ghita akhdar. The so-called great Rahma al-Hud." She pauses. "Ah, I see you're surprised that I went looking for other accounts of you. I did not want to be drawn off guard again. A girl fighting in Akko. A soldier who saved a little orphan. A village benefiting off the thievery of a kingdom."

"You have discovered much," I say.

"Yes, and when I'm through with you here, you can be sure the village will be razed to the ground and that child will lose her grandmother just as surely as she lost her mother and father. Perhaps she shall lose her little brother, too. Who is to say how magnanimous I will feel after this."

I admit, this rattles me. I strain against the chair.

The queen of Jerusalem just laughs. "You think you could best me? Outsmart me? When I am queen of all this land?"

"I did think it worth a try," I confess.

She pulls a stiletto from the chatelaine along her robe belt and points it toward me. "Badly done, girl. Add that to the list of other foolish things you have done. I will kill you. But first, I must reclaim the keys to the Holy Sepulchre. I will have what was mine."

But I'm not distracted by her knife or her threats—the seal to the crown of Jerusalem also hangs on the chatelaine along her robe belt. "I see you mean to reclaim your stolen kingdom."

She nods. "Stolen by you and your godless heathen dog king, Saladin. You will die. And he will die. And even Richard will die. And this land will be mine again. Do you want to know how?"

I do not, but she seems rather bent on telling me, for she doesn't wait for my answer. "I will keep all of these men fighting like dogs against one another. And when they are out of money and troops, I will sit again on that throne, dangling the keys to a holy site of pilgrimage for my people. No one will refuse me my birthright. So you see, girl-thief, you have lost. And everything you hold dear will be destroyed in the fire of my retribution.

"I will let this be burned to ash, just so that it might be mine again. You've already played into my plan; I can now blame my own men for rebelling against me, for hiring that spy of yours that you came to claim. I can now tear my lord husband Conrad's court apart from the inside out."

"You would destroy everything," I ask, a little in shock that the heart of her is thus, "just to steal the crown?"

"Yes," she says, and the light in her eyes is truly haunting. "So, I ask you—where is my treasury, and where are the keys?"

But I've got fight still left in me. "Come now, Isabella, is that the best that you can do?"

At the use of her name with no title, the queen rounds on me. She comes inches from my face, holding that stiletto knife of hers. But she doesn't put it to my neck just yet, and that is her mistake. "I will slit your throat myself, do you hear me?"

"Loud and clear," I say.

But before she can back away, I headbutt her, hard.

She goes reeling across the floor. Her dagger clatters to the ground.

And now I loosen the ropes that bind my hands. As I had held arms taut when they tied me, I could have escaped at any moment. Untying my legs is trickier, though.

The queen's furious; she's clawing for her dagger. She really will finish me now.

I have no time to untie my legs, so I hop in her direction. It's even slower going than it sounds and she's nearly got her dagger again by the time I get to her. I sweep her to the ground by rotating around and hitting her with the chair.

This also sends me crashing into the ground atop her.

Humdulillah she told the guards to expect noise, or I'd never make it out of here alive.

For a moment I'm stunned by my own success—and the pain across my back and the pain in my legs and the scrape across my cheek. But I can take no longer than a moment to register that pain, for I must sit up, despite all the aches across my body.

I can easily pull the leg of the chair out from my bindings. And in a minute, I'm free from the ropes and the chair.

What you must understand is, this is the moment I've always meant to escape.

I could not go, not before this. Not before getting within these walls.

The queen is knocked out cold on the dirty floor.

I pull out the original peace treaty deep from my own robe pockets, along with the true key to the Holy Sepulchre, which I attach to her chatelaine. I bury the treaty deep in the recesses of the pocket where she keeps her stiletto knife. I pray she doesn't find it there.

Then I have one last thing to steal from her: her royal seal.

And now it is time to run like hell and escape this desolate and brutal fortress in the middle of the desert.

CHAPTER FORTY-SIX

In like Flynn

I'M HUNGRY AND A LITTLE BIT BANGED UP AND WORSE for the wear, but I am still standing on my own two feet.

There were five men who brought me down here, and I can only assume there are at least as many on the other side of the chamber door.

I know they did not lock us in.

I do a knock, as though I am Queen Isabella, ready to exit. Then, as they swing the door open, I hide behind it.

"Get help!" calls one guard. "The queen is down!"

Two more run into the cell. "What has happened?" asks one, bending over.

"The witch is gone," says another.

He's got keys.

I leap out from behind the door, kicking over the man who was bent. He goes crashing into another guard and they go crashing onto the queen.

I'd laugh, but I've still two more to fight in this room alone. Who knows where the fifth guard has gone.

I throw the queen's dagger at one of them, hitting him square in the shoulder. This will slow him, but I doubt it will stop him. The one with the keys gets a good swinging punch into my stomach.

I hit the ground hard, but I scramble up before the men can kick me while I'm down. I've seen enough of soldiers and war to know that such men would delight in that.

As I'm getting up, I grab for the keys. Ah, they're in hand.

Now I've just got to continue to dodge his sword.

Oh, and the man who took the dagger in the arm? He's back and he's got the weapon in hand. And then the fifth and final guard enters the room, his own sword drawn.

I am outnumbered and outsized and out-weaponed. In every sense.

But while there are several of them and only one of me, I'm using each of them as a shield to block and get in the way of another. They strike toward me and I step behind another of them. They stab at their fellow soldier and I duck beneath their swing.

It's exhausting work, but at least I can use their advantage to my own.

It's a pretty dance—a bloody one, too—but they're the ones who wind up injured and I am the one who is dodging and weaving through them all.

"Come now, is that the best you can do?" I taunt. Men are so easy to taunt.

One guard grunts and takes another stab. He's so enthusiastic in the gesture that he doesn't think of what would happen if I were merely to step out of the way. He goes staggering past and runs straight into the wall. He's lucky to have avoided his own sword, truth be told.

Soon they're all on the ground.

I need to retrace my earlier steps down into this cavernous maze of tunnels, but first I must find all my belongings. Luckily, I discover they've put them in the outer cell. I grab my cloak and my hip bag, my bow and quiver of arrows. Then I break into a run.

Why I always seem to be running for my life, I suppose I'll never know.

Humdulillah I am fast.

I've got most of the men knocked out, but I've got to find my way through this fortress before I'm discovered. I take what I need out of my pack and stick to the shadows of this cavernous place.

There are guards everywhere, and staying out of their line of sight would be easier if I had a disguise, but I've no time to strip the armor from one of the guards and change. And I wouldn't wear the queen of Jerusalem's kirtle and robe. I'd rather dress up as a Templar than as her.

There's no time for costumes. I must get out of here. And I must find transport so that when I escape, the guards cannot catch me up and return me to my cell here. This castle is surrounded by desert for miles and miles.

I must steal another of the queen of Jerusalem's horses.

And here's a horse that seems good enough for the taking, tied up to a post in the courtyard.

As I'm undoing the knot of the tether, I hear a shout. "There she is!"

I have no time for introductions or formalities. I just have to hope that the beast is so used to being ridden that she'll take off running.

And humdulillah again, for she does.

I'm charging across the bridge as they're desperately trying to raise it and I'm bobbing and weaving because I can feel the whizzing of arrows around me at my back as I'm changing tack—

And by Allah—

They mean to trap me—

The bridge is being lifted—

And I hope this horse can make a leap for we've not time to stop—

It's a long moment as we lift into the air—

This horse and I—

and we go soaring—

I release my legs' grip on her saddle, for as much as you want to clench tight during a jump you must stay loose and not bring the horse to any kind of abrupt halt—

Especially when you don't know how big of a jump you are making and how big of a jump the horse can clear—

And then with a resounding *thud* that brings relief to my whole body as it vibrates through me and rattles every ache and pain that I've acquired in that damned castle, the horse and I land on solid ground. Her back hooves are about a hand away from the water, but it's just enough.

I stop her briefly, giving the horse a hearty pat. "That's a good girl."

She harrumphs as if she knew she could do it all the while.

The men on the other side are still firing and they're back to lowering the bridge.

But I've got one more trick up my sleeve.

I take some of those little clay pots in my quiver—the ones given to me by Viva—and I lob them against the walls of the castle. They break open and land in the moat.

As they crash against the citadel walls and set fire to the whole ring of water—and the giant bridge—I think to myself that Viva really does make a brilliant Greek fire.

They'll have a time and a half trying to get out of there now.

I take off, back across the desert.

My friends are still outside Jaffa, and we have unfinished business to attend to.

Back outside Jaffa

In the camp of Richard
of England

CHAPTER FORTY-SEVEN

Somebody Once Told Me

IF ANY GOOD HAD COME FROM THIS, FROM RICHARD'S point of view, it was this: Saladin had lost control of his troops. Of course, that was also the *problem*. Saladin's men had ransacked the city, saying it was their recompense for the massacre outside Akko.

Well, Richard was not one to wait anymore.

He had brought his own troops back to outside the walls of the coastal city, and as Saladin lost control of his own men, Richard would regain his own grasp of Jaffa once more.

His men were growing weary of such battles. The French troops left by Philip were dwindling, and Richard was running out of the money that Philip had left to pay the men.

Richard's own men were no longer fresh, and time was no longer his friend. He had to strike back.

But Richard felt as though he'd already lost his chance at Jerusalem. He'd removed his troops from there, while Saladin had stationed his own back at the city of Jaffa.

This was a game of chess, and Richard still hated the game.

He was beginning to regret not making use of the winter. He was beginning to regret not taking on Jerusalem when he could have.

Conrad refused to send troops again. Not until Richard instated him as king.

Richard could not backtrack now. That would be a show of weakness.

But he needed the troops.

First, he would take back control of Jaffa. Then he would find his way to Jerusalem.

And there he would wage a holy war like none the world had seen before.

Meanwhile, between
Jaffa and Jerusalem . . .

CHAPTER FORTY-EIGHT

A Life Span with No Cellmate

Zeena is not pleased to see me.

I'm not sure why this surprises me, but it does.

"I cannot believe you set Teni on me and would not let me fight!" she's shouting.

I am so exhausted I can no longer count how much time has passed since we were ambushed in the makeshift court of the queen of Jerusalem in the middle of Jaffa, but Zeena remembers this like it was yesterday.

Time has passed by for me in fits and starts, the way it is wont to do when you are held captive. I dismount the horse. "I cannot believe you thought I would let you stay and surrender for me."

Teni greets me with, "I knew you could do it."

I see that Teni has John's sword at her hip. I look at her questioningly.

"I lost my sword in the crowd," she admits. "John said I could have his until I found a replacement."

I look over to John, but he's politely ignoring us both. I can see that his ears are red, though.

And Majid? He just offers one of his lopsided smiles. His total confidence in me brings such a lift to my heart that I've no words to offer him. Nor do I seem to need them. He simply winks at me. "Thank you, by the way, for coming to rescue me."

His voice sends a little zip of energy all down my spine and I'm doing all that I can to stay still and calm. "Of course."

Those are the only words I can manage. I look him over, just to be sure he isn't further injured. His hair is still short, but his beard has regrown a little. I swallow. The rest of him looks as uninjured and handsome as I can remember right now. Before I can think to say anything else, Majid returns my look with such intent, I'm not sure what he means to do. My face flushes with heat all the way down my neck. I feel for my collarbone, wondering if it is as hot to the touch as my whole body seems right now.

Viva, however, is paying no attention to any of this. She is insistent on one thing and one thing only: "Did the fire work?"

"Like a charm," I say. "And lit up the little water around the castle in such a spectacular fashion."

Viva claps her hands, joyful that she got her alchemy just right. "Oh, that's splendid. And without having to light it first?"

"Exactly that," I say.

It's the happiest I've seen her . . . next to when she's holding hands with Zeena, that is.

I hand the horse over to John, who has finally returned to a normal shade of pink. "And how is our resident healer?"

He looks at me and frowns. "You're injured."

"Aye," I say. "I need every poultice you've got for bruising. I'll be black and blue tomorrow."

John continues to frown, but he sets about gathering things from his apothecary kit and setting them over the fire to make a solid paste.

"You speak of swords and bruising when you could have been *killed*!" Zeena continues to shout.

"Come now," I say. "I would have thought you had time to cool off by now."

"You think I would cool off when you go out and resign yourself to death?!" she says.

It feels as though she's always shouting. And always at me. I cannot take it any longer. I've just stolen the Seal of Jerusalem. I've made it out alive from Kerak Castle. I've bested the queen of Jerusalem, though she has no idea in how many ways yet.

I have won a great victory and Zeena is *yelling* at me and I cannot keep my cool any longer.

"And had you not resigned yourself to such a fate when you signed up for war?!" I demand. "Do you not think that I worry about you and such a fate every day we are here? That I would not like you safe and home, where we climb date trees and help Baba on our land?"

Her rage boils over. I can tell because she's no longer shouting—she's whispering, like a venomous snake ready to kill. "You think that's what I want? To go home and to die slowly? To marry a man and be bartered off for the sake of family politics and watch my life slip away? When I know who I am? I'd rather die."

The rest of our crew has gone silent.

Now it is my turn for my fury to boil over. "You came to Jerusalem to die?!"

"How dare you—"

But I don't let her finish. "No, you did, didn't you?"

She turns away from me, refusing to meet my eye. "You know nothing, Rahma al-Hud."

"I know some things. I know I'd kill anyone that came between us. I'd kill every single one of them to protect every hair on your head."

"That is not your job."

But I won't let her out of this. And I won't calm down, not now.

Not so near the end of it all. Not when we could be halfway home by now, if she had just listened to me when we had left Akko in the first place. "You're a grand liar. It's always been my job."

Zeena snorts, but it's not half so powerful as usual. She knows I am right, despite her protests.

I give her no quarter. "I just never knew I had to protect you from yourself."

She whips her head up, staring directly at me. "Tell me, oh wise younger sister. Do you see my future clearly at home? Would you choose that for me?"

I know what she means. She's got an active disposition. She's a fighter. She's meant to be on the road, in the open air. I know this of her all too well. "I would not."

"Then what would you have me do?"

"I do not know."

Zeena looks satisfied and sad all at once.

But I won't let her have this victory, not when we've been through so much together. "But I'll fight for you. I always will. We were born fighting, sister."

"Then what does this future look like? Why must you drag us both home?" Her voice is brittle and fragile.

I know I should not push her, but I do. "I don't know! But if it saves you, it's worth fighting for. It always was."

And then I see something I have never seen. Not in my entire lifetime.

Zeena begins to cry.

Not heavy tears of rage. Not screaming wails of grief.

Just tears. Quiet sobs.

She's been broken by this.

When I step toward her, she steps back.

She's never stepped back before, not in all our years. She yells and she wails and she gives me no end of grief. But she's never flinched away from me before.

The effect on my heart is catastrophic. I wonder if I know my sister at all. If she knows me.

If I am who I've always thought I was.

I was never the girl whose sister shrank away from her.

"I love you," I say. It's the truest thing I know, the *only* thing I know right now.

"Would you, if you knew all?" she asks, her voice a hoarse whisper.

I miss her hissing. I miss her vitriol. I cannot bear to see her so.

"I do know all, sister," I say. "We've been through hell together."

"But not love."

"Tell me who you love and I will love them, too," I say.

She looks at me strangely. Her eyes are lit with some sort of passion I do not understand.

"And what if I told you I love Viva?" she says finally.

It's a challenge. She expects me to reel, I think. To throw her out or to admit defeat.

"I already love Viva, sister, so I've no quarrel for you there," I say.

I look over to Viva. Her eyes are shining and bright like she's just heard all over again that her Greek fire worked like a little miracle.

And perhaps it is a little miracle. A brilliant stroke of alchemy, when God finds those who love us as we are and we can love them back. They say that God made us in pairs, in zouj. I smile at the thought.

I look at my sister and she's watching me with great apprehension.

"Do you mean it?" she whispers.

"I have many faults," I say. "But you know that I have always said what I mean."

She nods. And a resolution crosses her face.

And then she's taking Viva's face in both her hands and pulling her in for a kiss.

"Your sister always had a flair for the dramatic."

I startle and look to my side. Majid is there, still grinning that silly grin of his.

"Yes, well . . . She's got the al-Hud strike, it's true. The eyes and the stubbornness. But I think she gets the drama from our mother's side. They're Chalabis."

Majid laughs. John and Teni laugh alongside him. We are all merry at the sight of love, in the midst of so much war.

"Come now," I say to the rest of our friends. "Let's give the lovers a bit of privacy."

"And after that?" asks Teni, as soon as we're a little ways away.

"First, I would love a hot meal. I've eaten next to nothing for days." I look around at my band of merry misfits. Viva and Zeena are missing, of course, but they'll be back. "Then I'd love some of John's lovely balms for all of these damned aches."

"That I can do," says John.

"And then?" asks Teni.

"And then," I say, "I promised Zeena—we're going to Jerusalem. We've got to steal a negotiation out from under a king."

Back at Kerak Castle

In the court of the queen
of Jerusalem

CHAPTER FORTY-NINE

When the Sun Goes Down

ISABELLA COULD NOT BELIEVE THAT NOT ONLY HAD the thief attacked her, but her men had lost that girl yet again.

She was starting to think she was surrounded by a level of incompetence that could never be rectified. She had set so many pawns in motion, she could not be stopped now. She *would not* be stopped.

But she'd also discovered that if she wanted a thing done, she had to do it herself.

So be it.

She would gather her troops. She would gather what men there were left that she trusted.

And she would ride to Jerusalem.

And there, she would convince Richard that while she spoke to treat with him on behalf of her husband, what she meant to do was make war.

Isabella would not fail. Not now. She'd come too far.

Outside Jerusalem

CHAPTER FIFTY

Wonderwall

"HOW MANY SIEGES MUST WE GO THROUGH IN ONE lifetime?"

It's an excellent question, and one for which I have no answer.

"As many as it takes, I suppose," I say. "You're the one who got us into this mess."

"And you're the one, I suppose," says Zeena, "to see us out of it."

"Precisely." I wink at her because I know it will annoy her.

Teni laughs.

There are no walls around this Jerusalem. Perhaps that is what gives me the most hope. That for all the war and all the fighting, the city itself is open and free.

There are no walls to keep out those of another faith. I hope there never will be.

Perhaps all roads lead to Jerusalem in some way, this open and sacred space. Though, by my count, ours was a winding path to get here indeed.

This time, I wear no disguise. I am Rahma al-Hud. I am the girl with the green hood, and people part as I make my way through to the city.

Not everyone has the chance to be captured by the queen of

Jerusalem and live to tell the tale. But I have, and it has started to inspire a little bit of awe in those around us.

"Excuse me," says a small voice.

I look down and there is a small girl walking alongside Fouzia. I startle when I recognize her. "Hello there, Farrah. What brings you to Jerusalem?"

"Jedati came to pray at the church. She heard the Nasrani were allowed back," she says. "She has taken my brother with her in hopes that the church will open soon."

"And you?" I ask.

"I came to see the Green Hood again. May I come on adventures with you?" she asks.

I suppress a laugh, for I remember what it was to be such an age and to think that everyone older than I was always laughing at me. "Not quite yet. We are on a quest."

The girl gasps.

"But you might be able to help us."

Farrah stares, wide-eyed.

"Might you know where we can find the head camp of Richard, the Faranji king?" I ask.

She nods.

"Lead the way," I say.

Chapter Fifty-One

Watch the Throne

I INSTRUCT THE REST OF MY CREW TO STAY BEHIND, even Zeena. I tell them to set up a tent in between this camp of Richard's and the camp of al-Nasir beyond.

This next part I must do on my own.

Majid stops me for a moment. "Must you go alone?"

I reach out and put my hand in his. "I must."

Majid pulls my hand to his lips and kisses it. "Come back in one piece, Trouble."

I smile, a flush creeping across my cheeks. "I always do."

And then my hand is my own again, and I head straight for the largest tent in the camp.

"Enter," calls a voice from within the tent.

A guard opens the flap for me, and I bow low as I step inside.

"Who are you?" asks the same voice.

"A messenger," I say. I look up and there before me is the Faranji king—Richard. He is tall and lean, in the prime of his life, though he looks a little ill to me. Like he has been worn down by these wars as much as the rest of us have.

I never thought I'd see a butcher thus.

And when I look over, there beside him is Isabella, false queen of Jerusalem.

She shrieks when she sees me. "Get this imposter out of here! She's an assassin sent to destroy you!"

I bow lower still. "I have come with a treaty for peace, sire. I do not come to make war. I have no weapons on me, but feel free to have your men search again."

Perhaps it is the honesty in my tone, but Richard motions his men to check me.

I submit to the search without protest.

"A treaty for peace?" he asks. There is a smile in his voice, like he knows something funny that I do not.

Of course, I know what is funny. But I must act as though I do not.

"Yes, sire, from Salah-a-Din, if I might be so bold." The words taste like ash in my mouth, but I must call everyone by their proper titles if I am to get through this.

"Indeed?" Richard raises an eyebrow. "And what say you that this lady, queen of Jerusalem, has come to bid me treat with her?"

"I know not," I say. "I am all amazement, sire."

"How so?" he asks.

"For I have it under great intelligence, from my own lord, al-Nasir, that it is she who has stolen the keys to the Holy Sepulchre. It is she who has withheld the treaty from her own husband, Conrad of Montferrat. And altered it when he was unaware."

And then I look to Isabella, who has a murderous look in her eye. "It is she who wishes you to continue with this war. A war without end."

Richard stares, looking over me and then Isabella carefully.

By this time, Queen Isabella has gone purple with rage. But when she speaks, her voice is icy calm. "Lies."

Richard turns to her. "You would not mind submitting to a search, then?"

"I am the queen of Jerusalem," she says. "No man may search me."

Richard's expression grows hard and unimpressed.

"If I might be so bold," I say. "I believe she has both along her chatelaine."

I point at the pouch where she keeps her stiletto.

Richard moves quickly. He spots the key in an instant, behind the pouch. And he pulls out the stiletto and the treaty in one swift movement. He uses the knife to slice open the seal.

Richard looks up at me. "This is the true document." Then he looks at Isabella with something akin to disdain. "And the messenger speaks true. There is an alteration here in the parchment. And all the while, you brought me a forgery in your own terms, against your husband. You kept the keys to the holy church, kept out good Christian pilgrims."

"I would never," protests Isabella. "This is some hideous trick by that brat. She's a thief! The Green Hood. Ask her—she's stolen my horse, my coffers, and now my very kingdom!"

But Richard takes the keys to the Holy Sepulchre and the original treaty and sets them aside.

She looks at me in disbelief. "This cannot be. Those keys were not on my person, not even—"

Ah, and here she remembers. That she'd had me in her prison. That while she'd awoken with what she'd thought was all her goods along her chatelaine, she hadn't thought to check them. She'd assumed I hadn't had the presence of mind to take anything from her. That I had merely wanted to escape with my life.

Which is what she gets for assuming I was more of a fool that she was.

She lunges for me. I step out of the way as the guards take hold of her.

Richard levels her with a glare. "Leave. Now."

The guards immediately unhand her, for though she is not their queen, she is still royalty.

Isabella straightens her back and stares directly at me. "This is not over."

"Yes," I say, quite simply. "It is."

And then she exits the tent in a proud rage.

Richard is looking me over for a long moment. But then he turns his attention back to the document. He's clearly thinking.

I dare not interrupt him. Here is the butcher of Akko before me. But the peace is worth more than his death. Though I am sorely tempted to get out one of the knives in my boot and slash his throat and be done with it. That's what Zeena would do, at any rate. All the better I'm here instead of her.

Before I can change my mind, another man comes in, dressed in full armor. "My lord king," he says.

Richard looks up.

"Saladin has arrived at Jerusalem," says the man. "With his personal company."

"I thought he might," says Richard, a grim expression on his face. But then he looks to me. "I thank you for your service to the peace of this land."

I bow again. "It is my duty to my own sultan."

"And what does he want, your sultan?" he asks. His gaze is unflinching.

"To treat with you," I say. "There is a tent set up, between your camp and his. The middle ground. No-man's-land. Meet him there. King to king."

And then the grim expression on Richard's face gives way a little. "Verdun, get me a translator."

But before the armored man can leave or Richard demands my exit, I make a light cough.

The men all look at me. I stay bowed low for what I must say next.

"Excuse me, sire, if you don't mind. But I speak the common tongue as well as your own. I would be happy to act as translator, if you would have me."

CHAPTER FIFTY-TWO

The Translator

I THROW ON THAT TRUSTY JUPON, THE ONE I STOLE all those months ago, outside Akko.

Funny that it should still serve me now.

I weave my way through the camp until I am all the way to the other side.

I can see that up on a little hill, my own company has set up the necessary tent. Good.

I work my way through al-Nasir's camp until I'm at the door of the tent of the great sultan himself.

Here I submit to another search, this time from the sultan's men. They think me a stranger, belonging to the other side.

And perhaps, at the end of the day, I *am* on another side. Just not the one they imagine.

I'm on the side of those I protect. Not just my kin. Not just my company. But the people. Those who have no voice in any of this. Those who were not born with the power or the means to fight.

Perhaps they need someone in the tent for them as well.

I am admitted, and at once I am struck by how small al-Nasir is. For a man with such an imposing reputation, I had not expected him to be so slight and so short. Or so old. He is long past the prime of his life. And still, he fights.

I bow. "My lord sultan. I bring with me a message of peace."

"Peace?" asks Salah-a-Din.

I bow lower, and hand over the forged treaty. I made sure to use the seal I'd stolen from Queen Isabella to close the scroll with hot wax.

"And how can I know that he means peace?" Salah-a-Din takes the treaty from my hands.

I look up and he is watching me, his eyes serious.

"If I might," I say. I reach for the copy of the key to the Holy Sepulchre and hand it to him. "Richard, king of England, found this in the possession of Queen Isabella. He sends it to you as proof of his peace."

The sultan takes the key, amazed as he looks at it. "To the Holy Sepulchre?"

I nod and bow again. "He hopes that you might bring them back to him, at the tent on the high hill. So that you two might be brothers in peace, rather than kings at war."

Salah-a-Din nods, and stands. "We shall meet your king."

I back out of the room before he can change his mind.

Outside Jerusalem: No-Man's-Land

At the end, again

CHAPTER FIFTY-THREE

Your Kind Is My Kind

IN THE STORIES OF THE DAYS OF OLD, THERE WAS ONCE not a king, but a thief.

That thief stole the very seat of power and took back a negotiation that should have belonged to lesser men.

But here we are, back at the end again. And there sits Yusuf ibn Ayyub, known to his enemies as Saladin. And across from him sits Richard, king of England. And between them is a translator of little import.

No one would have marked her. No one would even realize that she was a girl. But she is the go-between for these two men.

And she has stolen a great peace for this land. She had written her own treaty. She could not expel the invaders entirely, but that had been the price of peace.

These two men, who each try to outfox and outwit each other, have both been played by a young woman who speaks on behalf of each of them.

She does not mistranslate them, mind you. She simply gives each a good sense of the terms. She does not lie, for she is one who would, even while in disguise, speak the truth quite freely. And so when she has finished translating what the sultan has said, and she waits through the long silence that Richard gives, she is not filled with trepidation.

She knows what will come next. Peace, at last, in this sacred land.

Richard nods. He agrees to the terms. Richard will destroy the fortress at Ascalon. He will agree that the sultan is ruler of the Palestinian coast, from Tyre to Jaffa. Saladin will agree to have Christian pilgrims again in the holy city.

The two men accord and treat for peace.

They leave this meeting as though they are each other's brothers.

And they owe their peace to a wily young woman and her band of merry misfits.

Sometime later

In the cedar forests
of the north

CHAPTER FIFTY-FOUR

Home Is Wherever I'm with You

IT HAD BEEN TRICKY TO FIND A PLACE TO CALL HOME again.

Zeena did not want to return to the Sawad, and I found that I had not the heart to make her go. But nor could I bear to be in this world without her.

We did not stay in the Holy Land, with all its names for God and all its pilgrims and all its war. I could not rest until I was somewhere that, at least for a little while, was at peace.

We had gone north until we'd reached lush green mountains. The wadis below were filled with farmers and all kinds of fresh food.

I think for a moment, of that hermit in his cave. The wild mountains that surround him. These mountains, at least, feel peaceful.

Ancient, but in some way, our own.

We used the treasure of the queen of Jerusalem to buy land and to build our own little village, where any might find a place to call home if they come looking for us.

It's green here, but not the green like where the two rivers meet. Here the smell of fresh, clean dirt, cedar, and pine fill the air. I wish I could describe it better for you. But it smells not like an old home, but a new one.

The trees are a refuge, like our own little Carmelite caves.

People begin to come from far and wide. They hear of us, in our little mountain village. First it was just a camp. But now we have multiple homes and a common green.

It is my little slice of paradise, and I do not take it lightly. We traveled far and wide and fought many battles to get here, and I would not give it up for anything, not until another army came to invade. And even then, I'd only go if my sister felt called by the drumbeat of war again.

Viva and Zeena have set up a little alchemy shop. When Viva is in residence, most of the other villagers give the home a wide berth for fear that it could explode at any moment. The alchemy shop is closed on Friday so that Zeena might go to the little masjid and closed on Saturday so that Viva has her Shabbat.

John has set up his apothecary and does his best to make eyes at Teni. She pretends not to notice and tends to the herds of goats and sheep. And horses, our herd as motley a crew as our human one. She still travels, bringing messages and those seeking refuge to and from our little village. Each time she goes, I wonder if she will ride all the way back to her homeland. Each time, she's returned.

It feels like a miracle I don't quite deserve.

Even Majid Mirza has giving up his spying and has found his own peace here in the forests. He says one day he will return to the land of his father.

I'm not sure whether I believe him. I'm not sure whether he believes himself.

It is not all idyllic. Zeena and I still fight, and being in charge of a village is no mean feat.

But they are happy there. We all are.

At least until adventure calls once more.

THE BEFORE

The Land Where the
Two Rivers Meet

The Domain of al-Hud
Safar, 581 Hijri

Hallelujah

THERE IS A PAIN IN MY CHEST. I'M RUNNING SO HARD
I think my heart might burst.

But I must beat Zeena.

She's the faster climber and she was down the tree so much quicker
than I was. But I'm the faster runner. I push and push with all my
might to catch up to her. She's just ahead of me. The dates are in her
hand. I try to be careful not to squeeze the dates in my own. It's forfeit to give Baba crushed dates.

This is a game of strength, but it's also a game of wits. You must
be faster than the other. But you must also see your task through to
the very end.

Allah, but she's ahead of me still. My feet are scraped from shim-
mying down the tree; so, too, are my palms. Perhaps one day, I will
learn to climb without making such a mess of myself.

But it's not today.

The wind whips through my hair and part of my braids comes
undone. I can feel that the cord keeping my left braid tied has come
loose.

But I've no time. I must keep going.

She's three strides away.

Now two.

Now one.

We're neck and neck and I'm pumping my arms and pushing my legs and my whole body tells me there is nothing left.

But I push just a little bit harder.

I'm running so fast that I don't see where I'm going, and as soon as I make it through the door, I crash into someone.

Big arms catch hold of both of us. "Habibti. Habibti." Baba has a good grip on Zeena and me. "I should have known it was you two."

I'm out of breath, but still I must speak first. "We've brought you dates! Here, have one!"

"No, have mine!" shouts Zeena.

Baba must know what we're up to, for he lets go of us and motions to the table. "Put them on the platter there."

It's difficult to hide my disappointment. But looking at Zeena, she does an even worse job.

"Sit here," says Baba. He's motioning to the thick, plush carpet beside him.

Zeena and I each take a seat, her to his right and I to his left.

"I must tell you two something very important," he says.

Zeena and I both lean in.

"It is good for you to play games," he says. "But you must remember, you are each of each other's tribe. You belong together."

I deflate slightly. I look over, chancing a glance at Zeena. Her own anger has subsided. Her expression is cooling, leaving behind her usual air of intensity.

"It doesn't make sense now," he says. "But one day, you will see. You'll need each other."

Zeena snorts.

Baba stares at her until the skepticism dissipates from her face.

I look over at my sister. I cannot imagine her annoying me any less than she does today. I cannot imagine a world where we are not fighting, where we are not competing.

It would be a strange world. I'm not sure one I'd want.

But as I look at her—the long, sloping, proud nose, and the wild tangle of hair, and the way her eyes refuse to give way to anyone or anything—I feel a surge of pride.

For she is my sister and I am hers. And we belong together.

A Timeline of the Third Crusade

---◆---

Jun 1191 CE—Jumada al-Awwal 587 Hijri
The Crusader armies of Philip II of France and Richard I of England arrive at the siege of Akko via the Mediterranean.

12 Jul 1191 CE—17 Jumada al-Thani 587 H
Richard I of England captures Akko.

Aug 1191 CE—Rajab 587 H
Philip II leaves Akko and returns to France.

20 Aug 1191 CE—19 Rajab, 587 H
Richard I of England orders the execution of twenty seven hundred Muslim prisoners on the hill of Ayyadieh.

7 Sep 1191 CE—15 Sha'aban 587 H
Richard I of England defeats Saladin's army at Arsuf.

Jan 1192 CE—Dhul-Hijjah 587 H
The Crusader army led by Richard I of England arrives within sight of Jerusalem but decides not to attack for fear of a counterattack by Saladin.

Jul 1192 CE—Jumada al-Thani 588 H
Saladin takes Jaffa.

Aug 1192 CE—Rajab 588 H
Richard I of England retakes Jaffa.

Oct 1192 CE—Ramadan 588 H
Richard I of England returns home but is shipwrecked in the Adriatic Sea. He is found, captured, and imprisoned by Duke Leopold V of Austria. (And, incidentally, this is where the traditional Robin Hood legends begin).

4 Mar 1193 CE—27 Safar 589 H
Death of Saladin, sultan of Egypt and Syria.

Author's Note

———— ◆ ————

HOW STRANGE IT IS, TO SIT HERE WRITING THIS TO
you.

You see, I grew up reading historical novels. Especially historical
adventures. I fell in love with the genre with *The Witch of Blackbird
Pond*. And then *The True Confessions of Charlotte Doyle*. And then, of
course, my first foray into the medieval genre, with *Catherine, Called
Birdy*.

I fell in love with history through all of those books. So much so
that when the time came, I studied art history in school and tried to
become a professor.

But perhaps that is a story for another day.

The story now is this—if you read enough historical fiction, you
know that this is the section where the author puts lots of little notes
on history that didn't make it into the story. Or, perhaps, the histories we changed along the way. Proof that we did our research. That
we know what we're doing.

But I confess I'm not going to do that.

The truth is, I hope you go out and look up the history of the
Third Crusade. It was a brutal period. But I hope you learn to investi-
gate the story on your own. I hope you don't take my word for it.

In fact, I hope one day I meet you and you tell me all the little
details that I got wrong.

For that's the beauty of history. It's always there, waiting to be discovered.

And rediscovered.

Acknowledgments

◆

THESE HAVE TO BE THE HARDEST ACKNOWLEDGMENTS I've ever written. Not because nobody helped, but because so many people helped throughout the entire process of writing this book.

This book started out the one I wrote during the pandemic. When the world went on lockdown and we all held our breath. Then it became the book I wrote when the people took to the streets and demanded justice. Then it became the book I wrote as the Hummers came rolling down Sunset Boulevard, with the National Guard marching through with their guns and their helmets and their fatigues. The book I wrote as the choppers circled overhead, their spotlights flaring into my bedroom window as I worked late at night. The *whoompa pop whoompa pop* reminding me of the police over and over and over again.

Then it became the book I wrote during the fires. When, like some badly formed Joan Didion metaphor, a gender-reveal device set off one of the most destructive fires in a century. The windows were closed. We had already been wearing masks. The power went out. And the world got smaller. And the choppers still circled overhead. The jasmine on my balcony nearly died. The people still marched. Justice was still demanded, needed. The world continued to keep going and continued to stand still all at once.

Then it became the book I wrote while I was diagnosed with cancer. While I went through chemo. That I raced to finish before I went in for surgery.

This book. This goddamned book.

I love this book.

I would not have had the opportunity to write this book had Emily Settle not come to me with her brilliant idea: "How would you like to write a classic retelling of Robin Hood from the perspective of the Muslims?"

As soon as that email hit my inbox, Emily, I knew I had to tell that story. It wasn't just our mutual love of Robin Hood or the fact that you are always willing to make a *Leverage* reference in the notes. You gave me a space to tell the story of the women in my family. The ones I'd heard about my whole life. Who had been the daughters of local tough guys and the granddaughters of tribal maliks. Those were the stories I'd heard from my father. And you gave me the space to share those women with the rest of the world. You've been wonderful to work with. And you pulled a dream from my mind that was so deeply buried, I hadn't even known it was there. Thank you, from the bottom of my heart.

Lauren. The first time I wrote an acknowledgment, I believe I called you a "beautiful, noble poetic land mermaid." That is still true. You have been my biggest advocate from the start. You have known what I was capable of and you've never let me sell myself short. I love that you sent me a magic tree for luck and I love that you watch old movies with an enthusiasm that honestly inspires me. You've given me so many people to work with that I'd only classify as good peoples, because you are good peoples. The best of peoples. It's probably because you've got a dachshund and love *Romancing the Stone*. I do that thing my father does where I brag about you constantly behind your back but never to your face. This is me bragging to your face. I'm so proud I get to work with you. Thank you.

Tara Timinsky. I am so grateful you were the one who read *Not the Girls You're Looking For* all those years ago. You've always gotten the heart of that book and the heart of my work. I've said it before, but I'm so glad we met—two Texas transplants in California. I'm so glad I've had the opportunity to work with you. I'm so glad I had someone to see *Cats* with just before the world shut down (incidentally, the last film I saw in theaters, if you can believe it). You are part of my dream team. I can't wait to watch a slew of bonkers movies with you when the world opens back up. Thank you.

Thank you to everyone who contributed to making this book. Rich Deas, the cover designer. Amir Zand, the brilliant cover artist who brought all of my characters to stunning life. I'm still dazed, looking at this stunning cover. The entire team at Feiwel and Macmillan, Kim Waymer, Kathy Wielgosz, Helen Seachrist, Jessica White, Mariam Syed, and Marielle Issa. Thank you all for your wonderful work.

Morgan Rath, my publicist extraordinaire for four books now. Thank you so much for finding a spotlight for all of my books. Thank you so much for all of your work and all of your kindness. Brittany Pearlman, the other half of this book's PR dream team. Thank you for your work and all of your efforts. This book makes it into the hands of readers because of you both.

Kat Brzozowski, thank you for organizing that care package. I drank all the tea, did all the crossword puzzles, and wrote so much of this book swaddled in that blanket. Thank you for being there for me. Thank you for listening.

Thank you to Aaron at the Ryerson Reference Center for answering my questions about medieval armory. Thank you to Jessica at the Costume Institute for also providing so many resources. Doing research during lockdown was particularly tricky, so thank you for making your institutions accessible, even when they were closed.

Thank you to Diya Mishra, for organizing a digital community and still running writing sprints in the BV, even when we couldn't go to the BV. Thank you for your beautiful enthusiasm and your love of stories and the written word. You're a champion.

Thank you to Somaiya Daud, for pulling so many JSTOR articles for me when I dropped into the group Discord as I panicked about the fact that I couldn't access anything beyond the abstracts. Thank you for answering my extremely long-winded emails about Arabic transliteration and when to use the en-dash. You are a scholar and a gentlewoman. I admire you immensely. Thank you so much for taking the time to help, every time I called and asked for it.

Thank you to my agency siblings, Valerie and Jodi. Thank you, Valerie, for the lovely tea care package. You're all heart.

Thank you to Emily Aaronson at the Studio City Public Library for organizing all of those Jeeves readings. They got me through.

If you know me at all, you know one of my favorite movie franchises on planet Earth is *The Fast and the Furious*. The running joke about those movies is that "they're all about the family": Dominic Toretto's wild, weird, thieving family that is both by blood and by adopted kinship. I could not have gotten through the year without my own family, both my blood and my chosen kin.

Thank you to my mother, Deborah, my brother, Joe, and my father, Hazim. My third parent, Annette. Mama J, who would listen on the phone. Alex, who would swap cat photos to keep up my spirits. John, who was willing to speak of his own experiences with me.

Another particular thank-you to Baba, who sent me more articles than I could have possibly read, who mailed me every book he had on the Crusades, and who told me every single family story I needed to hear. About my great-aunts who walked the streets unchaperoned and armed during the early twentieth century. Who, when catcalled, turned around, pointed their weapons at the offender's balls, and told the man to say that again to her face. The stories of my Bebe, wrestling snakes with her bare hands. Of Ama Hookum leaving her marriage when she was done with it and deciding she would stay with every family member she felt like, for as long as she felt like. The stories of the land you've told me since childhood. They're all in here, in one way or another.

I had never known the idea of the oppressed Muslim woman until so much later in life, because you told me about all the women of my line. The ones who fought alongside the men. The ones who ran their villages and their land. You told me I was tough and you called me sheikha as a little girl. You taught me to love stories and history and you made me resilient—more so than I ever realized. I think I know what you were trying to tell me now. Thank you.

Bridget, Emily, and Austin. Who took me to appointments. Who were the first to know. Who listened when I needed and who laughed at my dark humor and encouraged me when it was hard. I'm so glad we all ended up at that apocalyptic Sparrarow Lodge out in the desert, those years ago. There were many things I had to do on my own this year, but I never felt alone because of y'all. I don't have friends, I have family. Thank you feels like an inadequate word, but it's the best one I've got. Thank you.

Selina and Leslie, who I have known for over two decades now. Thank you for the baby photos and the dog photos and all of the FaceTimes and all of the calls. Thank you for reminding me of all of the life that was waiting for me once I was through with treatment. Thank you for including me as both of your families grow. It means the world that we were all girls together, and I've gotten to see the women you've become. Thank you for your love and your friendship.

Steven, darling Steven. I promised you adventure, though I'm not sure this is what either of us had in mind. But still, you took this adventure in stride just like the rest of them. You kept me going. You reminded me of joy every day. You sat with me through the worst of it. You are the best and most decent person I've ever known. *If I loved you less, I might be able to talk about it more.* You deserve a swimming pool filled with maple-glazed donuts. I'd even go to Krispy Kreme for you.

The sea and those who sail it are far more dangerous than the legends led them to believe . . .

This remix of *Treasure Island* moves the classic pirate adventure story to the South China Sea in 1826, starring queer girls of color—one Chinese and one Vietnamese—as they hunt down the lost treasure of a legendary pirate queen.

They will face first love, health struggles, heartbreak, and new horizons. But they will face it all together.

In a lyrical celebration of Black love and sisterhood, this remix of *Little Women* takes the iconic March family and reimagines them as a family of Black women building a home and future for themselves in the Freedmen's Colony of Roanoke Island in 1863.

THANK YOU FOR READING THIS FEIWEL & FRIENDS
book. The friends who made *Travelers Along the Way: A Robin Hood Remix* possible are:

Jean Feiwel, Publisher
Liz Szabla, Associate Publisher
Rich Deas, Senior Creative Director
Holly West, Senior Editor
Anna Roberto, Senior Editor
Kat Brzozowski, Senior Editor
Dawn Ryan, Senior Managing Editor
Kim Waymer, Senior Production Manager
Emily Settle, Associate Editor
Erin Siu, Associate Editor
Foyinsi Adegbonmire, Associate Editor
Rachel Diebel, Assistant Editor
Helen Seachrist, Senior Production Editor
Kathy Wielgosz, Production Editor

Follow us on Facebook or visit us online at mackids.com.
Our books are friends for life.